Gypsy Kisses
and
Voodoo Wishes

Denise N Tapscott

ISBN: 978-1-5356-0245-7

I dedicate this story to everyone who believes in Magic, and the power of Love.

Acknowledgments

I would like to take a moment to thank my angels (both seen and unseen) and the good Lord above. They remind me often to follow my heart.

Whitney Houston and Amy Winehouse were humans with the voices of angels. When each passed away, my heart broke into a thousand tiny pieces. Who would take their places in the music world? What would happen to the songs they were meant to sing that we hadn't heard yet? They're gone, but not entirely forgotten, at least not yet. After hearing about their deaths (and the deaths of countless other talented folk, including Robin Williams and Prince, to name a few) it was imperative for me to publish my novel. If I died suddenly, who would enjoy my stories? Would anyone ever meet Grandmother Zenobia and my vivid cast of characters?

If you, dear reader, died tomorrow, would there be anything you could leave us, or would your talent, your passion, fade away with you? I encourage you to do whatever it is that makes your heart sing.

Along my writing journey, I have discovered that goals and wishes do come true, with lots of hard, but enjoyable, work. Without the valuable help and input from Paul Gaston, Jeovantay Jones, Corey Garrett, Ricardo Torres, Johann Jansen Van Vuren, Marlene

Dinetz, Tori Hubbard, and Matthew Wilson, along with a few friends who prefer to be anonymous, as well as my beloved best sister in the world, Victoria, the story would not be nearly as interesting as it is today.

I appreciate all the help and guidance from the people at BookFuel. Without them, the story would just be a tale told only in person, every so often, and it would fade as time grows.

In a way, this story is also a love letter to the city of New Orleans. I love all of her mystery, her drama, her history, and her amazing food. For better or for worse, she is my home away from home.

I want to thank my mom and dad, whom I adore. When we were a lot younger, my dad gave my sister and me the same advice that one of his elementary-school teachers gave him when he was just a little boy. *"Hook your wagon to a star and you will always go very far."* I have heard other people say that too, but it means the most to me coming from my Papasan. Speaking of my parents, they have loved each other since they played together as young children. To this day, their love is stronger than ever, no matter what comes their way. It is that kind of amazing passion and commitment from one soul to another that inspired me to write *Gypsy Kisses and Voodoo Wishes*.

Lastly, if ever you are in a situation where you have to choose between love and something else, I vote that you always choose love. Not everyone finds it, and not everyone gets to keep it.

Contents

Part One: Gypsy Kisses

Chapter 1/Pralines

August 17, 1889

Dear Zenobia Jalio,

Thank you for your continued generosity and donations to the St. Augustus Church. My wife thanks you again for your jambalaya recipe. She hopes everyone will enjoy her version as much as yours at the summer potluck next week. Don't feel obligated to bring a dish, as she will be making plenty of jambalaya for everyone.

It has been brought to my attention that you are still giving Tarot readings and special "treatments" to members of the church at your home. These practices are works of Satan! I demand you stop practicing your Voodoo ways immediately. As it is written in the Old Testament, "Do not practice divination or sorcery" Lev. 19:26.

Provided that you can follow the ways of the Lord, and not Satan, you and your monetary generosity will always be welcomed at St. Augustus. Otherwise, I will be forced to ban you and your family from the church.

By his grace,

Reverend Eugene Milton

"Why did you bring that horrible letter with you?" Will asked as he snuck a peek at Grandmother Zenobia. He watched her shove the wrinkled letter into her pocket. "I don't understand why you've carried it around with you for almost a week. It just makes you mad."

"The nerve of that man!" Grandmother snarled as she shifted uncomfortably in her seat. "How dare he quote a Bible verse at me! Somehow, he managed to overlook 'Do not have sexual relations with your daughter-in-law.'"

As Will guided their horse-driven carriage down a dusty road, Grandmother fussed. Her head pounded. She was cranky that she'd had to scold Will all morning about his chores. For once she wanted him to do less, but he kept trying to do more. The horses needed to be brushed but he insisted they needed a full grooming, including changing their shoes. Eggs needed to be collected from the hen house but Will complained the entire chicken coop needed to be cleaned. Grandmother wanted the front porch swept but Will said he'd need time to sweep the entire wooden perimeter of the house.

Grandmother questioned why she even chose to leave the house. The Louisiana sunshine was too bright, even though she was shielded by the large brim of her favorite pink Sunday hat. She had been cross all week about that asinine letter, and now her headache added fuel to her anger.

"Grandmother, are you making that up?" Will asked carefully.

Clearly she was agitated. The carriage's haphazard bouncing on the dirt road didn't help much either.

"Honey, it's right there in the Good Book. Leviticus 18:15."

"Seems to me you know the Good Book better than Reverend Milton," Will snapped back.

Grandmother was about to scold Will for his flippant attitude when she noticed his small smile. Lately he seemed to be more outspoken, which she didn't care for. It was, however, an unexpected treat to see his dimples in his soft chocolate-colored skin.

"You might be right, Will. I do have a way with Bible verses."

"You have a way with many things, Grandmother," Will chuckled.

Grandmother answered his chuckle with a shrug of her shoulders. Then she chuckled too.

"Grandmother, are you actually laughing?"

"Will, it's rare that you ever joke about anything. Hearing you laugh makes me happy."

The buggy shifted as they bounced along the dirt road. Grandmother looked over at her grandson as he focused his attention back to the two Cleveland bay horses and the rugged path the carriage rode on. He went back to his usual quiet, serious self. As a teenage

5

boy, Will had the demeanor of an adult. To the best of her knowledge, and she took pride in what she knew, not once had Will experimented with alcohol or sex. He hardly ever rebelled against her. They would have lively discussions, but they never really fought. The young man was reserved and insightful. She often wondered if he was ever happy.

The throbbing headache she'd woken up to faded slightly. Grandmother had noticed, when they first left home, that Will was about as uncomfortable as she was. She assumed it was due to the overstuffed, hard seat of the carriage (which she wanted to scold him for because he hadn't follow the directions she had dictated earlier that morning), but as they talked, she realized she was mistaken. Will didn't want to go to the church picnic any more than she did. He'd tried his best, unsuccessfully, to get out of going with her. He had run off a sizeable list of things that absolutely needed to be done around the house and farm before they left. He had insisted that he needed to take care of everything that very morning, rather than escort her to a church function. Grandmother, however, would not take no for an answer from her grandson. Now it all made sense.

"I'm sorry about snapping at you earlier. Sometimes those church people get me worked up," Grandmother said.

"So then why do we bother with those church people? The whole thing seems foolish."

"Well, it's important to be social and get to know folks. Wouldn't it be nice to make some new friends, or for you to meet a pretty girl?"

Will grumbled.

"I want the best for you; that's all. As much as I scold you, you do take great care of the farm. Everyone around town loves what you create at the bakery. Hands down, you make the best upside-down pineapple cake in the French Quarter."

Grandmother smiled when he sat up a little taller, and held his head a little higher.

"I worry that you spend so much time alone," she said.

"I'm fine."

"I'm just saying that it would be nice to have folks over sometimes. I could bring out the good china. We could share stories and enjoy each other's company."

"Are you feeling okay? You never want to bring out the good china," Will said.

"Maybe today's lesson is to not judge others, like the reverend, for example, and for us to be generous to others."

"Is that in the Good Book too, or did you read that in your tarot cards?"

"Sometimes I think you're too smart for your own good, Will Jalio."

"I take that as a wonderful compliment, coming from the smartest person I know."

Grandmother squeezed Will's bony hand gently as they laughed.

"We won't stay all day long, I promise."

"Yes, ma'am," Will answered obediently as he guided the brown-and-black horses up a small grassy hill in the summer heat.

Grandmother admitted that the both of them needed to be more social. Back when she was a young girl, her tribe had big feasts under a new moon, celebrating new beginnings. She missed her grandmother's soft hugs and sweet kisses. She missed her father's bold laugh, and her mother's subtle grin. She missed her cousins dancing rhythmically in a drum circle. Life by the Nile was very different than in Louisiana. Although Zenobia had changed throughout the centuries, she still yearned to have family and friends around her again. She often dreamed of big Sunday dinners, where everyone ate too much and laughed until their faces hurt.

The problem was that, as much as she tried, she just didn't like people anymore. They didn't "act right." People were annoying. People were too noisy. People were messy. People were smelly. People meddled in other people's business. People were judgmental. People were cruel. People killed loved ones, like her family.

Since becoming an immortal, there were a few things Zenobia could manipulate. When people were cruel and caused harm to others, she believed it was her duty to intervene. She had the power to correct them. Grandmother Zenobia conjured lessons for evildoers. Sometimes they needed to learn humility, and sometimes they needed to suffer.

Usually she chose to be benevolent to the mortals of Carrefour Parish. She liked living in Louisiana. Not only did it have an interesting past and vibrant culture, but it also (especially Carrefour Parish) had a certain energy to it. It had, and would always have, a subtle vibration only felt when you were there.

Grandmother cast smaller spells that didn't cause too much harm, though she was capable of much more. Sometimes she would hex livestock to wander off the victim's property for a few weeks, forcing the owners to lose income. Sometimes she would cast spells that affected the victim directly, such as upsetting their stomachs. The victim couldn't hold any kind of food or water in their belly for three days. With some preparation and planning, the spells were easy enough to perform, and usually the evildoers changed their ways.

Because of her reputation as a Voodoo High Priestess, Grandmother had many visitors for her services. She saw people by appointment, all of which were discreet, of course. Tarot cards, love potions, and gris-gris bags were always at hand. Handmade candles could be provided too, all for a small fee.

Zenobia also knew it was imperative to respect the power of the universe. There were some things she knew she wouldn't dare interfere with. Actions with ill intentions always had a price, large or small. Whatever you reaped, you sowed, just like the Good Book said. If she chose to do something seriously harmful, some of her life force would ebb away. Still, there were times she was tempted to help the universe along. She didn't mind the few gray hairs or wrinkles that appeared because of her actions.

Grandmother also knew that people like Reverend Milton would be horrified at the real power she wielded. She could do much more than a few silly card tricks. There were tribes, back in ancient times, who feared her name. Her likeness was scrawled in the walls of a long-lost pyramid. She cringed when she remembered her short time in Asia. Her apprenticeship with brother and sister shamans to learn the dark arts had ended badly. Many people died because the witch and warlock doubted her strength. An ancient dragon was awakened before its time. She wasn't sure if she'd ever be allowed back into China, not that she wanted to return anyway. The list of her escapades was a long and colorful one.

The less Will, Reverend Milton, and his naïve congregation knew about her, the better. She was good at keeping people at a distance. By pushing people away, however, she would never have her large, laughter-filled Sunday dinners. Neither would Will. Grandmother's "people problem" troubled her a lot; she felt like a dog chasing its tail.

"Grandmother, are you okay?" Will asked, interrupting her thoughts. She didn't like his frown as he spoke to her.

"Sorry, I woke up with a terrible headache. Too much on my mind, I suppose."

The carriage stopped at the top of a green, grassy hill overlooking a pale, dry plateau below, speckled with a few large oak trees. In the center of the flat land was St. Augustus Church. The small, two-story sanctuary seemed harmless and innocent from a distance.

However, it was strange to some folks that grass had stopped growing on the church property. Grandmother wasn't the least bit surprised. She knew the reverend had been up to no good over the last year or so. The land wouldn't flourish until he saw the error of his ways. Grandmother looked up at the baby-blue sky, noticing a few cotton-ball clouds slowly pass by. As she focused her sight on the pointy white steeple, her temples pounded.

Without speaking a word, Grandmother and Will looked at each other and nodded in agreement. The horses led them slowly toward the potluck. Music and laughter filled the air as they bounced down the road.

"Look how nice everyone is dressed," Will said as they drew closer. His soft voice snapped her out of her mental fog. "I feel like I'm staring at a big, beautiful painting." He paused and then mumbled, "I sure am glad you didn't let me leave the house in my work clothes."

Grandmother chuckled. "It was a fight to get you to wear your suit. I see you wiping away beads of sweat from your forehead and twisting about in it." She stifled a hearty laugh as he tugged at the cuffs of his thick jacket. "But now you see why I insisted."

"You were right, as usual."

She turned her attention to what Will was looking at.

"My goodness, look at all those folks in their Sunday best. The hats alone are a sight to behold."

She surveyed the congregation as they drew closer. It might be Saturday, but everyone dressed in their finest church clothes for the annual summer potluck. Most of the men wore three-piece suits. The woman wore different shades of every color one could imagine, with hats of different shapes and sizes to match.

"It's nice to see everyone in high spirits."

Her headache lessened to a steady, low thud in the base of her skull as the carriage came to a stop. Bad headaches plagued her when something unusually negative or destructive was about to unfold around her. They were her personal alarms. The last time she remembered having a headache like this one had been when Will was seven years old.

That day, he'd wandered a little too far from the house and come across a Louisiana black bear. The bear, severely wounded by hunters, was a shape-shifter named Pallaton. He was a member of the lost Chapitoulas tribe and son of Zenobia's trusted friend, Chief Qaletaqa. His instincts led him to Grandmother's land to hide on her property for sanctuary. Pallaton, stuck in the form of a bear rather than his human form of a small boy, attacked and almost killed Will. That day was one of only a handful of days in her lifetime that Grandmother felt helpless. Her land was protected with magical wards. Her grandson should have been free to wander and play on a nice spring day. Pallaton was hurt and frightened. Chief Qaletaqa and his tribe were always welcomed on her land. There was no real villain in the situation and there was nothing she could have done to change the circumstances of the day. Eventually, with Chief Qaletaqa's help, both boys were healed.

"What could possibly go wrong at a church function?" Grandmother mumbled.

"We could be bored to death," Will said.

"Maybe I'm not myself because I skipped breakfast. I'm saving my appetite for the potluck."

"As soon as we get settled, I'll fetch you something to snack on."

"Thank you. I don't say it enough, but you are growing up to be a fine young man," she said as he helped her off the carriage to the ground.

Before she had both feet planted firmly on the ground, a cluster of Sunday school kids swarmed her, catching her off guard. She drew in a very deep breath to calm her nerves as children of various ages and sizes giggled and danced around her. They all knew that Will worked at a local bakery, and rumor had it he was bringing a special dessert to share. Their energies around her were loud and energetic, like a flock of birds overhead. The older children loomed a few yards away. Will left to park the carriage. While he was gone, she considered that maybe she wasn't ready to spend the afternoon with so many people.

They are just children, innocent spirits. You're safe, she told herself.

She took in another deep breath and patted her favorite amulet, a copper ankh, for good luck. It was a gift her father had given to her when she was ten years old. She wished her dog Ahy was by her side, but the church frowned upon people bringing pets to church functions.

"Now, children, what did we talk about just minutes ago?" asked Miss Weston as she approached, interrupting the frenzy.

The Sunday school teacher, only a few years older than Will, held her head high as she addressed the children. Her dark hair was neatly pinned under a smallish pale-blue hat, which matched her pale-blue dress. The dress was modest, but still accentuated the young woman's small waist and delicate arms. As Miss Weston spoke to the children with authority, Grandmother found the young woman to be bossy, but didn't mind her interruption.

None of the children spoke, but instead froze where they stood. The older children tried, unsuccessfully, to slink off. Miss Weston pointed at them and they shuffled back toward her.

"Where are your manners? How do we greet our elders, especially Grandmother Zenobia?" she warned.

All the children lined up obediently before Grandmother. Their energies calmed down.

"Good afternoon, Grandmother Zenobia," they announced together.

Grandmother was surprised at their obedience. She didn't expect them to be so respectful for Miss Weston. But then again, she was fairly certain no one really knew of Miss Weston's sins.

"Good afternoon, children. Thank you for the warm greeting."

One little girl not old enough to understand what manners were managed to wiggle through the line of children. Against Miss Weston's orders, she waddled right up to Grandmother. The sixteen-month-old furiously waved sticky hands in the air to be picked up. Her dress was covered in whatever her mother had tried to feed her for breakfast. She continued to squeal and clap her sticky hands while Grandmother stared down at her.

"Cookie!" the little girl managed to say.

Grandmother took a deep breath and looked around for help. Will was still parking the carriage.

"I do not want to touch this messy child," she said softly. "She probably needs her diaper changed."

"Cookie!" the little girl said again and did a little dance, asking to be picked up.

Grandmother swore the child was drooling. She looked over at Miss Weston, standing with her arms crossed, and noted a hint of smugness. She looked down at the child, who still insisted on Grandmother's attention. She gave in and bent over to pick up the sticky little girl.

Grandmother watched Miss Weston flinch when she raised the little girl in the air.

"My goodness, you are as light as a feather and smell like lavender."

As she held her close, the girl kissed Grandmother's cheek. The meddlesome headache vanished.

Grandmother removed a floral handkerchief from a pocket sewn into her dress and wiped the girl's delicate little fingers.

Will finally showed up at Grandmother's side with two large black wicker baskets.

"Sorry for the delay, Pip and Estella were restless. It took a few sugar cubes to get them to settle down."

He eyed Grandmother as she held the child in front of a young audience, and a huge smile lit up his weary face.

"I see you have made a few new friends, Grandmother."

"Yes indeed, and soon they will be your friends too." She smiled back. "Boys and girls, this is my grandson, Mr. Will."

"Good afternoon, Mr. Will," the Sunday school children all chimed.

They were mesmerized by the large baskets at Will's feet. Some giggled. Some stood with their mouths agape. Their excitement was contagious and Will giggled too.

"What's your name, little one?" Grandmother asked her new little friend in her arms.

"Cora," interrupted Miss Weston, who seemed uneasy as Grandmother and Will talked to the children. Her arms were crossed tightly around her chest again.

"Cora," the girl said, echoing Miss Weston.

"Well, Cora, because you and all of your friends look so lovely, all dressed up, and you all seem so well behaved, Mr. Will and I brought you some of my favorite treats."

"Cookie!" Cora squealed.

Will slowly approached Miss Weston, never looking directly at her, and opened one of the heavy, mysterious baskets. Her stiffness melted and was replaced with the same joy as that of her Sunday school charges.

"Pralines!" Miss Weston beamed.

"My goodness! What a delightful smile you have," Grandmother said. "Please help yourself."

She hadn't seen Miss Weston smile genuinely since well before the girl's husband had died last year. He had been involved in a strange printing-press accident. It was a shame that poor Eugene Milton Jr. was crushed to death. Grandmother made a mental note to invite the young woman over for some tea and a nice sit-down in the future. Grandmother would need to do a little more investigating before she continued to judge her. As much as she'd like to conjure up a lesson or two for Miss Weston and her attitude (not to mention the rumors of her seducing the reverend, Walter Milton Senior), she believed it would only be proper to look the young woman in the eye first.

"We brought pralines and chocolate-praline candy for everyone!" Grandmother announced.

Grandmother and Will laughed as the Sunday school children cheered in excitement.

"Enjoy the sweets, children!" Grandmother said as she fed a small piece to Cora. Grandmother loved seeing the children dance, laugh, and sing as Will passed out the candy.

"You see, this is why we came today, Will."

Will nodded.

"Miss Weston, would you mind helping me with the baskets?" he asked sheepishly.

"I'd love to," she said while nibbling on a praline.

Grandmother grinned as she watched Will chat with Miss Weston. Could this be the beginning of a new friendship? She couldn't get a clear read on either her grandson or Miss Weston, but she liked that her grandson was engaging someone else in conversation. His current friends were characters from books, and the farm animals named after them, not living people.

As a person grew older in the world, it became harder to read them from a spiritual point of view. Unless they were actively open to a reading, people generally created a protective layer around themselves, made up of their beliefs, hopes, dreams, and fears. A spiritually tuned being, such as Grandmother Zenobia, could see a person's aura, or life energy. Everyone on the planet was a little psychic, whether they knew it or not. However, it took a certain dedication, a certain mindset, to develop spiritual and psychic talents. Reading a person based on their social standards (like some so-called psychics did) was very different from experiencing a person's true nature. Grandmother Zenobia could focus on a person's energy to get information about them. For her, it was like seeing the color of their energy but also feeling their emotions. In some cases, she would smell certain scents and taste certain flavors. In special cases, she could see flashes of a person's past in her mind.

Younger, innocent souls were easier to read. They were still developing who they would eventually become. They had basic wants and needs.

This was the case with Baby Cora. Grandmother sensed a sudden change in little Cora's spirit as the girl twisted in her arms. The baby strained to look over Grandmother's shoulder. Sadness vibrated though her. It felt cold to Grandmother. A hue of dark blue vibrated around the baby's skin.

"Mrs. Jalio, I see you and your grandson have arrived," boomed Reverend Milton.

Grandmother slowly turned around to see the reverend in his expensive pinstriped suit. His aura was dark brown, like day-old chicory coffee. Grandmother expected his aura to be dark; the man didn't like anyone challenging his authority. He looked disapprovingly at the children while they ate the sweets. Miss Weston and Will had already started off toward the picnic tables to add the dessert to the rest of the feast.

"Call me Grandmother Zenobia, if you would please, Reverend Milton."

"I didn't think you would make it out to today's function," he said, ignoring her tone.

"We thought we would bring something sweet, seeing how you insisted last month that I not make my big pot of gumbo. Your letter was very clear for me not to bring my jambalaya either," Grandmother said.

Miss Weston was clearing space for the rest of the sweets and Will was inspecting the different dishes people had brought when he heard Grandmother's tone, off in the distance. Grandmother was still where he'd left her, with the baby in her arms. Miss Weston noticed that he stopped in his tracks and looked back. The two watched fearfully as Grandmother squared off with the large man while holding Baby Cora. Will swiftly passed the second basket of pralines over to Miss Weston. He noticed that her smile faded and her shoulders drooped at the sight of Reverend Milton.

"Sorry, Miss Weston, I have to go. This looks bad," Will said as he turned and walked toward Grandmother.

His walk turned into a jog as he approached. Miss Weston quickly followed behind him.

"Why are you holding my daughter?" he asked.

Grandmother gritted her teeth. The last thing she wanted to do was talk to this man, and here she was holding his child.

"Clearly, your daughter likes Will's pralines, although she seems fussy at the moment." Grandmother narrowed her eyes as she spoke. Cora fussed more as Grandmother held her on her hip.

"The children shouldn't be eating sweets before the main meal, you should know that."

Before Grandmother could snap back at the reverend, Cora burst into tears.

"Olivia, come get your daughter!" Reverend Milton bellowed.

All the picnic festivities seemed to stop at the reverend's outburst. Miss Weston ran faster, passing Will, and approached Grandmother Zenobia and Reverend Milton. She stood behind Grandmother Zenobia.

A meek Mrs. Milton rushed away from the potluck food and came up to her husband as quickly as she could manage. She was heavyset, like her husband, and running was hard for her. Her aura was a clouded red color, which meant she was holding on to a deep-seated anger. There were also flecks of pink, which represented love in her life. The pink flecks sparked when she drew close to Cora. Grandmother noticed the woman's dark-blue dress had food stains on it, from when she'd fed the baby earlier that morning.

"Grandmother Zenobia, I am so glad to see you. I see my precious Cora found you!" she said breathlessly, and took her wailing baby in her arms.

Grandmother noted that the baby's spirit flickered back and forth from happiness and sadness as she relinquished her.

"Olivia," said Grandmother, though she never broke her stare.

As Will approached, slowly but carefully, he watched Olivia stand between Grandmother and the reverend in hopes of appeasing them both. Grandmother was a tall woman, almost at eye level with the reverend. If anyone looked closely at her body language, they would have seen that the reverend didn't know whom he was messing with. The word "Grandmother" was more of a courtesy title for Zenobia. She wasn't frail. She wasn't decrepit. She had a small sprinkling of grey hairs tucked under her pink hat. Had Will not been around, no one would have suspected she was old enough to have a teenaged grandson.

"Good afternoon, Mrs. Milton," Miss Weston said coldly as she stood behind Grandmother Zenobia.

"Charlotte, be a dear and take Cora," said Reverend Milton.

Will looked at Miss Weston and then at Grandmother.

"Charlotte? You just called her *Charlotte*, so casually in front of everyone?" marveled Grandmother. The reverend ignored Grandmother. His demeanor had changed at the sight of Miss Weston. Grandmother growled at his crocodile smile.

"The baby needs to be cleaned up. Olivia seems too busy to attend to her own child," he continued.

Olivia Milton's eyes grew large, but rather than fight her husband, she just looked at him. As Miss Weston reached out to take Cora, Olivia relaxed her arms to her sides, like a rag doll. Without any care, she let the baby go as if she held a sack of potatoes. Will dropped to his knees and caught the child before she hit the ground. Miss Weston helped Will, with the baby in his arms, up to his feet. Once he grounded himself, Miss Weston took Cora from Will and fed her a small piece of praline. They walked off to join the potluck.

Grandmother roughly grabbed Olivia by the arm and escorted her away from Reverend Milton. They rushed past the potluck area, to the church.

Once inside the quiet, cool sanctuary, Olivia cried her heart out to Grandmother Zenobia. Her sobs echoed off the walls. Grandmother didn't like the large statue of Jesus staring down at her from the pulpit. Even though she practiced Voodoo and other magical arts from time to time, she believed that God was more inviting than the gaunt alabaster statue pinned on a cross.

"I am so thankful you are here, Zenobia. I'm losing my mind," Olivia managed to say in between sobs.

"You are one of my closest friends. I'm happy to be here."

The pew the women sat on creaked every few moments. Grandmother handed Olivia one of her favorite, soft handkerchiefs. Olivia's tears drenched the hand-stitched red roses on it.

"Olivia, we talked about this. You need to take care of yourself and that baby."

"I thought that Cora would make things better between me and Eugene, but instead things are worse. He hasn't come out and said it, but he hates me. All he wants is that Miss Weston," Olivia grumbled.

Grandmother didn't know what to say. She knew that Olivia was right. She put her arms around the large woman as she cried. Olivia was soft and smelled like lavender, just like Baby Cora.

"All he talks about is 'Charlotte said such and such' or 'Charlotte did such and such.' That is, if he talks to me at all."

"Olivia, you should focus on the things that make you happy. Like your beautiful baby, and your other wonderful children. I envy you and your large family."

"Cora was a mistake, and you know it. I never should have asked you to cast a fertility spell for me. I'm too old to be a mother now."

"But it's what you wanted."

"I thought he wanted a baby. He does, but not from me. The reverend is mad that he hasn't gotten Charlotte pregnant yet."

Grandmother grimaced.

"I wish I knew how to fix this situation for you. I understand that you're lonely. I get lonely too, but I find things that make me happy and the loneliness goes away. Think, Olivia – what else makes you happy?"

Olivia cried harder.

"What about cooking? You always enjoy a good meal," encouraged Grandmother. "How did my jambalaya recipe come out?"

"He insisted that the skinny little witch make it with me. It was horrible. I tried so hard to be happy around him. I tried so hard to be a good wife to him. Yesterday, the three of us stood in my kitchen and they acted like I was never even there. I was pushed off to the side to clean the shrimp. The reverend was so helpful to her with cutting up the vegetables and preparing the andouille sausage. It was disgraceful. They looked like newlyweds, the way they were so cozy. In my kitchen!" Olivia was at her wit's end.

"Olivia, no! That's horrible."

"No, Zenobia, the worst part is that this morning, before coming here, I found a letter that he wrote to her. It wasn't finished, but he's inviting her to live with us. He said she could have Junior's old room."

"Eugene Jr.? Miss Weston and the family buried him only last year."

"Yes, Zenobia."

"But Miss Weston is technically your daughter-in-law."

"Yes, Zenobia," she repeated.

"Why does he think she would want to do that? That sounds like a terrible idea." Grandmother shook her head with disbelief. She was shocked at the reverend's boldness. The whole time she'd thought Miss Weston was a home wrecker. She hadn't envisioned that the reverend was the root of problem.

"He doesn't care who knows about it. He insists that we need a live-in nursemaid. Everyone knows Miss Weston is great with children, so I can't argue against it. There's nothing I can do. I'm stuck with this horrible man, until death do us part."

As the words passed through Olivia's thick lips, Grandmother's headache came back full force. Heat flared in her temples as the blood vessels pounded away. She looked at Olivia, who sat up and stopped crying. Her eyes were cold and unfocused. Olivia slowly stood and Grandmother reached out to take her hand. Blinding psychic pain from Olivia flashed through Grandmother's body. Chills ran through Grandmother as she absorbed the despair that gripped Olivia's broken heart. She smelled like a wet dog caught in a thunderstorm.

"We'll figure something out," Grandmother tried to reason with her.

"You have been so sweet to me in the past. I appreciate you," Olivia said, her voice a monotone.

"I'm sensing a bad energy from you. I need you to sit back down. We can do a reading right here if we have to. We'll find a solution for you."

Grandmother panicked. Something was very wrong with Olivia. Her bones ached as the chills continued to run their course.

"Let's go outside and get some fresh air."

"Whatever you say, Zenobia."

Grandmother led Olivia outside, back to the festivities, into the bright sunlight. All around, people were enjoying themselves. The choir sang a few lively hymns, the children played, and some of the deacons and older men sat around in clusters, having helped themselves to small snacks. And yet, in the midst of all this happiness, Olivia looked like a soulless corpse lumbering around in a graveyard.

"I need to check on the jambalaya. I'm sure everyone is ready to eat, and I need to make sure it's ready. I'll come find you," Olivia mumbled.

Grandmother nodded in agreement, trying to shake off her headache. She looked for Will, who'd found a resting place in the shade under a lonesome oak tree, away from the congregation. At least he was safe, away from the reverend.

"I need a moment to collect my thoughts," Grandmother gasped. "How can I make this better?"

Olivia lumbered obediently back to her.

"Everything will be okay now," Olivia mumbled, dusting white powder from her hands.

"I hope you didn't add too much salt to your dish," Grandmother said, noticing her hands. Olivia didn't acknowledge her.

Grandmother gestured for Olivia to sit down at a vacant table and fumbled through her pockets. Members of the congregation were starting to help themselves to the potluck. Olivia just sat, despondent. Grandmother's fingers found a small victory. She pulled out a worn deck of tarot cards. The cards were ivory with black swirls and tiny roses.

As if a light had been turned on, Olivia became alert and looked directly at Grandmother, hoping for help.

"I need you to think of something that makes you happy. Don't tell me what it is. Keep it to yourself while I shuffle these cards."

Grandmother was desperate. She hoped the cards would reveal an answer for Olivia's dilemma. Olivia squeezed her eyes shut.

"Olivia, I've been looking for you. I helped myself to your jambalaya, and it doesn't taste right. Maybe it's the rice. I don't know. Even Charlotte noticed. You need to fix it before we serve it to everyone."

Grandmother cringed at the sound of Reverend Milton's voice over her shoulder. *Damn it!* she cursed to herself. She tried to collect the tarot cards, but she'd been distracted by Olivia's dismal energy and hadn't sensed him until it was too late. His shadow loomed over the two women, blotting out the sunlight.

"What is going on here?"

The reverend was furious when he saw the cards.

"I can't believe my eyes! You wicked woman! I cast you out, Satan!! In the naaaaaaame of all that is holy!" he yelled.

"Reverend, I can explain…" fumbled Grandmother. "Your wife, she's not well and I was…"

"Leave this place, and never return!" he interrupted. Everyone within earshot immediately stopped what they were doing and watched the reverend as he yelled.

The reverend barked orders for someone to fetch Grandmother's carriage. Miss Weston collected the empty black baskets while Baby Cora cried in her arms.

Will saw the commotion and rushed over.

"But you don't understand!" Grandmother shouted. Elders of the church grabbed her by the arms and escorted her away from Olivia.

"Thank you for all you have done for me, Zenobia. Thank you for being my friend. No one else understands. No one cares about me," muttered Olivia. She had grown distant again. The reverend stood over her, yelling at her as if he were scolding a child. The dark colors of their energies mingled with one another.

As Will caught up to the elders, they released Grandmother. Before she could think of a fast way to retaliate against the men who treated her like a prisoner, Miss Weston approached to return the baskets, now empty of pralines. Will accepted the baskets, but never looked directly at her. The men took a few steps back, guarding their territory, like armed soldiers daring them to re-enter the potluck. A younger teenage boy managed to bring up Grandmother's carriage. Their horses stomped their hooves angrily in the dust. Will pulled a few sugar cubes from his jacket pocket and fed them to the agitated horses in hopes of calming them down.

"Grandmother Zenobia, I'm sorry for how everything turned out today. I'm especially sorry for the way the reverend behaved. It's probably for the best that you both leave," Miss Weston said. She reached out and touched Grandmother apologetically.

Grandmother Zenobia was surprised at how genuine the Sunday school teacher was. Baby Cora, however, didn't stop crying. She grew more upset.

As Miss Weston's fingertips brushed Grandmother's arm, a psychic flash in ultraviolet colors burst through Grandmother's mind. She saw, in vivid images, an overbearing, masculine energy forcing himself upon Miss Weston. His aura was thick and black. Grandmother could only see Miss Weston clearly, but she recognized the toxic energy around her. It was the reverend. He charged at the young woman like a bull when they were alone in his office at the church. He'd pressed himself against her in the kitchen of his home after Olivia left. Grandmother continued to see bursts of moments of Miss Weston fighting off his sexual advances. She also saw Miss Weston crying herself to sleep, many nights.

Grandmother understood that she'd been wrong about her. Miss Weston was as much a victim as Olivia, in their tangled love triangle.

The flashes stopped. Pain shot up and down Grandmother's back. Her knees weakened.

"Lord above," whispered Grandmother. "I thank the heavens for those visions. Thank you for revealing the truth about Miss Weston."

"Grandmother, are you okay?" asked Will as he held her steady.

"No, but I will be. I had one of my visions," she said.

Grandmother would be sure to leave an offering for her Guardian Angels once she got home. She would also be sure to conjure up something awful against the reverend. He needed to be dealt with.

"Miss Weston, if you ever need anything, feel free to call upon me. Will and I would love to have you out to the farm sometime."

The young woman, with Baby Cora in her arms, managed a sad nod and reluctantly went back toward the reverend and his wife.

"Grandmother, please. We should go home," Will said quietly.

Grandmother nodded slowly as her head continued to throb. Whatever was going on with poor Olivia, there would be no visions like there were for Miss Weston.

There was only the constant pounding in her head and dreadful emotions.

Grandmother climbed up and into their carriage without a word. There wasn't anything she could do.

From a distance, she watched as the picnic festivities slowly started up again. Miss Weston approached the reverend, who continued to berate his wife.

Baby Cora jerked, writhed, and screeched in Miss Weston's arms. Dark-red blood spewed from her small lips. Olivia snapped out of her zombie-like state as Miss Weston shrieked in terror.

"What have you done to my baby?" Olivia howled at Miss Weston.

"Nothing!" she yelled back hysterically. But then she stopped, with a peculiar look on her face. She pressed her lips shut and staggered.

"Oh Lord, I'm going to be sick!" warned Miss Weston.

"Will, don't move the carriage. Something's happening," Grandmother said as they continued to watch from the distance.

One of the nosy church women, eavesdropping near the reverend, quickly ran to Miss Weston's side and took Cora from her.

"Someone fetch Doctor Evans!" a voice yelled from the small crowd that had gathered around.

Miss Weston violently vomited hot, dark blood. Rice, shrimp, and sausage, mixed with pralines, poured out of her mouth and littered her beautiful pale-blue dress. As she retched a second time, more pralines splattered on the ground.

"You fed Cora some jambalaya, didn't you!" barked Olivia. Her meekness faded away and was replaced with the rage of a bear. "You should never feed a baby that kind of food! What's wrong with you! She was never meant to have any of the jambalaya!"

"Don't you talk to Charlotte like that!" Reverend Milton said.

He raised his hand as if to slap her. She cringed, bracing herself for a blow she was well accustomed to. But the blow never landed. Instead he grabbed his stomach. Bloody vomit spewed from his lips, and his bowels loosened.

"I see you didn't just taste the jambalaya, did you?" asked Olivia. She straightened herself as her husband doubled over in pain. "Looks like you helped yourself to a healthy portion."

Grandmother Zenobia and Will sat motionless in their carriage and watched the scene unfold. Reverend Milton doubled over and collapsed. He thrashed on the ground at everyone's feet. Baby Cora continued to scream at the top of her lungs. Miss Weston was also on the ground, clutching her stomach. Olivia stood nearby and berated the young woman.

Grandmother frantically looked around.

"I don't see Dr. Evans," she said to Will.

"There he is!" Will pointed in the direction of the choir.

Dr. Joshua Evans was sitting with a few of the men near the choir. Grandmother respected the quiet, thin man because she knew he had an earnest desire to help people. With a little uninvited, unexpected assistance from Grandmother and her ways, his practice had flourished. Grandmother loved that he had a servant's heart and always made a point to let him know he was appreciated.

The eligible bachelor with a bright smile was relaxing with a handful of the deacons and a few older men who gratefully avoided their wives. They were sitting in a small circle close to the choir, gossiping and telling stories. Every few minutes a young boy would offer them snacks and coffee. Dr. Evans munched on the pralines Will and Grandmother had brought, and sipped a steamy cup of chicory coffee.

He and the men were listening to the choir sing until the music was interrupted by a frantic woman in a bright-green dress. She rushed from the choir over to him, pointing and screaming as she approached. At first Dr. Evans couldn't make out her hysterics, but then he saw the crowd circling Miss Weston and Baby Cora. He, along with some of the deacons, dropped whatever they were snacking on and rushed to the bloody scene.

Horror crept across his thin face as he looked at Baby Cora. He examined her little body carefully as she cried and vomited pralines. More members of the congregation sheepishly crept up to the scene. A few of the ladies tried to attend to the ailing Miss Weston. The men tried to hold Reverend Milton's body still as he violently thrashed about. Blood bubbled from his nose and lips.

"Please, save my baby!" wailed Olivia.

"Is she allergic to anything?" he questioned as he looked at the baby's eyes. Her pupils were large although they stood in the bright sun.

"She wasn't supposed to have any of the jambalaya!"

"What do you mean?"

"The jambalaya. It was just for the adults. The poison…it was just, just for…"

A new batch of tears flooded Olivia's puffy red eyes. She broke free of the crowd and ran inside the church in a panic. No one followed after the large woman.

"Poison? Mrs. Milton, wait!" he shouted. Still, no one chased after her. "Someone bring me my black bag!" Dr. Evans ordered.

Two younger men ran off to the doctor's carriage. Dr. Evans examined Miss Weston as she continued to expel praline cookies, bits of rice, and blood.

"Has anyone else had the jambalaya?" he asked frantically.

Everyone looked at the food area and saw that the tainted food wasn't set out with the rest. Surprisingly, the large casserole dish rested all alone, on a table separate from the other entrees. It had been the reverend's idea to display it, for everyone to see and enjoy. To his dismay, the pralines were the stars of the potluck.

Once his bag was delivered, he rifled through it until he found a bottle with charcoal.

"Someone bring me a few cups of water!"

Cups were handed off quickly and he sprinkled the charcoal in it.

"I need you to give some to the baby to drink," he said to the woman in the green dress.

Dr. Evans rushed over to Miss Weston. He cradled her carefully in his arms, and poured the concoction down her throat. Once she drank enough for his liking, he gently wiped away the vomit from her face.

"Dr. Evans, the baby…" Miss Weston started to say.

"You and the baby should be okay," he said to Miss Weston.

"Thank you, Dr. Evans."

"I need to tend to the reverend," said Dr. Evans.

He signaled for one of the ladies of the church to attend to Miss Weston. He took off his blood-soaked jacket and turned to Reverend Milton. A few men sat the large reverend up slowly, but as they did, blood poured from his eyes, nose, ears, and mouth. Dr. Evans shook his head in dismay. He knelt before the body and felt for a pulse, but he knew that the reverend was dead.

"Ladies and gentleman, the reverend has passed away," he announced to the congregation. Someone placed a tablecloth over the reverend's body.

Dr. Evans returned to Miss Weston's side.

"I think that, based on what came up, both you and the baby ate mostly pralines and very little jambalaya. The sweets should have absorbed a lot of the poison. The charcoal and water will help with whatever else might be in your system. You'll need lots of fluids and bed rest."

"We should do something," Will said as they looked at the crowd from the distance.

Will watched the few elders who still stood before them. They were distracted by what was going on with the reverend.

"There's nothing we can do," Grandmother said. "I think it's…

Before Grandmother could respond further, people shouted and pointed at the roof of the church. Grandmother heard a sad moan fill the air. Wailing echoed from the steeple.

"Stop! Mrs. Milton, don't do it! Somebody do something!" one of the congregation members yelled from the ground below. But no one ran into the church. They all shouted, pointed upward, and watched.

Olivia Milton stood clinging outside of the window of the steeple.

Grandmother looked over at Will with tears rolling down her cheeks. Will fiercely wiped away his own tears.

"Will, I feel so helpless!"

"There's nothing we can do," he said.

Grandmother didn't want to sit and watch like everyone else.

What Grandmother Zenobia wanted to do was summon a great wind to catch Olivia Milton. She wanted to conjure a wandering soul to pull the distraught woman back into the church. She wished the church would shake her friend back inside the tower. There were many things Zenobia could do, if only she wasn't so emotionally attached to Olivia. The people around her were a distraction. To exercise great power, she needed time. She needed to draw power circles on the ground. She needed turtle bones and chanting. She needed many things, most of which were not at her disposal as she sat in her carriage. She could use her raw, uncontrolled power, but her actions would make a scene. Her magic would draw more unwanted attention, which would make things bad for her and Will. She would be the scary witch people believed her to be, not the upstanding citizen of the community she wanted to be.

Zenobia envied Guardian Angels. In times of trouble, no matter what they wanted to do, how much they wanted to intervene, they obediently stood by until called upon. When called upon, they created miracles.

Olivia Milton turned her face up to the bright sun in the cloud-speckled Southern sky. She outstretched her hands as if giving an offering, and jumped.

Grandmother and Will embraced, not wanting to watch as her friend fell. No matter how many mortals she met, she was compassionate when some of them suffered. Grandmother's headache disappeared as soon as she heard the sickening crunch and thud of Olivia's body hitting a wooden picnic table. Her bloody body rolled to the ground as the congregation cried, shouted, and wailed.

"Take us home," Grandmother said.

As Will guided their carriage away, they heard Baby Cora's squeals in the distance. Grandmother smelled lavender on her hands, and she wanted to cry.

"Today's lesson was to not judge others, like the reverend, and to be generous to others," said Grandmother. The potluck had turned out to be much more than they'd expected.

Chapter 2/All Grown Up

August 23, 1889

Syeira, my love,

Please see me tomorrow night right after sunset. I can't go much longer without seeing your beautiful face. My heart burns for you.

Love always, Will.

WILL SIGHED DEEPLY. HE PERCHED on the edge of the porch of his Louisiana home, thinking about the day. After all of the drama at the church potluck, he didn't want to just let life happen to him.

"Ahy, I can't keep doing the same thing day in and day out, every day," he said to Grandmother's favorite dog. The tan-and-white basenji sat at his feet obediently.

Not a single word had been spoken between them on the ride home. After they arrived, both Will and Grandmother changed into more comfortable clothes. Grandmother replaced her big pink hat and church clothes with her favorite dark-purple turban, soft cotton housedress, and apron. Will was overjoyed to kick off his dress shoes. It was wonderful to be comfortable again.

He was free to be barefoot. He almost danced after he put on his favorite button-up shirt and pants.

In the silence, he thought over and over about how he needed to make a big change. He didn't want to do the same things over and over, stuck on Grandmother's farm. The change would include the love of his life, and he didn't want to wait any longer.

Will slipped his hands into a pair of heavy leather gloves. He whistled four short notes three times and held out his right arm. A small brown peregrine falcon who sat on top of a nearby oak tree answered his call. It flew at record speed until it landed, digging its sharp talons into Will's leather glove. The basenji hid under a wooden rocking chair, away from the predator.

"Hello, Miss Bennet, thank you for joining me," Will said.

With a great deal of effort, he tied his love note onto the leg of the falcon with a scarlet ribbon from Grandmother's sewing basket. Grandmother had taught Will that birds of prey generally weren't good messenger birds. Sure, they were fast and could do amazing tricks in the sky, but the large birds were better at hunting prey than recognizing people or targets. Miss Bennett was an exception. When she was just a few years old, she'd ended up on Grandmother's porch with a broken leg. Will (with Grandmother's help) nursed the bird back to health. Miss Bennett, along with various other kinds of animals and birds in the vicinity, had taken a liking to Grandmother and Will.

"I am so lucky to have found the girl of my dreams," he said to the bird as it squawked at him. "I found my mate, kind of like you and Mr. Darcy." Will glanced up at the oak tree that Miss Bennet had left. A larger, male peregrine falcon eyed him.

Will was head over heels in love with an exotic, raven-haired gypsy girl named Syeira. More often than not, he found himself daydreaming about their whirlwind romance. They would meet at their secluded hideaway in a bayou. Anyone who stumbled across the area saw only a thick gathering of trees. Will was proud of his secret, even if it was just an old, abandoned shack. He guessed that it had probably been used as a hideout for lost or injured soldiers during the Civil War. For Will and Syeira, the single small room was their personal sanctuary. They shared their fears, dreams, and ideas about life.

Will tried to clear his head. He released the falcon, sending her on her way. His daydreaming wouldn't fade away.

"I wonder if Romeo and Juliet would have lived happily ever after if they'd just used birds to talk to each other," Will said, mostly to himself.

He squinted his hazel-brown eyes as he watched the female falcon fly off into the distance in the afternoon sun, jealous that it would be touched by Syeira's soft, warm hands. He hoped that she was having a much better day than his. Little did Will know that birds would not have saved the famous star-crossed lovers, nor would they save him.

As Will continued to dream about Syeira, Grandmother's dog came out from the safety of the rocking chair. He interrupted Will's thoughts with sloppy dog kisses.

"Should we find something to eat, Ahy?" he asked the dog as if it were his best friend.

He was the only animal on the property that Grandmother had named herself. Will had named the rest of the animals after characters in books he read. The dog wagged his tail and jumped up, trying to lick his face again. He scratched the dog's head, stood up, and stretched.

Will decided he was done wasting precious time. His heart was set. He loved Syeira. She was a real treasure. Life with her was all he thought about, especially today. After Mrs. Milton jumped to her death, he was painfully aware that life was short. There were no guarantees. Grandmother constantly nagged him to save money from his job for a faraway, distant future. Now he understood that every dime he had saved would be for him and Syeira.

"What if my distant future is now? With my girl?" he said.

At first, being together would be a little rough, but he would do everything in his power to always make her happy.

Ahy wagged his tail playfully and scratched at the door, insisting he be let inside.

"All right, all right, we're going inside."

Will gently opened a squeaky screen door, and Ahy scrambled inside. As he closed the front door, he noted a slight drop in temperature. He didn't know how, but Grandmother's home always managed to block out the Southern humidity. When Will turned toward the kitchen, however, his knees started to shake.

"My next challenge is to talk to Grandmother about Syeira," he said to himself. The dog growled back at him as if he had heard.

The idea terrified him. He could talk to Grandmother about books, the farm, what he saw in town, and so on. But this was different. He valued her opinion and wanted to make sure he made a smart choice. Grandmother was very set in her ways. She was also very wise. Surely she would have the best advice for Will about what to do with his life.

How can I talk to Grandmother and not sound foolish? He was driving himself insane with all the thoughts that bounced around in his head.

Will did his best to remember what was true in his heart. As he stepped into the kitchen, he encountered savory scents that made his mouth water. Other than praline cookies, he hadn't had a bite of food all day and his stomach now reminded him of it. He crept up to the kitchen entrance.

Grandmother hummed to herself as she prepared dinner. Her gumbo took time; all of its flavors needed to marinate awhile before it turned into a pot of deliciousness. To make sure every meal was to her satisfaction, she always used the freshest ingredients. Will was usually summoned to run to the market at sunrise, because Grandmother liked to create culinary delights early in the day. Even after the tragedy of this day, Will knew that dinner would be as tasty as ever. He preferred Grandmother's gumbo to anyone else's food any day of the week.

She had already started with her roux when Will came in. She mixed flour and oil in a large cast-iron pot to create a savory sauce. It was a light-tan color, but she would stir relentlessly until it transformed into a dark, chocolate-looking sauce.

Without looking over her shoulder, Grandmother sensed Will.

"Yes?" she asked.

Will was frozen with fear. He cleared his throat and looked down at his feet.

"Speak up."

"Nothing, ma'am."

"I heard you saying something to Ahy when you were outside. Is he okay?"

Grandmother was the only family Will had, and he loved her very much. He wasn't sure why, but he couldn't shake off his panic. His heart pounded in his chest. He couldn't stand still for fear of dropping to his knees. He shuffled from side to side, causing the hardwood floor to creak underneath his feet.

"He's fine. You know how I like to talk to all the animals around here."

Grandmother continued to stir the roux, watching its color turn to a medium brown, making sure it wouldn't burn.

"I see." Grandmother focused on the hot liquid in front of her. "Would you mind going back outside and putting out the red slipper? I was thinking that although I couldn't help Olivia, maybe there's a chance somebody might come by looking to receive a blessing or two. I'd be happy to do some readings, if anyone passes by."

Every so often, Will watched people stop by Grandmother's house to get spiritual advice. He knew she preferred that people schedule appointments with her, but she did offer open hours for readings in her prayer room. When a ruby-red slipper was displayed on top of a wooden fencepost outside the entrance to her home, people were welcomed on Grandmother's property. If the slipper wasn't displayed for people to see, no one was allowed without an invitation. Trespassers were dealt with harshly.

"Yes, ma'am," Will said. He grumbled to himself as he exited the house. He grabbed the red slipper that sat in a basket on the porch, and dragged his feet all the way to the wooden fence.

"She could have done this herself," Will said. "She could walk out here and put out the stupid shoe."

Will spun around when he heard Ahy yodel at him from the porch. He thought he'd see Grandmother standing back with her hands on her hips, waiting to scold him for mouthing off. He was relieved when he saw it was just the dog, still waiting to be fed.

I don't know why I'm so scared to talk to her. Just because everyone around town is scared of her doesn't mean she's scary.

The locals whispered that Grandmother Zenobia did things no other person could do. They feared her because they didn't know where she came from or how long she had been in Carrefour Parish. There were no local folk named Jalio. They say that one day she just appeared, seemingly out of nowhere, and had a home built on several acres of land. According to her, the land had belonged to "her people." They believed that if anyone crossed Grandmother, bad things would happen. And, just as surely, that if anyone asked her for blessings or healing, she could help. Good or bad, there would always be a price.

When the red slipper was out, Grandmother made a small profit from their hopes and fears.

Will believed she had a few psychic abilities, and that she was fantastic at intimidating people, when she wanted to. Supposedly she cast spells on people, but he thought they were parlor tricks. He wasn't allowed in her prayer room, and was scolded for laughing at customers who came to her for help. This past week he had seen the lady who played the organ at church sneak by the side of the house for a reading. She was so worried about being seen at Grandmother's house that she didn't watch where she walked and twisted her ankle when she left. Honestly, he didn't care about whatever nonsense went on. If people were foolish enough to pay Grandmother to tell them stories and to scare them a bit, so be it. It made him sad, though, that the same people she welcomed into her home avoided her in public places. She could be a warm and loving person when given the chance.

Will trudged back to the house. Once inside, he snuck Ahy a piece of meat from the icebox in the kitchen. It wasn't time yet to feed the animals around the farm, but the dog was insistent on a treat.

Will believed his fear had faded until he looked at Grandmother. He watched her hum while she cooked.

She looked content doing what she loved. Butterflies filled his stomach. He needed to talk to her.

"May I help you cut up some vegetables or something?" he asked nervously, and shooed away a few chickens, who also loitered in the kitchen. His hands were sweaty and starting to shake a little. He plunged them into his pockets, trying to calm them.

Grandmother never turned away from the hot stove. She constantly stirred her roux.

Will was still terrified to have a sit-down with Grandmother.

He was not good with people, and neither was she, really. However, he needed her opinion about Syeira and his future. Syeira was everything to him, and he wanted to make sure he was planning to do the right thing. He also wanted to make sure the girl didn't trick or take advantage of him.

Will thought about Syeira and her beautiful emerald eyes again. Their first kiss had been magical. One lazy summer afternoon, while he was teaching her how to fish in the bayou, Syeira simply leaned over and softly kissed him. He was electrified! He had never kissed a girl before. Every hair on the back of his neck had stood up and his ears buzzed when her soft pink lips pressed against his. There might have even been a blue spark, not that he could prove it.

It has to be true love! It just has to be… he believed. If it were some cheap trick, he would just die. That kind of deception would break his heart.

Choosing to be with a gypsy girl could have bad results, but with some luck and a prayer or two, maybe not. Both he and Grandmother were aware that racial tension in the South grew every day. Every time he went into the French Quarter, there was talk of the whites accusing a black man of doing something wrong. There were reports of black men missing, only to be found days later, hanging like rotting fruit from a tree.

But he was clever and minded his own business. He was practically invisible. An errant thought poked relentlessly at the bubble of love around his heart: marrying a girl who wasn't black—marrying a gypsy— would change all that…and quickly. The people of Carrefour Parish loved to gossip.

Will believed that Grandmother would be honest with him. She always stood by the truth, whether it was scary, wonderful, painful…in the end, it was still the truth.

"Will!" Grandmother snapped at him.

"Sorry."

"What's gotten into you? I feel you stalking me like some skinny bear that hasn't eaten for months."

Will shrugged.

"I know the last thing you want to do is help in the kitchen. I should make you cut up some onions just to toy with you, but your energy would mess up my gumbo. The trinity of celery, onions, and green peppers should be chopped with love." She tapped her spoon on the pot three times as she spoke.

Will only cleared his throat, pushing Grandmother's patience further.

"What do you want? Speak up when you talk to me."

Will took a deep breath and walked closer to Grandmother. For some reason, language escaped him. The best he could manage was a weird, moaning "uuuuuhhhh."

"I'm glad I didn't stop stirring my roux," she mumbled. "Nothing's gonna ruin my gumbo."

She added chicken stock along with the trinity, and stirred it a few more times before adding chicken, andouille sausage, and ham.

"Hand me my large spice jar," she said without looking at her grandson. She tossed in a huge chunk of butter and a few cloves of garlic. She switched hands and continued to stir.

Will obeyed.

Her large metal spoon never stopped as she added copious amounts of her secret spice to her creation.

Once satisfied that her gumbo wouldn't burn if left unattended, she tasted her creation. Will liked that she nodded with approval. When she stepped back from the large pot and turned her full attention toward her grandson, his heart fluttered like the wings of a hundred hummingbirds. He clutched his chest, hoping his heart wouldn't burst.

"Grandmother, I am very very very very very much in love with a special girl," he finally said.

Grandmother unconsciously retreated a few steps from the tone of Will's response.

"She means the whole world to me, Grandmother. I would be so thankful for your advice. I don't think I could live without her. But I can't live without you, either. You are my family. I trust you with my life. I love her so much. Did I mention that?" The words poured from Will's lips.

"What?" Grandmother's sharp tone did not ease Will's nervousness at all.

"Nothing. Never mind..." Will looked down at his bare feet, defeated.

"I'm confused. You met someone? And what? Do you need something?"

"It's just, well, my girl, she ain't from…"

"She isn't from," Grandmother said. She always corrected his language when she got impatient with him.

"Yes, ma'am. She isn't from around here and people might not like us being together. If you were in my place, what would you do? I have never felt this way about anyone."

"Okay. I need you to slow down. Take a breath."

"Yes, ma'am."

"So you are telling me you have a sweetheart?"

Will nodded obediently.

"Who is she? Where did you meet her?"

"Grandmother, she is just…wonderful. Her name is Syeira. The first time we met was at the French Market, back in February."

Grandmother settled in and listened to the story of Will's first encounter with a girl named Syeira. She noted that he was very animated. He was usually stiff, and low key. Standing before her, her grandson seemed taller. He waved his hands around. His voice was a little higher, and he spoke quickly.

I was at the usual stall toward the back of the market, helping Mr. Carmichael put out cakes and cookies to sell that morning. He noticed we were missing the loaves of French bread, so he went back to fetch more.

While he was gone, I saw a girl with green eyes across the way. I have never seen eyes that green before. They stopped me in my tracks. She was looking at bracelets and scarves. There was something special about how she moved. It was as if she was dancing; her body slowly rocked from side to side even though there was no music. For a minute, I forgot where I was. Then she looked up at me and smiled. I thought I would fall out, right there. I hadn't thought she'd seen me. People don't seem to notice me in general, which I like.

I guess I was staring too hard at her, because one of the Rayford sons, Rufus, the short fat one, saw me watching her. He came right at me and said I had no business looking at some girl. He told me that 'I should get my life together.' He offered me a job working for his family on their tobacco farm. I said no thank you to his offer and that I liked working for Mr. Carmichael at the bakery.

Rufus was in a nasty mood. I could smell whiskey on his breath when he talked. He kept saying his family needed strong black men such as myself to work for them. Mr. Carmichael still hadn't returned and I didn't know what to do. Rufus came up real close to me and said that if I didn't volunteer to work for him, he would find some other means to get me out there. Slavery or no slavery, he would find a way to make me work on my hands and knees in those tobacco fields. His face was red, and spit flew out of from his flabby mouth when he spoke.

The next thing I knew, the girl with the green eyes shows up and stands right next to me. She was shorter than I expected. She smelled nicer than I expected, too. She poked Rufus with her finger, square in his chest, and said to him, 'Don't you talk to this man like that. He said he doesn't want to work for you. Nobody does.'

Rufus was just as surprised as I was. The girl was so bold. She should not have been talking to a man like that, but she didn't care. Her black curly hair bounced when she shook her head at him. Rufus started to threaten her, saying nasty things about what he wished he could to do her behind closed doors.

It felt like everyone stopped and watched what was going on.

I swear that for moment I lost my mind. I couldn't stand for any of it. I yelled back at him, and told him to leave her alone.

I stood between her and Rufus when I spoke my mind. I was so scared, until I felt her touch my back. Then I was ready to let him have it! I mean it! I don't know how to fight, and I didn't care. I was gonna defend this girl at any cost. Rufus started to back off. I didn't know that her brothers were behind me too, in case things got out of hand. Mr. Carmichael finally showed up. He brought Officer Bodie with him. Officer Bodie warned Rufus to stop threatening people to work for his family. He said everyone knew his father Lawrence was an upstanding citizen in the community and would hire people fairly. It would be a shame to ruin the Rayford name, and even worse to get an ass-whooping from the fine folk that stood around him. Rufus mumbled something and Officer Bodie told him to move along before he arrested him for being a public nuisance.

I was shaking like a leaf, but I introduced myself to the green-eyed girl. Her name is Syeira. Her family is new to Carrefour Parish and that day was the first time she visited the French Market. Her voice is soft and sweet. Mr. Carmichael offered her and her brothers one of my pineapple *upside-down cakes as a way of saying thank you for trying to keep the peace. He gave Officer Bodie some pound cake too.*

I had never felt so scared and so brave as I did that day. After that, Syeira would come by our stall at the market almost every day. She loves my pineapple upside-down cake more than anything else. I always feel so excited and nervous when she's around. I love her and I want to be with her all the time."

Will didn't notice his hands clutched to his chest, nor his enormous smile that lit up his face.

"I've never seen you this carried away about anything," Grandmother said as she covered her mouth. She tried her best not to laugh at his sappy words and sing-song tone.

"Grandmother, please don't laugh at me. I'm very serious about this girl," Will said. He winced as though she'd struck him.

"I'm sorry. I've never seen you wound up like this before. I wish you would have told me about Rufus Rayford sooner. He's the laziest man I've ever met. He's only trying to get folks to work for him because he's too lazy to work for his father. I'd like to give him a piece of my mind."

"That's why I didn't tell you about it when it happened. I wanted to be a man and deal with it myself. Plus, Officer Bodie was there. He's one of the good ones."

Grandmother studied Will's face, and considered his story before she spoke.

"All right, let me take a really good look at you," she said.

"Yes, ma'am."

"I'm checking to see if you have been affected by a love potion or spell, okay? Sometimes ladies will sneak cheap potions to catch a good man."

"I don't think she…"

"Have you felt any dizziness, or headaches?"

"No, ma'am."

Grandmother placed her hands heavily on Will's face.

"Stick out your tongue," she ordered.

Will obeyed.

She pawed at his face a bit, poked and prodded him.

"Look up at the ceiling," she demanded. "Let me see the whites of your eyes. Oftentimes when people drink potions, their eyes turn yellow and their pupils dilate."

"Dilate?" Will didn't like the sound of that at all.

"Their eyes get really big and dark. Now look down," she ordered again.

Will looked down at his nose.

"When large doses of love potions are given, there's also delirium and hallucinations. People get loopy in the head and see things."

"I have been daydreaming about her a lot," Will admitted.

"Now look left and then right." She took a close look at his eyes, which were clear and focused.

Will did as he was told, and then looked at Grandmother. He noticed a few gray hairs poking out from underneath her cloth turban. Then he looked directly into Grandmother's face. He didn't remember the last time he'd looked at her like that – boldly into her dark-brown eyes.

She stared back at him, no smile across her lips. She looked tired and, judging by the redness in the corners of her eyes, as if she had been crying about Olivia.

Grandmother raised one eyebrow, never blinking. Will swore he saw something more. He knew it was his grandmother who stood before him, but as she looked back, she was someone else. It was the way she looked back at him that scared him. He couldn't put his finger on it. He didn't recognize this person. She was someone powerful, magnificent, and terrifying. The small voice in his head whispered softly that she was much more than his fussy Grandmother.

The floorboards of the house vibrated softly until Will and Grandmother broke their gaze.

"Did you feel that?" Will asked as he looked around nervously.

"Feel what?"

"The floor…what was that?"

Grandmother smirked.

"It's just the house settling. It does that sometimes."

Will started to question what he knew about Grandmother. *Could she do more than see someone's future by looking at chicken bones or the palms of their hands? Could she do more magic than silly parlor tricks in her prayer room? That would be weird.*

"Um, you know that story about you and Madame Laveau? That didn't really happen, did it?" asked Will. He looked at the floor when he spoke.

"What story?" asked Grandmother as she checked Will's fingernails.

"There's that story everyone tells about when you and Mama, when she was a little girl, had afternoon tea with Madame Laveau and her daughter, in the French Quarter. They say you all sat for hours with the Queen of Voodoo, sharing stories and laughed loudly. They say your waiter was rude and tried to rush you out of the outdoor café. They say he insisted that other customers had waited too long for a table. They say you stared at the waiter in disbelief because he spoke to you all with a disrespectful tone. Madame Laveau waved him off like he was an annoying fly. They say Mama and Mademoiselle Marie laughed and pointed at him."

"Oh really?" Grandmother Zenobia rolled her eyes. "Is that what they say?"

Will thought about the story he was recalling to Grandmother. *Nah, it can't be true, it's a silly story. People like stories. I don't know what I was thinking. There's nothing weird about Grandmother.*

"Yes! It's what they say," Will continued, with a melodramatic tone. "People swear they know someone who knew someone else who actually witnessed everything. The waiter turned to call his boss, when suddenly he clutched his chest, made a strange squeaking sound, and fell down dead on the spot. They say you continued your conversation as if the waiter had never existed."

"Well that's some story, all right."

"Yeah, I didn't think it was true, right?" Will winked at Grandmother.

Grandmother didn't answer him. Instead she poked his stomach.

Will's nervousness rushed back.

"Grandmother, why are you so serious? Am I sick? Maybe that girl did poison me. Maybe I'll never find real love. What if there's no cure?"

"Did you eat any of the food at the potluck?" she asked.

"No, Grandmother. I only had the pralines that we brought."

"I see."

Grandmother stepped away from Will. She added more butter to the large, steamy pot and stirred it around a bit before turning the temperature lower for the gumbo.

She tapped her wooden spoon three times for good luck before turning her attention back to Will.

For an older woman, she moved lightly across the hardwood floor. She then settled at the handcarved wooden kitchen table.

"Sit with me, Will."

Will sat next to Grandmother and tried desperately not to fidget. Grandmother looked thoughtfully at the young man.

"Stop slouching."

"Yes, ma'am."

Grandmother's interrogation commenced.

"So, this girl, where is she from?"

"Like I said, I met her at the French Market a few months ago."

"Where is her family from?"

"I don't know. She said something about growing up in Texas. Her family moves around a lot."

"Is she respectable?"

"Yes, ma'am," Will answered as he stared at his hands. He wasn't ready to look at Grandmother again. He wasn't ready to hear that he had been poisoned. He didn't want to die from a broken heart.

"Is she having your baby?"

Will looked shocked at Grandmother's bluntness. His nervous behavior stopped dead.

"No, ma'am. We haven't done that yet."

Will regretted having this conversation. He squirmed as though his skin crawled, embarrassed that Grandmother had brought up sex.

I NEED TO KNOW THE TRUTH he yelled at himself. He drew in a deep breath to calm himself and sat up taller in his chair as courage began to awaken within him. He looked Grandmother directly in the eyes and no longer wavered.

"Grandmother, I respect your opinion. Just tell me the truth. Did she poison me? Am I going to get through this? If it's all a trick, I swear to you, I will die of a broken heart. I'm very serious about this girl. We're sitting here now, talking about her, because I wanted to know what you think I should do. I feel strong and secure when I'm around her. My heart says I need to be with her, no matter what her family says. I know in time I could provide for her. We would be very happy together. Being with her is different. I know I can be anybody I want to be. I can do anything I want to do and not be judged because I'm black."

Grandmother stared at Will. She reached out and held his hands.

"You haven't been poisoned. It's worse."

"Worse?"

"Honey, you are in love," Grandmother laughed. "You're all grown up, right before my eyes. You're a hardworking, smart young man. I have always known that you could be anything you want to be. It was a matter of time before you knew it too."

Will noticed Grandmother relax her shoulders and sit back in her chair. She nodded slightly. Her eyes twinkled when she looked back at him. Whatever residual nervousness fluttered around in Will's body faded away.

"I give you my blessing. You have searched your heart and you know that this girl makes you happy. Being the good person you are, I think she'll respect you. As long as you take care of her and respect her as well, there is nothing on the face of this earth that can come between you two. Love is a powerful force." Grandmother got up and moved away from the table. "I have to do something for you."

She walked down the hallway, passing Will's bedroom on the right, the bathroom on the left, and the small prayer room where she performed readings for clients from time to time. She continued into her bedroom at the end of the hall.

Things had turned out better than Will had hoped. He could hardly wait to see Syeira. It would have been horrible if he had been poisoned. Will shuddered at the idea of the disgusting remedies Grandmother would have made for him had it been true.

She must be looking for her Bible that she usually keeps in the living room area. I bet she's going to say a big blessing, he thought. He heard the footsteps of her basenji and other furry friends as they followed obediently behind her.

Grandmother Zenobia's bedroom was the largest room in the house. A rainbow-colored pile of blankets draped her huge bed. Countless decorations clung to the walls, different-sized glass jars, dusty figurines, and ornate religious items were stuffed on shelves, and trinkets were shoved in every corner. The knickknacks circled all around, including stained-glass stars that hung from the ceiling overhead. A large, shiny black ceramic urn secured with thick rope sat precariously by her bedside. Things fell, thudded, and rattled as she rummaged through her closet.

Will giggled to himself when he heard her growl in frustration.

"Aha!" Grandmother cheered.

To her satisfaction, Grandmother found exactly what she wanted and placed it in the pocket of her apron.

She came out of her room and returned to her seat next to Will. He liked that she smelled like cinnamon, regardless of what she cooked. For a moment, Will found it unsettling that the footsteps of dogs, ducks, a raccoon, an occasional goat, and other animals in her entourage were heard on the hardwood floor, but that Grandmother never made a sound as she walked around their home. Will was not sure how old Grandmother was, but she moved comfortably in her body. She always wore a hat or turban to hide her thick, nappy hair, and complaints about aches and pains were never heard in her house. Talk of old age was not allowed.

He watched her neatly manicured hands (which also seemed ageless) as she carefully placed a small purple velvet box in front of him. Will opened it slowly. A simple ring, a gold band with roses carved on the sides, glowed as it pressed against soft velvet.

"This was your mother's ring," she said.

She fought back the emotions that tried to escape. Will's eyes welled up too. He'd never gotten to know his mother, Angelica. Grandmother had a few photographs and pictures of her. His favorite image of his mother was a self-portrait Angelica had sketched, but it wasn't a good substitute for the real person.

"This girl, Sara?"

"Her name is Syeira."

"Keep her honest."

"Yes, ma'am."

"Have you met her parents?"

"Not yet."

"Then you need to get right on that. You have to ask her father's permission to marry her."

"I didn't think about that."

"You know what? I have a better idea! Invite them over here! I need to meet her people anyway. We could have a nice dinner together. How big is her family?"

"I'm not sure."

"Well, we can figure all of that out, before the wedding."

"Wedding?"

"Oh Will, it'll be wonderful. Obviously Reverend Milton can't do it, but maybe the associate pastor can perform the ceremony. We could have the reception in the French Quarter. I know a few people who would lend us a spot."

"Reception?"

"Will, you have to make this girl your wife before her folks think you are up to no good. When she says yes, and she better say yes if she knows what's good for her, start planning a specific future together. Make a real plan. No daydreams of 'somedays'. Make me proud. Give this ring to your bride-to-be, with my blessing."

Grandmother sat for a moment and looked up to the ceiling as if looking for an answer to a question she'd asked privately. Then she continued, "As a wedding gift, I would like to give you a portion of my land. The two of you could start your new life with a solid foundation."

"You mean it, Grandmother?"

"Of course! I would do anything for family. Plus, we wouldn't be too far away from each other. You and your girl could come over whenever you wanted."

"You'd be okay living here all alone?" As Will spoke, he realized the weight of his words. Not only was he worried about a future with Syeira, but he was also worried about leaving Grandmother all alone.

"I'm never truly alone. Ahy will always be at my side."

Sure enough, her dog was at her side as they spoke.

"Have you counted how many critters we have wandering around here? I am perfectly fine in my house with all these animals and such," she joked. "You have your own path to follow. We will always be family and I will always love you. Nothing could ever change that. Don't worry about me. Besides, after you get married, grandkids are sure to follow."

Will froze in his seat.

This is too much to take in. I simply want to live my life, with Syeira.

Will wanted to tell Grandmother to slow down. He needed to take things one step at a time. But instead he sat as she rattled on. He watched his grandmother chat excitedly about what it would be like to be a great-grandmother. She waved her hands around and laughed a lot while she spoke. She wasn't guarded or serious. She was excited about Will's future, and the idea of having more family around.

He waited until he thought she was done, or at least at a good place for him to interrupt her.

"Thank you, Grandmother. I love you and everything that you do for me."

"I love you too, Will."

Will hugged her, and then he pulled on an old pair of shoes.

"Where are you going?"

He knew she watched closely as he ran into the kitchen and frantically searched around.

"I have to get things together for when I see Syeira tomorrow! I can't wait another moment. Do we have a…"

Grandmother held out a large burlap bag, stopping him in his tracks.

"Be grateful that these summer days are so long," Grandmother said. "And while you are out, remember to stop by the post office and get my mail."

"Yes, ma'am."

Every month, in addition to letters she got from folks around town, she received a letter or package with no return label. Sometimes there were colorful, foreign-looking stamps on them. Will was forbidden to open any of them. He knew that sometimes they contained money, sometimes not. She made it abundantly clear that whatever appeared was for her eyes only.

Will rushed toward the front door.

"And after dinner, I will need you to take a bowl of gumbo to Dr. Evans and a note. I would rest easier knowing if Miss Weston and that little baby are okay."

"Yes, ma'am," he shouted as he ran outside.

"Will?" she shouted after him.

"Yes, ma'am?" Will stopped even though he was losing patience with Grandmother.

"At the first sign of trouble, you come straight home," she warned. "I mean it."

"Yes, ma'am." He nodded hastily. "Anything else? I need to go before it gets too dark. Like I said, I have lots to do before seeing my girl."

"I'll leave you alone," said Grandmother. "Godspeed."

Will watched Grandmother escape the warm air, slipping back into her cool home. She chuckled at Will's excitement.

Once Will had run off, Grandmother returned to her steamy pot waiting for her on the old stove. She reflected on the all the events of the day.

"Ahy," she said to the basenji at her feet, "I am absolutely heartbroken by Olivia's death. She was my only real friend, other than you." She sighed. "But I am grateful for Will. I can't believe he's in love! I hope the young lady feels the same way. I imagine that I'll have more family members in no time!" Ahy wagged his tail while she spoke. She patted him on the head and gave him, along with a few other members of the furry entourage, snacks from the cupboard. After she shooed away a raccoon that lingered too long for more treats by her feet, she hummed her favorite tune and turned back to making dinner.

Chapter 3/The Princess

SYEIRA CAMLO WAS A PETITE, headstrong girl. She usually got her way with whatever she wanted. Except when it came to rest. Sleep had not been a friend of hers over the past few nights. She was tired and irritable. Over the past week, her parents had pestered her constantly about her choosing a husband. She loved Will, but didn't know how to approach her parents about him. He was a gadje, an outsider. Until she could solve how to tell them the truth, she avoided them as much as possible. On this Saturday afternoon, she had no desire to spend time with her raucous, chatty cousins (many of whom were already married), and she did not want to be bothered with her daily responsibilities.

She snuck off, away from the tribe, to groom her favorite horse, Lyuba. It was a routine Will had shared with her a few months ago. Luckily for her, it was a pleasant surprise to her father. Syeira despised performing her regular chores and would often persuade someone else to maintain her horse. However, she had developed a new appreciation for caring for her horse after spending time with Will. He had explained to her that tending to Grandmother's horses wasn't really a chore. It was like spending time with friends. He named them Pip and Estella, after characters in one of his favorite books. Talking to them was an escape from loneliness. It grounded him. He told her that the dark, heavy thoughts that weighed upon him from time to time disappeared when he paid attention to a horse's breathing. He whispered his worries away in a horse's ear and the horse stomped them away. After a few ill-fated attempts, Syeira believed his ritual worked for her too. Being around her horse helped her to dismiss the annoyances of the day, and being away from the clusters of family helped her to clear her head.

On the border of the gypsy land was a small grove of trees where most of the tribe's horses were roped off in a makeshift pen. The trees provided shade and protection for the horses from the fickle Louisiana weather. The sun was low in the afternoon sky when she arrived with a brush and treats for her chestnut-colored friend.

As she whispered her troubles softly in Lyuba's ear, she brushed her horse's dark mane. The two of them were content until the horse was distracted. Instinctively, Syeira backed away. Her horse reared up when a brown falcon, with a note tied to its leg, landed on a wooden post next to Syeira. Seeing the scarlet ribbon, Syeira instantly knew the bird had sweet words for her. She carefully retrieved the note and fed an apple to her horse to calm her down.

Traditionally, Gypsy women were illiterate. A handful of the women in the Camlo tribe were an exception. They could read Latin when they wanted to conjure blessings or curses. Learning to read had been bothersome for Syeira until Will read stories to her. She found herself hanging on every word he spoke and insisted he teach her to read and write English.

Syeira's hands trembled with excitement as she read every word of the note slowly and carefully, as Will had taught her. She went over and over and over it until she memorized the letter. Her heart pounded in her chest.

"I miss him so much," she said to both her horse and the bird. Her voice floated away in the sunburned sky.

"Thank you, Miss Bennet," she said to the large bird, and sent her into the summer night. "At least you approve of Will," she joked as her horse nudged her for another treat.

Holding the note close to her heart, she considered her options. She couldn't bear another day of scolding and warnings from her parents about an arranged marriage. Will was her one and only love. After much thought, she made a firm decision.

"Tomorrow, I will declare my love for Will to my parents. I don't care if they banish me from the tribe.

I would welcome the freedom. I only hope he feels the same way. I would do whatever it takes to be with Will."

She left a few more apples for Lyuba and ran back to her tent. Hastily, she began her personal treasure hunt. The gifts she would offer to her parents were already in place, but some were hidden in vases, some in other people's tents, and some safely in trunks buried in secret locations. She needed to collect and organize them all for tomorrow's presentation.

She wished she could send a note back to Will telling him about her plans to make her declaration of love to her parents, but under Will's tutelage she was still learning how to write. There was something strange about this particularly long Saturday. She could not understand why, but in her heart she believed that now was the perfect time to start a new beginning. She wanted to appreciate every moment she could with Will, and she could barely wait for Sunday's sunset.

Sunday morning after breakfast, Syeira entered her parents' noisy tent. It was filled with the laughter and chatter of family and tribal members, enjoying each other's company as they avoided the bright Louisiana sun. Frankincense ticked her nose as she stood near the entryway of the tent, away from the commotion. She wore her favorite green silk dress, and a large copper ankh around her neck, both given to her by her father, and had adorned her curly hair with bejeweled handmade combs from her mother. She hoped they would take her seriously if she presented herself in an elegant but serious manner. As king and queen of their tribe, her parents expected to be treated with respect, especially by their children.

"Father, Mother," she announced carefully. "I have brought you some gifts and I ask for a moment of your time."

Her voice wavered more than she had expected.

Through the business in the tent, Syeira's father could see that his usually playful daughter needed to discuss something serious with them. Her frown suggested there was something that weighed heavily on her heart.

"Leave us. We have an audience with Syeira," he roared.

A messy litter of children and a cluster of adults evacuated the tent. The king's personal guards obediently stood outside the royal tent, keeping watch.

The royal residence had two tents, both of which were large enough to comfortably accommodate twenty adults. The community was very close and relationships were honored. Their homes reflected it. The first tent was perfect for social gatherings. There, Syeira's parents entertained family, spoke to elders, and shared knowledge and customs with little ones. At the entrance, there lay a thick piece of red carpet leading up to a platform that supported two large, overstuffed leather chairs and a hand-carved wooden end table between them. A golden family crest hung between the two chairs. When needed, the king and queen of the tribe would sit nobly to receive anyone who wanted an audience. To the left, there was a large table with several chairs where, once a month, elders discussed affairs of the tribe. Incense smoldered from an ornate bronze centerpiece. The larger secondary tent, which sat behind the first, was the Camlos' personal living space. It was where they had trunks of trinkets, clothes, and books. It was where only immediate family members slept, unless the parents did not want to be disturbed, which was rare.

Once the tent was cleared of onlookers, Syeira's parents officially took their seats. Dorian Camlo was a tall, handsome, muscular man with hazel eyes. As he looked down at his daughter, he smiled. Syeira knew he adored her. They had always been very close, especially when she was younger. He taught her how to make jewelry, something he had learned from his mother. As she grew older, as expected, they spent less time together. He was a strong leader and needed to govern his people justly. She was now a teenager and had her own duties and chores to attend to. But no matter how busy they could be, Syeira knew she'd always have a soft spot in her father's heart.

She watched Dorian run his large, tan hands through his curly, jet-black hair. He turned his attention to his wife, Patia, and watched her struggle to take her seat next to him.

Dorian and Syeira had had many "lively discussions" about Syeira's relationship with her mother. He insisted that she respect her mother as queen of the tribe, even though she didn't love Patia nearly as much as she loved her father.

Trying to bond with her daughter, Patia showed Syeira a few tricks and taught her a few small gypsy spells from time to time. Patia attempted to explain the power and mystery of gypsy magic, but she didn't seem to fully understand what she was talking about. It frustrated Syeira. Eventually, Syeira learned a few sleight-of-hand tricks to make snakes appear from eggs or blood appear in water. She didn't care much for Patia's games, but tolerated the time they spent together for her father's sake. If she needed to make money, she would choose to sell jewelry before she offered palm readings.

Dorian and Syeira continued to watch Patia as she climbed upon her throne. She always fought and fidgeted with her silk scarves, waving them furiously around her. After adjusting and readjusting her long skirt with its many layers, she eventually sat, finally ready to receive her audience. Patia was a few inches shorter than their daughter was and looked out of place next to her statuesque husband.

At first glance, Patia was drab. She was not conventionally beautiful to anyone in the tribe and didn't project much of a personality. Her pale, pinched face always displayed a deep frown, as if she constantly lived in misery and pain. Conversely, she was married to a very respected and honored man who provided her with anything and everything she wanted. It was odd to most people for her to appear to be so miserable. However, if anyone looked too closely at Patia, they would notice that her face would change. Sometimes her nose was too large, or too small. Sometimes one ear was higher on her head than the other. Sometimes her eyes were set too close together, or too far apart. Once, one eye was much larger than the other, and the colors didn't quite match. Sometimes her skin was alabaster and sometimes it was ruddy, no matter the season. Every so often, it would take on a light, greenish hue. Her face constantly changed on its own.

No one spoke of it, but there was definitely something unnatural about Patia's looks. Syeira figured some spell had probably backfired on her, causing her disfigurement. Patia seldom spoke to anyone without being addressed first, so she avoided as many people as she could, and they in turn avoided her.

Patia sat hunched over on her throne. She had no real interest in whatever her daughter was up to, but nodded that she was nonetheless ready to hear whatever Syeira had to say.

Syeira respectfully approached the pair as king and queen of her tribe, rather than her parents, and bowed deeply before them. Without a word, she presented a large basket, revealing their favorite snacks, a silk scarf, scented soaps, and, to Dorian's surprise, his favorite treat of all, Tokaji wine. The wine, supposedly consumed and enjoyed by Napoleon himself, was very expensive and hard to get. It was not just any bottle of fermented grape juice; it was wine with a regal and glorious history. Syeira never shared how she'd acquired it specifically, but knew her father would be secretly proud of her and her brothers. The proprietor of the Napoleon House, on Chartres street, didn't regularly check their inventory, especially dusty, forgotten items that would never be claimed by Napoleon himself.

With these gifts, Syeira gained their undivided attention.

"To what do we owe this pleasure?" said Dorian cheerfully.

Admittedly, Syeira was his pride and joy. Even at the age of fourteen, Syeira was his little girl, and his favorite child among his handful of sons. Only she had the power to coax a smile from his usually set jaw. Her mother said nothing, but continued to frown and examine the gifts that gleamed at her feet.

"Please accept these gifts with my utmost respect. It is an honor to be your daughter."

Syeira slowly rose from her offering and looked squarely at her parents, resting her hands on her hips. *Just breathe,* she thought. She knew she was about to kill her father's rare, handsome smile.

"I'll keep this short. I am in love with someone who is not one of our people. I demand that you stop your search for my husband. I want to be with him, and nobody else."

Dorian's smile collapsed into a scowl, and he sat taller upon his throne. He'd known something was wrong when his daughter addressed him so formally after everyone left the tent. He already disliked the idea of finding her a husband in the first place, and now she announced she had found someone on her own?

"You *demand*?" Dorian said. "Is this a joke?"

"Who is he? What tribe is he from then?" asked Patia carefully.

"He is a freed Negro, from around here," Syeira announced.

The words crashed down upon them all. Syeira's knees wobbled, but she continued. "I warned you. He isn't one of our people and I don't care. It is my life. I decide which man I want to be with. I love him with all of my heart!" Syeira held her stance, challenging her parents with her words.

She reminded herself to breathe. She knew that once she was done with her parents, she would see Will soon enough.

Dorian Camlo sat quietly, and stroked his beard.

"No," he said simply. "That is not the gypsy way. It's not up for discussion." Dorian's tone was dismissive.

Patia looked over at her husband in disbelief, surprised at his calm demeanor.

Syeira narrowed her eyes as anger flashed through her body. She stomped her feet and balled up her fists in fury.

"But Dati, I ..."

Dorian interrupted her, sitting high on his throne.

"Do not make me raise my voice," he warned.

"But it's my happiness, my life, and I want..."

"It's settled," boomed Dorian, holding up his right hand. "*We* will select your husband tomorrow, or the day after that. You should expect to be married in a week."

Syeira gasped in shock.

"You should be grateful for the freedom and privileges you have had as the daughter of a king! We all know that you should have been married off last year, or the year before. One of your younger brothers is already married! I've been too soft with you."

"You can't tell me what to do!"

"Yes, I can. I am your father. Boldo, Fonso, come in at once," Dorian roared.

The two men who stood guard at the door ran into the tent.

"Escort my daughter to Bee Bee Mirela's tent immediately!"

"No!"

"You will go to your aunt's tent and stay there until we call for you. I forbid you to ever see that Negro man ever again. I curse the day you two met."

"But…"

"The only way is the gypsy way!"

Syeira tried to fight as she was quickly escorted out. Patia dismounted her throne and feverishly examined the gifts from Syeira's offering. Dorian grabbed the bottle of Tokaji and turned, ready to set off in the opposite direction from Syeira.

"Is there anyone in particular you would like for your daughter to wed?" Patia asked, interrupting Dorian's exit.

"No. Find me three available men, and I will choose one for her."

Patia watched Dorian struggle with his anger.

"I trust that you can make this happen. I don't want to banish my daughter from our tribe. She must follow our ways."

"I'll fix this for you, Dorian," Patia assured him.

Dorian stared for a moment at his wife, nodded gratefully, and then stormed out of the tent.

Chapter 4/Just Desserts

ONCE LEFT ALONE, QUEEN PATIA took her time and enjoyed a few of the delicacies from the basket before her. She loved sweets. She was thrilled that Syeira had found her favorite dessert, baklava.

How can I fix this situation? I don't have patience for Dorian when he's upset, she thought as she munched on the small, flaky pastry filled with nuts, cinnamon, and honey. A delicious idea came to her. She could conjure up a curse to keep the Negro away from her daughter. She would have extra time to find three available men to marry Syeira.

Not wanting to share Syeira's offerings with anyone else, Patia snatched up the basket and headed to the family tent. She nibbled on a slice of cake, and saved a second one in her skirt pocket, before searching for a hiding place for her treasures. She stuffed the basket under piles of dirty clothes until she could find a better place to hide it.

She then rummaged around the tent, looking long and hard for something else she had hidden away from the rest of the tribe. Her back ached and sweat rolled down her neck while she hunched over several trunks. She was about to give up when she found what she searched for: a heavy leather-bound tome. It was a large book of spells handed down to her from her own mother. Flipping through the old, worn pages, she found a few spells to her liking, but nothing specific to conjure up. It was times like this that she wished she had paid more attention to what her mother had taught her. She was reminded that women were not allowed to read, as most tribes forbade it. Nevertheless, her mother had tried to teach her to read and write Latin. Only a few of the spell-casters were entitled to dabble in Latin. When she focused, she was almost fluent. After her mother died, she had rarely made an honest effort at it.

The cover page had many scribbles and notes from women, who handed the book down to their daughters when they were ready to pass on tradition. The last inscription was in short, tense letters, addressed to Patia. *"My sweet Chavi Patia, no one will love you the way I love you, Jaelle."*

Patia regretted never telling her mother how much she appreciated what she'd shared with her.

The first chapter of the book had a spell that would turn a man's hair white. She liked the idea, but had no personal effects of the victim to use for the spell. There was one page bookmarked with the tail of a rat. There, she saw a paralysis potion that grabbed her attention, but there was a long list of ingredients and she was too lazy to collect them all. As she continued to rifle through the book, she saw a few pictures that appeared threatening, but the handwriting was hard to make out.

Patia felt foolish. She considered letting the spoiled girl run off. It would be easier to do nothing, but Dorian would not stand for it.

Patia thought about giving up for now and having a snack. She could finish the second slice of cake that rested in her pocket. She could savor more of Syeira's cookies to her heart's content. She mulled over her various options, but found herself staring at Dorian's leather workboats as they stood guard by the opening of the tent. She decided to focus and push forward with finding a spell. She didn't want to face Dorian's rage today.

Patia turned the pages in frustration. In desperation, she went to the last section of the book, where her mother had scribbled a few pictures, rather than write in Latin. To her relief, she found what she needed. There were directions explaining how to systematically create a brand-new spell.

She quietly thanked the heavens. She decided to name her curse the Poltroon Curse! She could create a spell that would make its victim a coward. He would be afraid of his own shadow. Syeira would see how annoying and disgusting he was.

Crab powder was first on her list. Because it came from crabs, she hoped her victim would walk sideways or backward. His strange behavior should embarrass Syeira. Had Patia researched the powder more, she would have realized it reversed spells and hexes.

Horsetail was on the list because when prepared properly, it made a nice pale-green dye for scarves and dresses. She hoped it would give the darker-skinned victim green-colored skin. Horsetail actually secured vows and commitments, assisted with fertility, and strengthened bones.

Patia would steal elderberry wine from one of the men when they were away and add it to the spell. She noticed that when some of the men drank it, they sweated, a lot. The victim would be so nervous and scared around her daughter, he would sweat too, from head to toe.

For good measure, she grabbed a handful of dandelions, simply because they annoyed her. She considered that dandelions would make the victim annoying as well.

There were other items used in basic spells she would collect later, but at the moment she was pleased with the new items for her new spell.

Next, she needed to know where the two lovers met. Her curse would create a small attack of some kind, which would frighten the suitor away from her daughter. Syeira already intimidated many of the young men in the tribe. It was one of the reasons it was so hard to find her a husband – she was bossy and demanding. She always spoke her mind. It was a struggle to get Syeira to do much of anything when she was in a stubborn mood, even when elders in the tribe ordered her.

Quite a few spells called for body parts of bats, but she only had two old, dried bat wings, which she used for her readings in town. She got lots of money from her clients when she revealed the wings in her elaborate presentation. She didn't want to waste them in her new potion, in case the curse didn't work.

Her thoughts were promptly broken up, distracted by the sound of laughter from small children who'd found their way back into the primary tent. As expected, the children annoyed her. The night before, she'd threatened them when they were throwing rocks at the sky. The children insisted that they were trying to hit birds that flew at night. She explained repeatedly that they were wrong. The idea that birds flew at night was ridiculous. When Syeira reminded her before bedtime that many birds, including owls, were nocturnal, Patia dismissed her.

Patia scowled at the memory. More tribe members followed the children back inside the communal tent. She grabbed her notes and went outside, away from the clamor. Looking up at the blue afternoon sky, she remembered seeing a small colony of fruit bats swirl in the sky at sunset. Patia laughed to herself when she finally understood what the children called night birds. Bats so small they could fit in your hand were always out at dusk, every night. She didn't need to waste one of her crusty bat wings, or to kill a bat or two. She just needed to guide the fruit bats to where the lovers met, to scare off the gadje.

The spell would begin when the couple was physically close to one another. It would be triggered once the man openly declared his love for her (whether he lied or not). Syeira had boldly declared her love for the Negro. Surely he would answer her in the same way. Certainly, Patia's spell could get the bats to swoop down upon him. After the attack by bats, the lover would appear weak before Syeira and he would flee the scene. The spell could work. Undoubtedly, his cowardly actions and peculiar behavior would be enough to convince Syeira that her parents had the best in mind for her. There would be no need to banish her from the tribe. Syeira would not be a disgrace to her people. Dorian would be pleased with Patia and all the hard work she'd done.

It seemed to her that the spell, although a bit confusing, should work perfectly. It would also give her a little more time to find her daughter a husband from a successful gypsy family.

Syeira's declaration of disobedience was no surprise to Patia. She should have predicted it and warned Dorian. Patia was secretly thankful that Syeira would be dealt with, married off, and sent away to have a life with new responsibilities. She loved her daughter but did not adore her as Dorian did. He doted on Syeira too much. Jealousy poisoned Patia's thoughts as she considered the possibility that Dorian cared more for Syeira than for anyone else in the tribe. Soon enough, Princess Syeira wouldn't be able to shirk her duties or get away with little things that no one else in the family could. Besides, if Patia couldn't have Dorian's heart, there was no reason her daughter should either.

Patia decided to get the curse in motion. First, it was imperative that Syeira reunite with her lover. She checked to make sure the small lemon cake was still in her pocket, along with notes for her spell.

"Boldo, Fonso," Patia said as she approached Bee Bee Mirela's small tent.

Mirela and her children had gone into town to get supplies. Syeira was alone in the stuffy tent. The men bowed as they stood guard at the entrance.

"King Dorian wanted to thank you for your loyalty. He appreciates all that you do for him. As a token of his appreciation, he wanted you to have a treat."

"Thank you, my queen," they answered obediently.

She could tell they were hungry by the way they eyed the small cake she held before them.

"Take a short break, enjoy yourselves."

"King Dorian was very specific with his orders to guard Princess Syeira, my queen."

Patia stared at the men and cocked her head to the left. Both guards avoided looking directly at her.

"Truth be told, I need to have words with my daughter. I will be just a moment. I am sure my husband would not mind me speaking to our daughter."

"Yes, my queen."

Patia usually bribed the guards with gold coins or furs for their services. Judging by their grumbling stomachs, it had been a few hours since they had eaten.

"I heard they were having some of that chicory coffee at the campfire," she suggested.

The guards reluctantly accepted the cake. Patia patiently watched as they trudged off.

Once the area was clear, she untied the opening of the tent. She did not enter but looked in at her daughter. Syeira had thrown a temper tantrum in her aunt's tent and created a huge mess. Clothing, handmade toys, and shoes littered the tent. Defeated, Syeira sat in the center of the chaos she had created with her face buried in her hands. Patia opened the tent slightly, exposing tempting fresh air, and quietly snuck away, leaving Syeira unattended.

Patia sidled into the tribe's common area, where some tribe members milled around in the hot Southern sun. She did her best to avoid the men she had just dismissed. After looking around, searching the faces of her subjects, she found a scrawny young boy, Gunari. He and his little brother Markos were crafty trackers, trained by Dorian and their father. The Shaw boys ran errands for Patia from time to time. They were always eager to please King Dorian, so they believed doing whatever Patia commanded would somehow honor him.

"Gunari, come here!" Patia snapped.

The scrawny boy came to her immediately and bowed.

"Yes, my queen?" he asked, trying not to show that he was scared to be near her.

"I need you to do me a favor. King Dorian is worried about where Syeira has been wandering off to lately. He needs to know she is safe. We believe she meets with someone we do not approve of. It might be someone dangerous to our tribe."

Gunari grimaced.

"We all hate the idea of Princess Syeira being in danger, yes?"

"Yes," Gunari said, avoiding Patia's gaze.

"Syeira was banished to Bee Bee Mirela's tent, but I bet she won't stay long. Track her once she sneaks off. When she is settled, bring me something from the area. Fill a small bag with dirt, flowers, and grass, whatever. Report back to me her whereabouts, with the bag, as quickly as possible."

"Yes, Queen Patia," Gunari said with a bow. "I'm happy to do anything for you and King Dorian."

She handed Gunari two sugar cookies and he ran off quickly.

Patia knew that, when no one was looking, Syeira would sneak off on her own. Like father, like daughter.

Chapter 5/Reflections

BEE BEE MIRELA WILL BE furious with me when she gets back. I don't care, Syeira thought as she eyed the mess she'd created. Realizing how childish she sounded, she bit her lip. Bee Bee Mirela was Dorian's favorite, closest sister. She was a full-figured woman married to a short, wiry-looking man; the odd-looking couple had many children. She always greeted Syeira with big hugs and kisses. She treated Syeira as if she were her own daughter. She was always honest with Syeira, and hardly ever put up with any of Syeira's bad behavior. Once the guards dumped Syeira into the tent, she'd had a ridiculous temper tantrum. Clothing, shoes, and toys were strewn everywhere. Ashamed at her own behavior, she hid her face in her hands.

How am I going to get out of this?

Aunt Mirela's tent was hot and stuffy. Mirela's musk oil hung heavily in the air, and Syeira couldn't think clearly through her frustration. Instinctively, she reached for anything close to her to throw in anger again, when fresh air tickled her back. Syeira sat up and looked over her shoulder. Quietly, she crawled toward the opening of the tent, expecting to see Boldo and Fonso stare at her.

They were nowhere to be found. A soft summer breeze kissed her face.

"I'm free!" Syeira whispered in a muted squeal. She snuck off into nearby tall grass. Once clear of familiar grounds (as Patia had hoped), Syeira ran off. She ran as fast as her feet would take her, to her home away from home.

"My parents do not understand what is best for me," Syeira said to herself as she continued to creep through tall grass and lurk around trees. "They are too old to remember what love is like."

Syeira tried to calm herself down once she was safe in the shack, but frustration and anger ruled her afternoon. Her normal reaction was to throw things around, but everything she reached for reminded her of Will.

"No, don't throw that book; it's old and one of his favorites, with the hunchback. No, that plate is the only one we have left. No, I made the pink pillow for Will, with the hand-stitched flowers. How could I possibly throw or break anything that Will has given me?"

She stopped and considered what Will would do in this situation. When Will was frustrated, he took quiet moments. He showed Syeira what it meant to have patience. He did not tolerate her flares of anger. He knew she was gypsy royalty, but understood the real person she was, too. Syeira closed her eyes, and held one of Will's favorite sweaters.

Breathe deeply, she thought. *The answer will come. Just breathe, as Will does.* The perfect idea came to her. Take a nap. It was the smartest way to calm her mind and get a fresh perspective.

About half an hour later, she awoke refreshed. Syeira reread the cherished love note she had tucked away. Her mood changed. Excited and hopeful to see Will, she cleaned and decorated their haven with wildflowers.

Unbeknownst to Syeira, the young trackers had been on her trail since she'd broken free from camp. Secretly, silently, the two tracked like wolves searching for large, wounded prey. They watched Syeira arrive at her hideout. Gunari signaled to Markos to lie low in the tall grass. They both observed Syeira until she lay down. When they were certain she was asleep, Gunari grabbed a handful of grass and dirt by the entrance to the shack. When he believed it was safe to leave his little brother as a lookout, he returned to camp. He needed to report to Patia. Time was of the essence. Syeira's location was thirty minutes from the gypsy camp by foot. Once he was clear of the hideaway, he sprinted as fast as his legs would carry him.

Little Markos stayed behind as his brother told him. He hid in the tall dry grass and continued to watch Syeira through a window. She was the most beautiful girl of their tribe. She was also the meanest. He liked how she hummed and danced around once she woke from her nap. Her happiness was infectious.

When the sun hung low in the summer sky, Markos spotted someone on a trail leading into the clearing opposite him. His older brother would be proud of how quiet he was as he hid. The man approaching wore an expensive-looking suit. He marched quickly toward the shack. When the man got close enough, Markos thought he didn't seem dangerous. The man was thin and had dark skin, but he didn't seem scary. The man smiled to himself. He carried pretty flowers, and he hummed a catchy tune, too, which Markos liked. Markos knew not to question Patia but didn't understand what she was worried about.

Back at camp, Gunari sought out Patia to report his findings.

"Queen Patia, may I have a word?" Gunari asked, interrupting Patia as she sewed with other women of the tribe.

Patia sat hunched over a quilt, not making much eye contact or conversation with the others in the women's community tent. Located centrally to the campground, it was where the women gathered daily to sew, get advice, and gossip. Gunari was uncomfortable in the women's tent. He shifted his weight from side to side, anxious to get out.

"What do you want?" she snapped, not looking up to see who addressed her.

"I have what you wanted," he said.

Patia perked up and looked at Gunari. He thought she attempted to smile at him.

"Excellent."

Patia pulled him aside, away from the other women. Gunari handed her the bag of dirt and grass. He leaned away from her as best he could. When she spoke, her breath smelled like rotting fruit.

"I found your daughter in the bayou. Markos is there now, keeping watch. I made a map of her location." Gunari fished out a crumpled piece of paper from his pocket. It had rudimentary drawings of where the shack was located. Patia snatched the map.

"You are dismissed for now," Patia said, reaching into her pocket. She held out her hand. When she opened her crooked, claw-like fingers, she revealed a shiny coin for Gunari.

The boy scampered away, relieved to get out of the tent of women, and away from Patia.

Chapter 6/The Curse

CREEPING BACK INTO HER OWN tent, Patia noticed Dorian was still absent. She gleefully gathered her notes for her personalized hex and a burlap sack. The contents of the bag included strands of Syeira's hair wrapped carefully in a handkerchief, grain, ingredients for her potion (including the stolen bottle of elderberry), candles, chicken bones, and a rabbit in a wicker cage. She was armed with everything needed for her dark magic.

She went out alone. She walked until she lost sight of the tents – she made sure she couldn't hear the voices of her people. She passed by a few trees and shrubs and continued until she found herself in a field of grass. Once certain she would not be disturbed, she prepared her potion and created a small shrine.

She drew a large circle around herself with grain. She knew she should have used salt, but grain was easier to take without anyone noticing. She lit a few stubby candles around her. She knew she needed new, fresh ones, but she assumed that the ones she had were okay. Whatever residual energies they held might work with her haphazard spell. She sprinkled the potion she'd mixed together with Syeira's hair, a few coins, dandelion heads, and other items listed from her notes in a metal pot. The mashed-up horsetail dyed her fingers green. Lastly, she poured in the elderberry wine, followed by the crab powder and clumps of grass and dirt Gunari gave her from Syeira's location. She set the trapped rabbit in front of the small shrine with Gunari's crude map. She didn't want to sacrifice a live chicken, so she used a few chicken bones and chose to use a rabbit instead. The area where they camped was full of rabbits, and they were easier for her to capture than running after a silly bird.

Standing proudly in her circle, armed with her notes, she commanded the curse into action.

"I demand that swooping fear from the heavens will fly down, on my command. May darkness scare the boy away, whenever he is in the presence of my daughter. On this day, whatever man is close to Syeira, declaring his love for her, will attract the curse. May he cower in fear."

She giggled at the idea of some boy running off, afraid of his shadow. She laughed at the idea of Syeira throwing a temper tantrum for not getting her way.

A soft summer breeze blew, but Patia dismissed the wind and waited for a specific sign. She watched, expecting the rabbit to roll over and die as confirmation that her incantations were heard by the powers that be.

To her dismay, nothing happened.

After her grandiose first attempt, she evaluated her words. She scribbled a few notes and tried her curse again. She considered that the first attempt wasn't serious enough. Her mother's spells were always poetic, so she tried to create the same feeling. She focused on the subject of her spell, and tried again.

"From the heavens above,

I command fear upon your soul, sparked by words of love.

I command darkness to surround you, shadows overcome you,

and the sun forsake you.

May you quake with fear, down through your flesh and bones.

By the master's doing, so shall it be."

Patia's words still came out dry and flat. Everything with the ceremony went wrong. The candles blew out and pages kept turning when she tried to read her notes. Her amateurish shrine fell apart. After accidentally spilling her potion everywhere, she grabbed the rabbit's cage. The bottom fell out, giving the rabbit its freedom. The grass irritated her nose and the sun hurt her eyes. Her back and knees hurt, and she wanted to give up, as she had done many times in the past.

Patia closed her eyes and growled. She thought about her mother, who insisted that Patia was gifted and powerful. Even on her deathbed, she insisted that Patia was special. Patia missed her mother.

"I will try this again."

She was determined to make the spell work.

"Once, when I was younger, I was special," Patia pleaded to the wind as she bit her lip. She was more emotional than she expected. "Let me be special again, just for now."

She refocused. She put away her candles and the makeshift shrine in order. Once properly grounded, she spoke again, this time earnestly, from her heart. Her words transformed from broken English and Roma into Latin. She hadn't spoken Latin since she was around Syeira's age.

"De cælo sunt desuper,

Timor mando animo excussum verbis amoris.

Ego præcipio tibi tenebras castellisque circummunire instituit, umbrae prævalebunt

et obscuratus est sol derelinquet vos.

Tu cum metu commoti sunt,

per os tuum et caro tua.

A magistris, ita erit."

Her words filled the air around her with resentment and bitterness. The more she chanted with passion, the more the energy grew around her. Her words changed, and came easily to her lips. She continued to shout her incantations repeatedly at the top of her lungs.

Her bitterness turned into loneliness, which was just a mask for sadness. As she raised her gnarled hands to the sky, her heart opened. As she breathed, she knew that her daughter's heart would be broken.

It is not my intention to hurt Syeira, she thought as the words continued to drone.

Unexpected tears coursed down her dirty cheeks. She remembered when she was Syeira's age. She was also madly in love with a boy from another tribe, and their relationship was never meant to be. She was crushed. His family arranged for him to marry someone with a bigger dowry than hers. *The gypsy way was the only way.*

Patia fell hard to her knees and cried harder and harder as Latin continued to pour from her lips. She was tormented with regrets and the loss of laughter in her life. Her emotional breakdown caught her off guard. Patia pushed through, insisting that the curse work. She continued her chanting, mixed with sobs. She remembered having a few moments of happiness in her life from time to time. She used to sing songs with her husband. She used to write poems and share them with him. She loved raising her daughter. She wished her mother could have met Syeira. Memories continued to flood her mind as she repeated her Latin.

The smell of rich, fertile earth filled her nose as her tears fell to the ground.

Patia finally stopped her chanting. She needed to catch her breath as she knelt, face down, in the dry grass around her. She placed her hands on her cheeks to wipe away her tears. She was startled by a change: her face was soft and smooth. She sat up and looked at her hands. Her fingers were long and slender. Warts and moles were gone. Her hands, by all appearances, were young and graceful. Frantically, she fished around in her pockets to find a golden pocket watch. Her hands, still slightly green from the horsetail, shook as she popped it open. Opposite the timepiece was a small mirror. She stared at her reflection. A woman with kind eyes looked back at her. As Patia attempted to smile, the reflection smiled back.

Patia barely believed what she saw. She stood up, strong, tall, and balanced. Her back was straight, and whatever daily aches and pains she experienced had vanished. She did not dare take her eyes off the reflection. Her teeth were straight. Her pink lips were soft and smooth. She continued to smile at the reflection in the mirror. For the first time in a very long time, she saw that it was alluring.

Syeira inherited my smile, not Dorian's toothy grin.

As she thought of Syeira and her natural beauty, anger and jealousy slowly crept back into Patia's heart. The small memories of her own happiness while raising Syeira faded away. Poisoned feelings and lies crept in.

"Syeira is spoiled. Syeira is too pretty for her own good. Syeira is disrespectful and ungrateful."

As poisonous thoughts continued to infect her, Patia's heart hardened. She was not aware that the source of the negativity was from a curse placed on her own head, by her mother.

She watched in the mirror as her eyes lost their brightness. Her body, starting with her fingers, cramped up. Warts and hairy moles popped up. She winced as her face pinched tight and wrinkles invaded her soft, creamy face. Her jaws ached as her teeth shifted around. Her skin turned coarse and dry. It slowly slithered across her skull. The familiar back pain and spasms throbbed. The sun was too bright, and the smell of dry grass was back, irritating her nose. Worse, she thought she smelled hints of horse manure. Once again, bitterness ruled her heart.

The candles Patia used with this hex were ones she used time and time again. They should have been cleansed with sacred oils or Florida water after every use. Salt, not grain, should have been used to absorb and cleanse psychic energy. Patia's lazy, makeshift spell created a healthy source of negative energy. The energy grew quickly with her intention to do harm.

Patia closed her pocket watch, refusing to look at her reflection any longer. She shrieked in anger with all her might into the sky.

"Damn her! Damn them all!"

She spewed the spell one last time and wiped her tears away in frustration. She felt the ground underneath her feet quiver, the summer breeze blow wildly around her, but she barely noticed. She gathered her few belongings and stomped back to camp. She never broke the circle for her spell.

The negative energy was alive, and waited for its victim.

Chapter 7/The Lovers

WILL NERVOUSLY HUMMED TO HIMSELF as he approached the shack. To his delight, Syeira sprinted out and greeted him on the path.

"Syeira, you're early! I was gonna surprise you!"

"I couldn't wait. I had to see you. Are you happy to see me?"

Syeira hugged him tightly. He loved the softness of her skin and the scent of jasmine that followed her when she moved.

"Yes! I'm thrilled to see you!"

Will embraced her, not wanting to let her go. However, he had a plan and had to stay focused. He would fight through his nervousness and his excitement, no matter what.

"Treats for my angel."

"For me?" Syeira squealed with happiness.

He stepped back and presented her with a bouquet of fresh flowers and a small pineapple upside-down cake, carefully wrapped in cheesecloth. It was one of her favorite desserts.

She hugged him again, almost knocking him over.

"I love you, Will," she said, looking up into his hazel eyes.

"Syeira, you are the world to me. I love you too." He leaned over slowly and kissed her lips softly.

A warm buzz ran quietly through him. He was savoring the moment when an eerie growling sound disturbed their kiss. The lovers looked up, trying to figure out where the noise came from. The sky above darkened and a colony of bats erupted into flight, swooping down on the two unsuspecting lovers.

Patia's curse unfolded.

Will instinctively dropped the cake. Instead of running away, he snatched Syeira close to his body as the creatures recklessly smacked into them. The attacking bats were disfigured. Some had heads too large for their bodies. Some had misshapen wings. Many had abnormal green spots.

"What's happening?" Syeira said as she clung tightly to Will.

The ground vibrated around the couple.

"I've never seen fruit bats act like this. There's something wrong with them," Will shouted over the growling creatures.

He felt Syeira tremble in his arms.

"You're safe with me. I promise."

He held her tightly. He felt her fingers dig into his skin and heard the bats screech in his ears.

Will swung the bouquet of flowers at the winged beasts, batting them away. He gritted his teeth as the bats scratched his forehead and nipped at his ears.

"We can't stand out here in the open like this," he said. "Listen to my voice and stay with me."

Syeira cried harder and buried her face into his chest.

"Sweetheart, I need you to listen to me. Be brave. We'll get through this."

Will hummed his favorite song and stepped carefully toward the shack. Syeira followed his lead. A larger bat smacked into Syeira's head, getting tangled in her hair. Will dropped the flowers and wrangled it free from her dark curls.

"Go away! Leave us alone!" Will screamed.

The bats acknowledged his command, and thinned out.

"Stay with me. They're flying away."

Will kept humming with each step closer to their refuge. As he stepped, she stepped.

The bats eventually disappeared.

Young Markos, the tracker, saw the attack and panicked. He sprinted away, expecting the bats would swoop down on him too. The disoriented little boy lost his brother's path. It would take up precious time for him to find his way back to camp.

Once safely inside, Will quickly slammed the door behind them. Syeira still clung to him fiercely.

"It's okay. We're safe, just as I promised." He slowly released his grip, but Syeira refused to release hers.

"We're okay. Open your eyes. Let me look at you."

Syeira drew in a deep breath, and let Will go. She quickly covered her face in shame.

"I've never been so scared in my whole life."

"Syeira." He carefully took her hands in his. "Let me see that beautiful face."

Syeira looked up at Will.

"You kept me safe," she finally managed to say.

"Of course, you are my girl. I've never felt so brave in my whole life."

Syeira hid her face again.

"Let me check you out, the way my grandmother looked at me."

Will peeled her hands from her face until she looked at him. Then he playfully frowned and grunted as he pretended to know what he was looking for. He nodded and shook his head. He made silly faces and strange noises until Syeira laughed. Satisfied that she was okay, he spun her around slowly, like a ballerina.

"I didn't know you could dance," Syeira giggled as Will continued to spin her.

"I didn't know I could either. But I can do anything when I'm with you."

Syeira changed direction and attempted to spin Will around too.

"I love your laugh," he said.

On another spin Will saw a bloody scratch on one of her hands. He abruptly stopped spinning her.

"You're hurt!"

"I'm fine. It's just a small scratch. It's nothing. What about you?" she asked.

Syeira realized she hadn't checked to see if Will was okay.

"I'm fine. Just a few pesky bats," he said casually, adjusting his suit. "The scratches burn a little, but I refuse to be defeated!"

"That was so weird. Those bats looked so strange and came from nowhere!" Syeira looked around nervously.

"Syeira, you and I together are unstoppable. I am fearless when I'm with you."

Will looked outside, grateful to see the sun slowly setting in the horizon. A few stars sparkled high in the sky.

"The bats are gone. I'll be right back."

"No, don't leave me!"

"It's okay." He pointed to the broken flowers strewn outside and the dessert, still neatly wrapped in cheesecloth.

"I want to get them before it's too dark out."

Will trotted outside. He grabbed the cake and picked up a few of the flowers that hadn't been destroyed. As he turned back to the shack, Syeira had joined him.

"We do things together." She smiled nervously.

Will offered his arm. "Let's go inside," he said.

Syeira looked at the stars winking at her in the night sky. Will escorted her, holding her hand softly. After lighting a few candles, Syeira examined Will closely. He'd suffered quite a few scratches.

Lost in her beauty, Will watched Syeira as she cleaned his head with some fresh water. She sat next to him on a large trunk.

"Other than that scratched-up face, you're very handsome today," Syeira said. "Why are you all dressed up?"

"I had a long talk with my grandmother," Will said nonchalantly.

"About what?" Syeira asked while she continued to treat his scratches.

"About you."

"About me? That's interesting," Syeira said, tickling Will's nose playfully with her washcloth.

Will grinned. He liked their game of cat-and-mouse. "How was your day?"

"I had a talk with my parents too. It didn't go very well."

Will saw that her eyebrows creased her forehead and her smile melted away.

"You just lost your smile. What did you talk to them about?" Will gently stopped her from treating his wounds.

"I told them to stop trying to marry me off. I said that I am in love with you and they cannot tell me what to do with my life."

Frustration crept into her melodic voice. She searched Will's face for his reaction.

"They banished me like a small child to my aunt's tent. They threatened to find me a husband over the next few days. So I ran away and now here I am, with you. I won't go back to them, ever."

"I guess the last day or two has been crazy for the both of us," he said. "Yesterday was horrible. I went to a church potluck with Grandmother. The reverend's wife poisoned her husband, accidentally poisoned her baby, and then jumped off the church roof. It was so sad. She was a lonely woman. There was nothing I or Grandmother could do to help her."

"That's terrible."

"It made me think a lot about my life and what I want and don't want. Life is short."

Syeira stroked Will's cheek.

"You say you won't go back to your family? Do you mean it? That's pretty serious."

"Of course I mean it."

Will did his best to keep a straight face. Rather than jumping for joy and shouting gleefully from the rooftop, he clenched his jaw and slightly pressed Syeira's small frame away from him. He placed his hands gently on her waist as she stood up. Syeira stepped toward him, but he pushed her away again. Syeira furrowed her brow. She expected him to hold her close, not push her away.

"Well, let me ask you this…" he started.

"What, Will?" Syeira snapped. She stood impatiently, tightly crossing her arms protectively in front of her and staring down at him. "I thought things were serious between you and me. I won't go back to them, and you can't make me."

Will awkwardly slid from the trunk he sat on in their makeshift kitchen onto one knee on the dusty floor. Still clenching his jaw to suppress his grin, he held out his left hand, summoning her close. She stood her ground. He haphazardly patted his chest with his right hand, searching for something.

"Will, what are you doing?" Syeira demanded in frustration.

Will motioned again for her to come closer to him. She stomped over, bracing for bad news.

He patted his heart and then sighed.

Will revealed a purple velvet box from an inner pocket of his jacket. Adrenalin raced through his body. He'd planned for this special moment. Time seemed to stop. As he opened the box, revealing a gold band, Syeira's emerald eyes welled up with tears.

"Syeira Camlo, you are my world, my everything. I promise you a life of love and happiness. Together I know we are unstoppable. Will you be my wife?"

"Yes! I will marry you! I love you with all my heart."

He placed the ring delicately on Syeira's left hand.

Syeira showered her soon-to-be husband with kisses. He kissed her back just as passionately. Out of the corner of his eye, he saw golden sparks dance around them. Their kisses grew more intense but softer, slower, and more passionate. The golden sparks faded. Syeira nervously led Will to a mattress covered with blue-and-green-colored quilts she had sewn for him.

"This is the best day of my life," she said.

"This is the best day of my life too," Will said as he slowly kissed the palms of her hands.

Taking his time, he undressed Syeira, slowly revealing her warm olive skin in the candlelight.

"You are more magnificent than I imagined. I am the luckiest man in the world," he said.

It was surreal for Will to see his chocolate-colored hands caress her soft body. The large copper amulet she wore around her delicate neck glowed.

The scent of pecans and cinnamon was all around Will, the same sweet smell that had surrounded him when Syeira first visited the cozy little bakery to see him. Syeira breathed in deeply, looking into Will's warm hazel eyes.

"I'm the luckiest girl in the world. I'm safe and sound in your arms."

"This is where we're supposed to be."

For the first time in their lives, they made love.

Afterward, the couple lay together for a while, looking through the window at a beautiful, starry night.

"Grandmother made a whole list of things we need to do, like places we should get married, food for the reception, and family stuff," Will said. "She insists on meeting your family. She was very bossy about the whole thing. Honestly, though, I don't want to wait to marry you. Is that okay?"

"My family will disown me. It will not matter if she wants to meet them or not. Tomorrow would be a great day to get married."

"Then first thing tomorrow, after I introduce you to her, we'll find a justice of the peace to marry us."

Syeira frowned. "What if she doesn't like me?"

"You make me happy. She'll like you."

"Are you sure?"

"I'm sure. Grandmother is a little rough around the edges, but she'll like you. She said she wants to give us some of her land to start a family."

"She does sound bossy," Syeira said.

"She's strongwilled, like you," he said and kissed her nose. "I mean that in a good way."

"People in the quarter say she's scary."

"Nah, they just don't know her. You'll see once you get to know her. I bet she would help us find someone to marry us, if we ask her very nicely. She'll have to understand about your family and that this is our future, not hers. The day we become Mr. and Mrs. Jalio will be the best day of my life. I plan to have many best days with you."

"I like that. We will have many 'best days' together."

Syeira giggled as Will drew her close to him.

The gypsy curse, however, was still active. It had different, dark plans for the lovers.

In the dark of the night, Will was restless. He kept shifting his weight and changing positions in bed. Syeira got up and lit a new set of candles. To her dismay, she saw that the scratches on Will's face were swollen and crusty with dried blood. Heat radiated from his body and the odor of pecans turned into a sickly, sweaty smell. In the candlelight, Syeira dressed, trying not to disturb Will, but he sat up anyway.

"Are you okay?" Will asked cautiously.

"I'm fine. I'm more than fine, really. If anything, I'm worried about you. You don't look good. You might have a fever." Syeira placed her soft hands upon his warm face and frowned.

"To be honest, I don't feel well, but I don't want to ruin our perfect evening."

"It's perfect and nothing can change that. Looking at your scratches, I think you need some medicine or some kind of help. What should we do?"

Syeira got a cloth soaked with cold water and placed it on his forehead.

Will's condition grew worse as the minutes passed. His head pounded and his stomach squealed. He hoped he would shake off whatever ailed him, but Syeira was right. He needed help. He put on his undershorts, which felt like sandpaper against his skin. As he struggled to stand, he realized he was too weak to put on the rest of his clothes. Syeira gently insisted he lie back down.

"Go to my house and talk to my grandmother. Don't call her ma'am or Mrs. Jalio. Call her Grandmother Zenobia. She'll know what to do. As a warning, don't just run up all willy-nilly to the front door. You have to ask her permission to come inside her house to see her. She can't stand when people show up uninvited. Tell her you are my girl. She'll welcome you into her home."

"Are you sure? Maybe I should just go into town?" Syeira suggested hesitantly.

"Ignore any of the stories you've heard about Grandmother. She's a good woman once you get to know her. I talked with her about you for a while yesterday. She knows all about you, and she gave us her blessing."

"She gave us her blessing?"

"Yes, she did. If you're going to be my wife, you're going to have to trust me."

Syeira chewed her lower lip.

"I tell you what. Give her this pillow and tell her it's a gift for her." Will struggled to sit up and handed her a pink pillow with hand-stitched flowers.

117

"But I made it for you," she pouted.

"I love it. I do. Give it to Grandmother as a kind of peace offering. When we're married, you can make me a thousand pillows."

Syeira reluctantly agreed.

"Take my pocket watch. It has a compass. Follow the trail east until you get to a large oak tree that stands alone in the woods. From there, take the fork west for ten minutes. You will find yourself at a small dirt road. Continue west on it, which will lead you to her home. Chances are you will hear dogs barking before you see a big purple door."

Syeira took the watch and kissed Will softly. Will noticed the air buzz softly around him. His body aches lessened.

"I don't want to leave you."

"I know. You'll be back before you know it, and you'll help me feel better."

Grabbing a small oil lantern by the door, she dashed outside. Stopping short, she turned back and approached the window.

"I love you, Will!" she called out.

"I love you too, Syeira, with all my heart," Will shouted back.

Syeira headed off to Grandmother's. She had barely taken five steps when she heard growling overhead. The scent of rotten eggs filled the air. She turned to look at the shack.

Something cracked overhead, through the growling.

"Not again!" Syeira panicked and crouched to the ground. This time the bats didn't come toward her.

She watched in horror as hundreds upon hundreds of bats swooped down from a nearby tree and circled the shack. They flew through the open window and flooded the inside of the small room. They flew toward their unsuspecting victim. The colony of bats attacked mercilessly. She heard Will's screams mixed with the screeches of bats.

"Will?"

"Syeira, run! Go to Grandmother! Please!" Will yelled.

Syeira ran away as quickly as she could manage. A few bats came her way, attracted to the lantern she carried, but she fought them off. Once she was at a safe distance, she looked back at the shack for Will.

Will managed to get out of bed and tried his best to fight off the bats. He wore only his shorts, so he was completely exposed. He had no weapon to defend himself. The bats eventually engulfed Will's body. They tore at his skin, ripping his flesh. The smell of rotten eggs was overpowering. The more he swung, the more agitated the bats were. More bats, even larger than the first wave, poured into the shack. They furiously attacked. Finally, Will stopped fighting, dropped to his knees, and tried to protect himself, covering his face with his hands. The bats were unstoppable.

Syeira heard his tortured screams. Terrified, she ran into the darkness. Will was in big trouble. She needed to get him help right away. She didn't know what to expect when she came face to face with Grandmother. She had heard many things about the old woman when she made trips into town for supplies from the French market. Her own mother was a mediocre palm-reader. Quite a few men and women practiced Voodoo around town. Aside from the Queen of Voodoo, Marie Laveau, Grandmother Zenobia supposedly had legendary powers. Will dismissed the rumors, but she still believed them to be true. The stories varied from Grandmother Zenobia striking people dead with a flick of her wrist to causing frogs to fall from the sky. Panicked and alone, Syeira had no choice but to make her way to the Voodoo High Priestess.

Chapter 8/The Rescue

WILL'S DIRECTIONS WERE HARDER THAN she expected. Syeira fought to catch her breath as she trembled in the night air. She found herself standing on a narrow, dusty road, looking at a small house with an oversized, purple front door. Just as Will had warned her, dogs barked at her in the darkness. She wanted to rush right up and bang on the door, but something stopped her. A distinct hum buzzed in her ears. It wasn't the usual hiss of June bugs or songs of cicadas. The hum was a warning.

"Hello? Grandmother Zenobia? Is anyone there?" Syeira called from the road. She lifted her lantern to get a better look around her.

A figure appeared indistinctly in the front window.

"Who are you and what do you want?" the voice said.

Syeira needed to do whatever it took to help Will, but she was scared out of her mind. The hum continued to vibrate in her ears. She wanted to run away, screaming her head off, back into the darkness. Syeira gasped for air, hoping to fight off the urge to vomit everything in her belly in front of the Voodoo woman's home.

"Ma'am, um, Grandmother Zenobia, is that you? We have not been properly introduced," Syeira squeaked. "My name is Syeira. I am…Will's friend. I am sorry to disturb you but…something very bad has happened to him and I need your help right away."

There was an uncomfortable pause.

"You have my permission to come on my property."

The humming faded away and the large purple door creaked open.

From the other side of the door, Grandmother watched a dark-haired young woman run up the porch steps and approach the doorway. The gas porch light shone brightly on her as she reached the top step. Grandmother saw a glint of gold on the girl's hand, and something pink under her arm.

"A gypsy is wearing my daughter's ring," she grumbled to herself. "Come in."

"Thank you. This pillow is for you. It's a gift…"

"Who are you, and why are you here, really? Don't bother lying to me," Grandmother said.

Syeira blushed and stopped in her tracks. She knew the truth was always better.

"Will is my soul mate, not just a friend," she admitted. "I made this pillow for him but he thought you would like it too."

Syeira looked up as she offered the pillow. Grandmother Zenobia stood before her, with her hands on her hips. The dark-skinned woman mesmerized Syeira. She was taller than expected. She had dark-brown eyes, unlike Will, that looked down and examined Syeira closely. She wore a headscarf that matched the purple door, a cream cotton blouse, and a long black skirt.

There was another awkward pause between the women as they stood face to face in the entryway of the home.

"Damned gypsy kisses. Why didn't I sense any of this?" asked Grandmother. "I thought that Will was in love with some black girl who lived far away, not a gypsy."

Syeira stood still as the Voodoo woman paced around.

"I should have known better than to get caught up in Will's excitement. What kind of future can you two have?"

Syeira was shocked. Will had said Grandmother was a good person. The woman before her sounded a lot like her own parents.

"Well, Will wasn't tainted with a love potion, so this must be real," Grandmother continued. "He loves you, and you are brave to stand before me on my property."

Grandmother closed her eyes and said a quiet prayer. She reminded herself that love was a powerful force and should be celebrated, not fought against. However, it still disturbed her that she had not sensed anything on a psychic level.

"I did give the two of you my blessing."

Ahy trotted in and inspected the girl. After a few sniffs, he licked her hands and wagged his tail.

"It seems Ahy likes you."

"So this is Will's best friend. It's nice to finally meet you, Ahy."

Syeira bent over to pet the dog when he howled. He jumped feverishly and pawed at her.

"What's gotten into you?" Grandmother asked the dog.

He looked at her and yodeled.

"Ahy, settle down," she said. Then she turned to Syeira. "You, have a seat."

Grandmother pointed at a small couch in the front room for the girl to sit on. Syeira tried not to stare at Grandmother. She could not help but notice that Grandmother was younger and stronger-looking than she'd expected. She'd assumed she would be a creepy, gray-haired old woman with crooked teeth who hobbled with a cane. Grandmother Zenobia was a tall, athletic-looking dark-skinned woman. She probably worked on the farm as much as Will. Syeira noticed the home smelled of pineapple upside-down cake. Her heart sank. Will had been there earlier, baking her favorite dessert.

Grandmother fussed at the hyperactive dog for a few moments before she turned her attention back to her guest, who stood by the small loveseat.

"Well, young lady?"

"Thank you for seeing me. Will always speaks very highly of you. I am honored to finally meet you," Syeira blurted out. She bowed, trying her best to show respect before she sat.

"Call me Grandmother," she replied coldly.

As the young girl perched on the edge of the loveseat, Grandmother recognized similarities between her and Will. She appeared to be so young, but had an old soul, like Will. She did not fidget like other young people did. She sat still, and observed her surroundings.

"What is your name again?"

"Syeira. Syeira Camlo."

Grandmother continued to observe the young woman. Another answer she did not expect. Grandmother was getting angrier by the minute.

"Why didn't I sense any of this? You're from the Camlo tribe?"

Grandmother was puzzled. She drew in a deep breath and tried to calm her nerves.

"You know my tribe?" asked Syeira.

"That's something we'll talk about another day. You make Will happy. No one has had that effect on him. He told me, repeatedly, about how much he loves you and wants to marry you. So I guess I'm fine with it too."

"It's an honor to be a part of your family," Syeira said. She twisted the golden band on her finger.

"So what's the problem? Where is my grandson? Is it the Rayford boy? I will go straight to his father and get things settled once and for all..."

Syeira interrupted Grandmother's rant.

"You won't believe my story. We were attacked. Will is hurt and he said you would know what to do to help him."

As Syeira stammered out her words, a large owl burst through an open window. It screeched as it flew at her. It jumped on Syeira's shoulders, digging its claws into her thick hair. Grandmother rushed to find a broom to scare off the bird. Ahy jumped and howled. Syeira struggled to get the screeching, clawing thing off her head. When Grandmother approached, armed with her broom, the owl hopped to the floor and revealed its prey. It was a large, disfigured bat. It had green bald spots on its body. Its eyes were misshapen and its mouth was larger than most of its head. The owl shook it fiercely in its beak. Ahy stood back and growled.

"Drop it!" Grandmother shouted at the owl as she wielded her broom.

The bird obeyed. Syeira stomped on the bat before Grandmother could smack it with her broom.

"Stop!" Grandmother warned.

Syeira stomped once more, for good measure, and backed off.

Ahy leaned into Grandmother and whined. She patted him on the head and quietly apologized.

"I thought you were going to tell me about some 'one' that fought my grandson, not some 'thing' that he fought," Grandmother said in a tone that ran chills down Syeira's spine.

Grandmother took a long look at the dead creature crumpled on the floor.

"This isn't a fruit bat. It's a vampire bat! Worse, someone has hexed it. It is a sign something dreadful attacked my grandson."

She was well aware that this type of bat was not native to the United States. With the right spells, they could be summoned, especially through the dark arts.

"A group of those things attacked us!" said Syeira.

"This is very bad."

Grandmother no longer had the luxury of hiding her magic.

"Child, brace yourself for what you're about to see."

Grandmother waved her hands over her head. She muttered a few words under her breath for protection and clenched her fist tightly. Syeira gasped as she watched the Voodoo woman work her magic. Grandmother waved only her left hand in the air, this time at the dead bat. The nasty furball rose in the air and sailed across the room. It was as if an invisible hand tossed it toward her empty, cold fireplace. She muttered a few more words as the creature slammed into the back of the chimney and burst into flames.

Syeira couldn't believe what she had witnessed. The women of her tribe talked about magic from time to time, in the sewing tent. They spoke of fertility spells and burned candles for protection. No one in her tribe could ever make anything sail across a room the way Grandmother did. No one she knew had that kind of power. She wondered if Will knew about his grandmother's ability. She wondered if he had the same supernatural powers.

"We'll discuss all of that later."

Grandmother rushed back to the kitchen. Hastily, she grabbed a burlap bag and threw in a few clean towels, a small bottle of red powder, a bottle of leeches, a box of matches, and another bottle with rubbing alcohol.

"Will is in serious danger. We have to leave, now!"

Grandmother stopped at the front door, Syeira right on her heels. Grandmother bent down and spoke to Ahy.

"Sweetheart, you have to stay here. It might not be safe for you where we're going. I promise we'll bring Will home."

Ahy lay on the floor by the door and whined.

"I almost forgot. Please, open that window."

Grandmother pointed at the large window by the front door.

Syeira did as she was told and then cautiously stepped back. Grandmother snapped her fingers. The door to the icebox slowly opened. From a ceramic bowl, a chunk of crabmeat for the next day's batch of gumbo rose in the air. It dropped on the floor before the owl. The door to the icebox slammed shut.

"A reward, my friend, for your help," she said to the large bird. "Come and go as you please."

"You talk to birds the way Will does," said Syeira.

"We'll have a nice sit-down once everything is resolved with my grandson. In the meantime, tell me absolutely everything that happened! Spare no detail," Grandmother said as the two women set off hastily to rescue Will.

Back at the gypsy camp, Patia met up with the two trackers who'd spied on Syeira. They'd showed up back at camp much later in the evening than they'd planned.

"Tell me what happened? What did you see?"

Young Markos fearfully repeated Gunari's story that he and his brother had found the place where Syeira snuck off to. He was starting to explain how they selected which grass and which section of dirt they collected when Patia cut him off.

"I know all of this. You try my patience," she threatened.

"Go on, tell her, Markos. Explain what you saw," Gunari said. He pushed his little brother forward, toward Patia.

"After Gunari left, I heard a scary sound in the sky and then a bunch of weird night birds attacked a black man with the flowers and Syeira."

"You idiot! They aren't night birds, they are bats!"

Markos trembled as she spoke, but Gunari encouraged him to continue. Markos felt his big brother gently pat his back.

"The black man protected Syeira from the bats."

"He didn't run away?"

"No, my queen. Syeira was very scared, but he protected her. I had to run away. I was scared they would get me too. I lost the trail for a while and was turned around. I came back to report what I saw as soon as I found my way."

Something went wrong with the curse, Patia thought to herself. The bats did not scare off the suitor. He protected her instead. Syeira didn't come home.

"Wait for me by the horses. I'll need you to guide me to Syeira. I have to bring her home at once."

The boys scampered away.

Patia rushed to speak to Dorian, who had eventually returned to camp. She found him drinking and playing cards by a fire. The boys saw that Patia approached the men and decided to ignore her orders. They circled around and followed behind her instead of going to the horses. They always enjoyed seeing King Dorian up close and personal.

"My king, I need a word with you," Patia said, bowing slightly.

Dorian waved in her general direction as if she were a fly buzzing around. The men laughed and continued their fun and games.

"Dorian, I need a word with you now," she snapped.

The men stopped and looked at her. Women did not speak to their husbands with that tone, especially to the King of the Gypsies. Dorian, undisturbed at her lack of respect, dismissed her.

"What do you want? Can't you see I am busy?"

"It is Syeira, she…"

"What about my daughter?" Dorian snapped back.

"Well, uh, you see," Patia hedged.

He leapt to his feet, knocking over his whiskey. Some of the men around Dorian looked away from him, while others stepped back. He grabbed Patia roughly by her arms.

"What is it?"

"She's in trouble. I tried to fix things, but something went wrong. I figured she would sneak away against your orders to see her lover. Which she did. So I cursed the young man to send her home. From what I can tell, it didn't work. The curse should have driven her home right away but she isn't in Mirela's tent as you commanded."

"I never should have trusted you. We'll find her and bring her home," Dorian roared.

"We know where she is," Gunari said.

Patia noticed the meddlesome trackers behind her.

"Those two know her location. They were supposed to be waiting by the horses."

Dorian shook his head at his wife. "You should be ashamed to use little boys to do your foolish work. Go back to our tent and I will deal with you later."

Patia lowered her head and retreated.

"Gunari, Markos, prepare my horse," Dorian ordered.

"Yes, my king!" they answered quickly. They were excited that Dorian called them by name.

"We need to go to the last place you saw my daughter."

The boys ran off once again to the horses.

"Boldo, assemble some of the men."

"Yes, sir."

Dorian dashed inside his tent. He retrieved a silver revolver from a wooden case and returned to the men by the campfire.

"We'll scare that boy the old-fashioned way and bring my daughter home," he said while waving the gun in the air for all to see.

"Yes, sir."

"And, Boldo, I'm serious. We do not want to kill the stranger, only scare him. Murder would bring extremely bad fortune on our people."

With assistance from the young boys, the men mounted their horses and rode into the night.

As Dorian with his men followed Gunari and Markos, an uneasy feeling of déjà vu settled over him. They reached a patch of trees quickly.

"We're here, Your Majesty," Gunari said as he bowed.

"What do you mean we're here? I don't see anything but trees."

"Right there." Markos pointed at the shack.

"Don't mock King Dorian, or you'll be punished!" barked Boldo.

"Calm down, Boldo. They don't mean to be disrespectful."

Dorian squinted. He still only saw a cluster of trees. He noticed his horse was agitated. He dismounted and felt the ground slightly vibrate under his boots. Then he saw exactly what the boys pointed to, a shack tucked in between trees and shrubs.

"Syeira, come out! I demand it!" Dorian declared as he approached.

There was no response, not even the chirp of crickets.

Dorian released his horse and continued to approach the shack.

"No. This cannot be happening. Not here." Over the years, the rickety wooden shack had been a sanctuary for several people, not just Will and Syeira. It held old memories for Dorian, from back when he was younger.

Dorian's knees buckled at his first glance inside. He clutched the doorway for support.

He staggered further inside the small room and frantically searched through it. There was no sign of his daughter. There was only the dead young man, and piles of dead disfigured bats. After retreating from the shack, Dorian covered his face and cried.

"Is it my daughter?" Patia asked, her voice creeping from the darkness. Against Dorian's orders, she and a few of the women had arrived behind the men.

"She isn't here. It's someone else, and they are dead."

Dorian looked at the dead body once more, and yelled as loudly as he could muster.

Patia knew it was Syeira's lover.

The onlookers questioned Dorian's reaction. Gunari and Markos, along with the other family members, stared at him. His grief and anger were personal.

"King Dorian, are you okay?" asked Markos as he approached. He smelled sulfur. As he drew closer, he saw dead bats scattered all around the ground outside of the shack.

Dorian wiped his face and rolled his shoulders back until he settled his emotions. He looked down at the small boy. He patted him on the head and intentionally blocked the boy's view of the body.

"Don't look, Markos. Something very bad has happened to a young man."

Dorian placed his hands on Markos's shoulders and turned to his men.

"Burn the shack and the body. Burn this entire area. Do it now," Dorian commanded.

The men searched for kindling. The handful of women who'd followed their men also helped. Patia lurked behind a tree, watching the entire scene from a short distance away. Markos strained to see what was so upsetting. In spite of Dorian's warning and physical efforts, the boy snuck a peek.

Through the doorway, he saw a young black man, his eyes and mouth gaping open. His body rested askew on a makeshift bed. Markos recognized handmade gypsy blankets. The young man was very still. He never blinked, and he never stirred. His skin was puffy, bloated, and covered with blood.

Seeing a dead body in general didn't frighten Markos. This one, however, was disturbing. It did not have a peaceful appearance, like the elders who had passed away in his tribe. They were dressed up and given gifts for the afterlife. They were celebrated and honored at funerals, for days at a time. Upon realizing the identity of the body, the little boy was overwhelmed. It was the nice black man with the flowers, who'd hummed a nice song. The poor man had suffered while fighting for his life. Markos buried his face in Dorian's pant leg and sobbed.

"Someone take this little boy back home to his father."

"Why are we burning the shack?" asked Gunari innocently as he came to retrieve his little brother.

Dorian looked around as everyone stopped, staring at him in silence.

"We are burning the shack because that young man was killed by a dark curse. One of our own people cast the hex. There is no telling what could happen to our people. Karma does not play favorites. Crops and livestock could dry up wherever we go. We could be infected with horrible diseases. Anything is possible when dealing with dark magic. The only cure I know is to burn cursed things and then beg the heavens for forgiveness."

Everyone present stepped up the pace and urgently searched for kindling, now understanding the importance of building a bonfire.

"Thank you, again," Grandmother said to Syeira. She clung tightly to the young girl's arm for support. Once grounded, she frantically wiped her hands on her dress. "I'm embarrassed that I keep stumbling around. I'm usually very surefooted around here."

It was the third time in less than twenty minutes that Grandmother had tripped and fallen. Syeira patiently helped her to her feet each time.

"Are you all right?"

"I will be once I see my grandson."

Grandmother continued to follow Syeira awkwardly in the darkness. She was frustrated. She usually moved gracefully everywhere she went, but this evening she was like a blind man without a walking stick, fumbling his way around in the bayou.

"I can't think clearly! I need to focus. When I get home I need to do my meditating."

As Zenobia followed the gypsy girl, she noticed she couldn't sense Will's presence. She was distressed that she hadn't sensed that her grandson was in any kind of danger. She always had a feel for Will – or so she thought, until today. She needed to dig deeper and tap into her mystical strength. Because she didn't use magic at full strength anymore, her power was haphazard.

There were hundreds of reasons she didn't use magic full force. One of them was that she didn't like lots of attention. Using her power openly, whether it be publicly or privately, with non-spiritual people terrified them. Back at the house, Zenobia had smelled fear rise from the young girl's skin, like a shark smelled blood from a wounded fish, deep in the ocean. Sure, there was a good chance that the girl was fearful for whatever Will was going through (not to mention that Grandmother hadn't given her a warm welcome). Grandmother saw the girl's grimace when the bat was hurled into the cold fireplace and burst into flames. She hadn't seen a grimace like that in some time. People usually gathered together and created mobs to attack when they were spooked by something they did not understand.

In the distance, an orange glow caught Grandmother's attention.

"Who's having a bonfire way out here?" she wondered.

As she continued to bumble along, a dull ache crept into her head. It started from the base of her skull and slowly leaked its way up and around to her forehead and between her ears. With each frantic step in darkness, the pain increased, shifting from an uncomfortable throb to sharp flashes. She winced and blinked as stabbing pain jabbed its way around her eye sockets and the bridge of her nose.

Syeira and Grandmother were still a good distance away as the gypsies burned the shack and the area around it. The dead bats caught fire easily. Grandmother strained to see what was happening.

Grandmother sensed the ground pulse. It was an indication that something malicious had happened. She stopped where she stood.

She shifted her weight, closed her eyes, and awakened her psychic eye. She wouldn't budge another step until she could sense her grandson. The small spot on her forehead in between her eyes pulsed. She drew in three deep breaths, feeling her lungs expand and retract. Her heart beat slower as her chest rose and fell. When she was ready, she slowly opened her eyes. Small clouds formed around the gypsies that were yards ahead of her. Their auras were muddied blues and grays. They all were panicked and afraid. The leader of the gypsies had tinges of dark yellow, a sure sign that he was fatigued from trying to learn something.

Zenobia looked over at Syeira, whose aura was bright pink. As the girl moved closer to the bonfire, the pink faded to a muddy blue. She sensed something was wrong too.

The Voodoo High Priestess looked once again at the bonfire.

"Will Jalio, reveal yourself."

There was no response, no sign of her grandson's life force. He was gone.

"We're too late," Grandmother moaned.

She felt a heavy weight on her chest. She nervously patted her heart.

"How could this have happened?" Grandmother was numb. At first, all she could do was blink in disbelief.

Grandmother's intuition was strong, unless she dealt with someone she was emotionally attached to. The closer she was to them personally, the harder it was to read them. Will was everything to her, so her supernatural sensitivity to him was muted. And now he was dead.

Once again, Zenobia was the only member of her family. Her tribe no longer existed.

She clenched her left hand and massaged her large fleur de lis ring. She drew in another long, deep breath. When she exhaled, she engaged her mystical powers. Her heart thumped in her chest and, slowly, a warm sensation coursed through her body. She welcomed the fullness of her strength. It was deliciously sad, like the sweet embrace from a long-lost friend.

She looked tearfully to the starry sky for answers.

I've suppressed my power for too long. I thought it was the right thing to do. How dare these people treat me and my family like this? They killed my grandson!

Zenobia clenched her teeth tightly. High above a thick mist collected and hid the stars. Dark storm clouds began to swirl overhead.

I should tap into the power from this land. I should demand the earth swallow every one of these people. My husband was right. Mortals are foolish. Mortals are weak. Mortals cannot be trusted.

A cold breeze picked up, waving the grass around her feet.

I should kill them all! It is what my beloved would do. I was stupid to think Carrefour Parish was the safest place to be. The earth's energies are strong at the crossroad in Louisiana. I thought hiding here as a Voodoo Priestess was a good idea. I should have chosen a small island instead, and called myself a healer. Damned crossroads.

Thunder boomed in the distance, miles away from where she stood.

My poor grandson didn't deserve this. He was a good boy.

The wind continued to blow. A mournful howl filled the air. Grandmother bent her knees in a warrior stance.

She summoned a spell, calling upon the elements of the earth to fuel her anger. She did just as her husband, the Egyptian god Set, had taught her centuries ago.

Flames grew taller and taller, lighting up the swampy forest. Cool wind whipped Syeira's hair around her face as she looked back at Grandmother. She didn't understand what the black woman had muttered, or why she cried.

"Why are you stopping, Grandmother?" she shouted through the wind. "Come along! We're almost there."

When Grandmother didn't respond, Syeira looked back at the glowing light.

"Why is my family here? Where's Will?"

She had been so attentive with helping Grandmother that she hadn't realized they had arrived. They stood yards away from her home away from home. She saw the shack ablaze, and her beloved Will was nowhere to be found. Then Grandmother's words were clear to her.

"We're too late."

"Nooooooo!" Syeira screamed.

The heart-wrenching cry broke Grandmother's concentration. Grandmother remembered she had uttered a similar exclamation of despair, centuries ago, when she was simply Zenobia of the Jalio tribe. Back when she was betrothed to the Egyptian god Set, her entire family was destroyed. That devastating loss, that painful heartache, that loneliness, always stayed with her. The belief that "time heals all wounds" was a lie. No one fully healed from the pains of death. The little gypsy girl would have to deal with that pain too.

Syeira's outburst was the only thing that saved everyone from Zenobia's wrath.

Destruction does not undo destruction.

Zenobia closed her third eye by massaging her forehead. She released her warrior stance. The cold howling winds stopped immediately and the clouds evaporated, revealing the stars. She looked down at her hands, noticing a new collection of wrinkles.

How much of my soul did I just lose?

The gypsy tribe turned to see Syeira with Grandmother when the winds died down. Syeira recklessly ran toward the flames.

A small group of women rushed to their princess. Patia, however, remained behind. Grandmother stood alone and watched as the women tried to hold Syeira back from the flames. Although she was thin, she was very strong. She fought like a wildcat. Syeira scratched and bit at the women until finally she slipped through the group and approached the burning shack. As she got unbearably close to the flames, she fell to her knees in despair.

Grandmother looked around at the fiery scene. There was something angry and bitter that tugged at her. It wasn't what made the ground vibrate, but the negativity hung thick in the air. Her eyes searched the shadows cast by the flames. She reached out both hands and focused her energy. The source revealed itself, the person who'd started the drama. Although she closed her third eye, a residual effect remained. A muddy green-and-red aura clung to a strange-looking gypsy woman. Grandmother waved her fingers in her direction.

In turn, Patia felt an energy push her. She stumbled back a few steps. She tried to figure out what had moved her when she saw an African American woman look right at her. Patia scrambled to hide behind some trees.

Concerned at seeing a large fire in the distance, Miss Weston, Dr. Evans, and a few of the locals came upon the scene. Miss Weston hurried to Grandmother's side.

"What's going on here, Grandmother?" she asked.

Grandmother flinched at first, not expecting anyone to come from behind her. She noticed that Miss Weston's color had returned to her cheeks, but based on the dark circles under her eyes, Grandmother knew the young woman was still shaken from the church-potluck incident. Grandmother stared at the fire as she spoke.

"Miss Weston, you should be home resting," Grandmother said.

"Young Kenny and his friends came by to see us. They told us that, as they were coming back from fishing and catching turtles, they saw a group of gypsies riding horses this way. The gypsies don't usually travel down this far in the bayou. We didn't think much of it until we saw smoke in the distance. Charles…I mean, Dr. Evans, thought someone should take a look around. He collected a few folk that live nearby and I insisted upon coming too. What's going on here?"

Grandmother sensed that a new relationship was quickly budding between Dr. Evans and Miss Weston. Under different circumstances, she would have been excited at the news.

"Grandmother, are you okay? You look so…"

"Something terrible happened to my grandson," Grandmother responded through clenched teeth. "Those people killed him." She fiercely wiped tears from her cheeks.

"Will is dead?"

Before Grandmother managed to speak, a few loud pops and crackles erupted from the bonfire. A wailing sound followed by the rustling of a mound of ashes caught everyone's attention. Will Jalio rose up, in a crooked stance, in the bright flames. He was lit from head to toe. The sickly smell of burnt flesh and hair filled the air.

"My love, where are you?" he moaned.

His corpse slowly stumbled out of the front door of the burning shack. His right eye popped and oozed its liquid as the flames engulfed the back of his head.

"My grandson!" exclaimed Grandmother.

"I'm here, Will! I'm here!" shrieked Syeira hysterically.

Patia couldn't believe her eyes.

"My spell did this? No, it's not possible. It was supposed to scare the boy off, not kill him."

She wouldn't accept that her deepest, darkest inner power had triggered one of the most successful curses she had ever attempted in her life.

Patia stumbled back further, watching in horror as the undead man walked toward the group. Several of her family members tried once again to pull Syeira back, away from the flames. Will cocked his head when he heard Syeira call out to him.

"Syeira, where are you? I'm in so much pain," he wailed. "I need you! Syeira, my love! Help me!"

A few of the tribal women cried, and the men howled. Some of the locals said prayers while others backed away in fear. Dr. Evans protectively wrapped his arms around Miss Weston. The area grew hotter and hotter as flames burned brightly. Dead bats scattered all around, sizzling and popping.

Syeira was restrained by her people and Grandmother was surrounded by the neighbors. Will continued calling to Syeira, pleading and begging to see her.

"Syeira, please…come to me."

The sound of his voice was distressing as he called out.

"I told you Grandmother would like you. Come, be with me."

Everyone around was terrified. Clearly, he was dead but continued to move, arms stretching out, searching for his love.

Grandmother Zenobia sobbed. Will was cursed and she couldn't save him.

Dorian Camlo, Gypsy King of the region, stepped forward, watching Will's haphazard approach. Dorian stood tall as he pulled out a handcrafted silver flintlock pistol, equipped with handmade silver bullets. Despite the copious amounts of whiskey he'd drunk throughout the day, his hand was steady.

Gunari looked over at his little brother Markos, who clung to their mother.

"Markos, don't be afraid. King Dorian will keep us safe."

Markos held tighter to his mother.

"Do you see that gun King Dorian is holding? When you were just a baby, Papa and I sat with Dorian and the other men around a campfire. He told us and the other men a story about when he inherited the gun from his father. It's made of 100% silver."

Markos loosened his grip and peeked at his brother.

"Why silver, Gunari?"

"Silver is very powerful. God favors it. His father taught him that it stops unnatural things of the world."

The flaming corpse screamed for Syeira again. Markos clung tighter to his mother, and Gunari wrapped his arms around them both.

When Will staggered out close enough to the crowd, Dorian pulled the trigger. The gun boomed like a thunderclap. His first target was Will's heart. The bullet ripped a hole the size of a grapefruit in the flaming chest area. Dorian reloaded and aimed a second time. He shot Will square in the head, partway between the eye sockets and the forehead, causing the back of his burning skull to explode outward. Will slowly dropped to his knees and fell, silently, lifelessly, onto the ground.

"We're safe now," Dorian declared. He watched as the locals rushed to put out the fire around the corpse.

Patia peeked out from where she hid and looked around. Her eyes locked onto Grandmother Zenobia again. Grandmother's eyes flashed when she looked back at Patia.

"I see you, gypsy," Grandmother spoke wordlessly into the woman's head. "I see what feeds your hatred, you selfish, bitter woman. You stole my family from me."

Patia's heart pounded fiercely in her chest. Faceless hissing sounds swirled around her head. She abruptly turned away from looking at the black woman across from her, gasping for air.

"Heaven above, save me," she prayed. "I did not mean to call upon the devil himself. Save me."

Grandmother heard Patia's feeble plea for help. "I will make you pay for this," she grumbled. She considered killing the gypsy where she stood.

Unexpectedly, the ground shifted under Grandmother's feet, causing her to lose her balance.

"Remember where you stand, Zenobia," said a voice from deep within. Grandmother gritted her teeth. The area she stood upon had unspoken memories and lessons for her.

Walk away, Zenobia. Be merciful, she thought to herself. *Whatever you reap, you sow, just like the Good Book says.* Grandmother dropped her gaze from Patia.

"I am so sorry for your loss," Miss Weston said through her tears as she approached Grandmother.

"Grandmother Zenobia, let Charlotte take you home," said Dr. Evans as he followed closely behind Miss Weston. "The rest of us will take care of your grandson's body tonight. You have my word he will be in good hands."

Grandmother was speechless. She'd never imagined that dark magic would steal her family away from her so cruelly.

"I can make it back home by myself," Grandmother said.

"Once we handle the situation, I'll notify the authorities. These people can't just kill someone and not get away with it. Tomorrow I'll stop by and we can talk about what kind of service you want," Dr. Evans said.

"Don't bother with the authorities. I will have a meeting with Officer Bodie. Other than him and maybe a few others, the police won't care about the death of a black boy. They don't care about gypsies either. I will deal with those people myself."

Grandmother turned her attention away from Dr. Evans, over to shouting she heard from the travelers. Syeira fought the women around her.

"Syeira, come here. Let me take you home," Patia said, finally revealing herself to everyone.

"Never!" she growled at her mother. "I hate you! I hate you all!"

Syeira tore free from the people restraining her. She pushed past Charlotte and the locals too. She rushed toward Grandmother with all of her strength.

Grandmother braced herself, half expecting the girl to attack her. She hadn't been nice to the girl when they'd first met.

Instead of an attack, Syeira desperately held on to Grandmother, sobbing hysterically into her chest.

"They killed him," she sobbed. "They stole him from us."

Grandmother paused and looked at Patia before fully embracing the girl in her arms. She consoled Syeira as if she were her own daughter.

"Yes, they did."

The young girl wept. Grandmother quietly consoled her as best as she could, while fighting back her own tears.

"I'm going home. Do you want to come with me?" Grandmother asked.

Syeira managed to squeak out a "yes" in between gasps for air.

Members of the Camlo tribe lingered in the dwindling light of the smoldering embers of the fire. They were shocked, and confused. Dorian stared hard at Patia. He knew this was her fault.

"Everyone, back to camp," Dorian ordered. "We need to leave before the muskers show up and take us all to jail."

Miss Weston and a few others began to prepare Will's burnt, motionless body. Grandmother and Syeira turned to leave.

Dorian, with his people behind him, jogged toward Grandmother Zenobia.

"Syeira, please come home," he beckoned.

Syeira shook her head furiously and held on tightly to Grandmother. Grandmother Zenobia spun toward him, held up her left hand as a warning, and shot a look that stopped Dorian dead in his tracks.

Without an utterance, she slowly withdrew her hand and turned away. Dorian watched as Grandmother disappeared with his beloved daughter into the bayou.

"Why are you just standing there? You're letting that woman take away your daughter!" Patia yelled at Dorian.

"Everyone, back to camp, *now*," Dorian ordered again.

The rest of his people mounted their horses and slowly, quietly, headed home. Dorian did not speak to Patia. He simply whistled for his horse.

Patia screamed at her husband like a brazen hyena taunting a menacing lion. She pounded her fists on his large chest. Dorian, unmoved, slowly pushed her away and held her off at arm's length.

"Control yourself. There is nothing else we can do tonight."

He figured the woman would eventually tire. Regrettably, he miscalculated her movements. Patia ducked and stepped to one side, avoiding his grasp, and slapped him hard across the face. For good measure, she spat at him. Warm, slimy saliva dripped on his face.

That was the last straw. Dorian smacked Patia to the ground with one blow.

"This was your fault. All of it!"

His horse obediently arrived and Dorian rode off back to camp, leaving his wife wallowing on the ground.

"My Syeira! She's taking my Syeira from me," Patia screamed into the soft, boggy ground. Some of the women helped her to her feet as everyone dispersed.

Chapter 9/Welcome to the Family

ONCE HOME, GRANDMOTHER PREPARED A potion to help Syeira calm down. Syeira curled up in a ball on Grandmother's couch. Grandmother mixed herbs and spices that were symbolic of the sun. Cayenne pepper was for warmth, sunflower juice was for happiness, and marigold petals were to combat darkness. She added elements of love, including rose petals. To complete the beverage, she added cocoa powder, which was Will's favorite sweet dessert, to ease her heartbreak. Blending them all together, she chanted a few Voodoo wishes over the potion.

This should bring energy to Syeira's spirit, she thought as she poured the concoction into a tall glass.

"Drink this," Grandmother said. "It looks horrible, but it's for your own good. It'll help you sleep."

Syeira sat up obediently and drank the lukewarm concoction. It was hard to choke down the lumps and slime in her glass.

Once she managed to swallow the last drop, Grandmother had the young woman stand on a white rug near the fireplace.

"We need to do a clearing, to make sure no other negative energy is with you."

"What?" Syeira asked. She was tired. She was sore inside and out. All she wanted to do was curl up next to Will, but he was gone.

"I'm gonna say a Bible verse, Isaiah 41 to be exact, and wave this feathered brush on you. It's supposed to brush away bad energies that might be around."

Syeira stared at the Voodoo woman.

"Does it hurt?" she asked.

"Not at all. Bear with me; it won't take long."

Grandmother Zenobia dashed down a small, dark hallway and into a small room on the right. When she returned, she held a fan constructed of a turkey's wing. She said the Bible verse loudly and clearly while swooping the turkey wing in a downward fashion.

"Was that it?" Syeira asked. It wasn't as bad as she'd expected.

Syeira's thoughts drifted back to Will. What would she do without him? How could she go on all alone? Her heart was heavy and her body was weak.

"I know it's hard to ask, but try to get some rest," Grandmother said as she led Syeira to Will's room. The usual furry menagerie followed them through the house. The room was rather sparse; aside from a nice-sized bed, there wasn't much except the bookshelves that lined each wall. Ahy whimpered at the foot of Will's bed.

Grandmother laid out one of her own nightgowns and a robe for Syeira to wear if she wanted.

Once Syeira settled in, Grandmother sat motionless in her small, stuffy prayer room. She tried desperately to hear her own heartbeat to no avail. It had throbbed in her chest earlier, but sadness now ate at her insides. Grandmother could hardly breathe.

Will was a good boy. He never hurt anyone and now he's dead. He was tortured by those bats. That gypsy curse got ahold of him.

It disturbed her that she had no idea what was going on.

Grandmother had done her best to raise her grandson. He was loved and protected under her care, and yet she could not save him from a curse. She had no family left, other than her faithful dog Ahy. She believed that the situation was somehow her fault. Tears finally escaped their prison, trickling down her warm cheeks. Moans crept into the smothering silence. To her surprise, the moaning came from the hallway, not her own mouth.

Something was wrong with Syeira. Grandmother's heart woke up and pounded thunderously in her chest. She broke away from her sadness.

Grandmother grabbed a silver bucket and some fresh towels in case the young woman was sick. She knocked on the door several times, but there was no response. She pushed through into Will's room. The room smelled like sweaty old clothes. The menagerie of animals was nowhere to be found. Grandmother lit a candle to see what was going on. Syeira looked horrible as she tossed and turned in Will's bed. Grandmother had left the girl alone for just a few minutes. Her once-beautiful face was puffy and pale. She looked bloated in her borrowed nightgown. Grandmother sat beside her and checked her forehead. Her temperature was high. Syeira moaned loudly and incoherently as she thrashed about.

Did my potion poison her? Grandmother panicked.

Syeira moaned louder, babbling away about bats and wildflowers, and clutched her stomach. Grandmother held the ailing girl's wrist to check her pulse. She noticed a few scratches on Syeira's right hand. They were inflamed and dark blood oozed from their crevices.

"This is not from my potion."

Grandmother retrieved her medical bag. After rifling through it, she found rubbing alcohol. She poured it on the girl's scratches, hoping to stop any infection that had set in. Syeira whimpered when the cold, clear liquid touched her skin and, to Grandmother's dismay, the scratches bubbled with an orange, foul-smelling foam. It was an indication of dark magic. Syeira was also cursed. The cleansing prayer hadn't worked.

Grandmother reflected back to the gypsy woman lurking behind the bushes and trees. Judging by her reaction and desperate prayer at the scene of Will's death, it was she who was guilty of the black magic. Syeira was cursed by her own cowardly mother. Dark, bitter energies exuded from that woman. Grandmother Zenobia didn't like her one bit. She'd figure out how to get the gypsy woman back for all she had done, but that would have to be once Grandmother knew Syeira was okay.

Grandmother fed Syeira a few small white flower petals from her medicine bag to induce vomiting. Syeira instantly sat up, clutched her stomach, and threw up a sticky orange puddle. She retched several times, spewing orange goo all around the room.

When Grandmother thought the young girl was done, Syeira began to gasp for air and clutch at her throat. She choked on whatever was left in her stomach. Grandmother managed to get the girl on her feet. Grandmother stood behind her, placed her hands under the girl's ribcage, and pushed several times. Syeira vomited again and growled as more goo splattered on the floor.

As Syeira leaned forward, a huge glob of orange goo slowly slid from her mouth. It revealed a large, black, sticky, spider-like creature. The monstrosity was six inches in diameter. It had several eyes, which rolled around its partially formed head. When it fell from Syeira's lips, it landed on its back, its legs twitching violently in the air. Three of the legs had deformed pincers on them. Four legs were stubby and short. A few others were long and had thorns peeking through sticky black hair. The beast eventually managed to roll over and sprung up on all of its sticky legs.

Zenobia should have been scared; most people in that situation would flee into the night. But not Grandmother Zenobia. She was furious. The creature reared, rubbed its front legs in the air, and hissed aggressively at the Voodoo priestess.

"Not in my house!" she yelled. Grandmother motioned with her hands and the creature was lifted in the air. The creature screamed like an overheated tea kettle. Grandmother howled as she slammed it, with gale-force strength, all around the room. It banged on the floor. It banged against the door. It bounced in between walls. Several times it was crushed on the ceiling. The twisted hissing finally stopped and the creature oozed a dark substance as it lay at her feet. Grandmother growled as she motioned her hands again and crushed it. Her rage took over, even after the creature stopped moving.

Grandmother's fierce outburst was interrupted by Syeira's sobs. The girl watched, terrified, as Zenobia wielded her magic. She tried to hide in the vomit-soaked bed linen. She vomited again, and bile mixed with blood all over the linens.

The creature, which Zenobia had thought to be dead, squawked. To make sure the beast was dead, Grandmother rushed over and with her own hands physically slammed the silver bucket several times upon it. She bashed it and bashed it until there was nothing but tiny bits left in a puddle of ooze. Syeira continued to cower, trying to hide.

"Syeira, I am so sorry you had to experience this. I promise you, I'm not the evil person people think I am."

She slowly approached the girl, who buried herself in a corner of messy blankets.

"Everything will be okay."

Grandmother was disappointed to see how fearfully the girl looked at her. Her own daughter, Angelica, had looked at her like that once, and it had broken her heart. Grandmother grabbed a few towels and carefully sat on the bed. She slowly removed the blankets around Syeira and carefully wiped her vomit-caked face with a clean towel. Syeira refused to move, frozen in the corner.

Zenobia left the smelly room, grabbed a tall glass from the kitchen, and filled it with cold water. Without hesitation, she went straight for the large black urn that sat at her bedside.

"If this doesn't work, nothing will," she thought as she collected two small pinches of red dust from the urn.

Grandmother Zenobia was the sole guardian of the Blood of the Ancients. It was a powdery red substance, contained in a large urn. It had stardust from a meteorite found in the Arabian desert. It had blood, ground-up bone, and flesh from two Egyptian deities – Ra, the Sun King, and his sworn enemy, Apep the destroyer and ruler of darkness. The samples were taken when both had assumed temporary human forms. Most importantly, it had a chunk of her husband's heart.

Zenobia was married to Set, god of deserts, storms, and chaos. The ancients fiercely believed the heart was kept with the body when it was mummified; the heart was the most important part of a person. When the soul returned to the afterlife, the heart would speak for the soul when it was judged. Set was so despised by so many deities that when he was trapped in human form, his heart was separated from his body. His spirit, his essence, was forced to linger in limbo for centuries until Zenobia discovered it. She was just a young girl, playing along the Nile river with her dog Ahy, when she found a jar that held his heart. She kept it with her, always protective of it. The majority of Set's heart was eventually added to the Blood of the Ancients. A small sliver of his heart, about the size of an almond, was kept in a black-and-gold compartment of the ring Zenobia wore day and night. Secretly keeping his heart close to her was a reminder that no matter how destructive Set was, he would always love her, and she would always love him.

Throughout many centuries, as Zenobia had travelled the world, she collected knickknacks, remnants, and remains to add to the Blood of the Ancients. The urn included samples of Roman Kings, royalty from the Far East, and a handful of powerful people whom Zenobia had encountered. It had the blood of virginal sacrifices, scales of a dragon, and ash from a volcano. She'd managed to trap a minor demon from hell. For good measure, it also had bits and pieces of mystical places of the earth. The urn, with all of its contents, was a reminder of who Zenobia was, whom she'd met, where she had been, and where she wanted to go. It was a twisted collection of her past.

The Blood of the Ancients had a powerful effect on mortals. Zenobia had figured out how to use it in very small amounts to heal people, but she only used it in dire emergencies.

After mixing the smallest pinches she could manage of the Blood of the Ancients with cold water, Grandmother went back into Will's room. Syeira was still dazed as she rocked herself and mumbled. Grandmother slowly approached her, humming a sweet song, which stirred Syeira slightly from her haze.

"That's Will's favorite song…" she whispered sadly. Her throat burned from all the vomiting earlier. Blood was caked on her lips and chin.

"It's mine too," Grandmother said, mirroring her soft tone. "Drink this, sweetheart. It will make the pain go away."

Syeira paused. She didn't want to drink anything else Grandmother gave her. She wanted to curl up in Will's arms.

Her stomach gurgled. She was too weak, too scared to leave. Even if she left Grandmother's home, she wouldn't go back to her people. Realizing she had nowhere to go, she figured she had no choice but to follow the Voodoo woman's directions. She swallowed the cold beverage. To her surprise, it soothed the throbbing pain in her throat and calmed her queasy stomach. Once Syeira finished her drink, Grandmother gave her a clean nightgown and removed the soiled bedding.

"Thank you," Syeira said as she sat on the bed next to Grandmother. She laid her head on Grandmother's chest like a child. As she did, Grandmother rocked her slowly and hummed, stroking her hair.

Grandmother missed quiet moments of bonding with another person. Happy memories of her daughter Angelica flooded her mind.

Grandmother whispered in Syeira's ear, enchanting her to sleep. Grandmother hummed again as Syeira closed her heavy eyelids and drifted off to sleep.

Once the girl was tucked back into bed, Grandmother looked around at the messy room. She was too tired to clean everything up by hand. So she waved her left hand, and a cool mist filled the room. It swirled about the room, highlighting orange goo, the remnants of the creature, and the vomit splattered around. As it swirled, colored flashes lit up the room like fireflies. The light burned away any residual negative energy that remained.

She opened the window next to where Syeira slept and the mist dissipated as it escaped into the night air.

Foolish gypsy woman, I know who you are, Grandmother thought as she watched Syeira sleep.

Patia Camlo, you will pay for what you've done. I would gladly give up twenty years of my soul to see you suffer! I should have killed you when I had the chance. Tension filled her body.

A photo of Will shook on a nearby bookshelf. Seeing Will's small grin reminded Grandmother that she was no longer the enraged, anger-fueled woman from long ago. She unclenched her teeth and drew in a cleansing breath.

I'm better than this. I will leave it to the heavens, like the Good Book says: vengeance is mine, I will repay, says the Lord. She didn't like it, but she knew that the Good Book was hardly ever wrong.

Grandmother believed that the young girl was relatively safe from any more curses or spells. Still, she sat dutifully next to Syeira's bedside. Every once in a while, the girl quietly moaned and clutched her belly. Grandmother stayed with her through the rest of the night. In the morning, the sun finally poked its way through ominous thunderclouds that hung in the August sky.

The evening's torment eventually melted away with the sunlight. Once the young woman seemed to be at peace, Grandmother proceeded to her own room to get a little rest herself. She paused at the bathroom mirror and was surprised that there were no new gray hairs.

Later that morning, as Syeira woke, she noticed she felt different. She sensed a quiet buzzing sensation from head to toe. She reached over and grabbed a small mirror with a multicolored border that Will had made resting on a nearby nightstand. She noticed that her eyes had changed color. They'd gone from emerald green to one eye dark brown and the other a beautiful deep blue. The change in eye color was shocking. Her vision was the same; she could see just fine. Everything around her still buzzed. She noticed a large bandage on her right hand as she pushed away sheets soaked in her own sweat.

"May I come in?" Grandmother asked softly after knocking gently on her door.

Syeira heard Grandmother's menagerie of pets, the many dogs and cats, ducks, and other animals who had adopted her as one of their own, waiting impatiently, barking, squawking, and scratching at the bedroom door.

"Yes, please come in," Syeira said softly.

Grandmother entered with a large tray of food fit for a queen. The animals rushed in, all insisting on being near Syeira and protecting her. They wiggled, pressed, and leaned their soft furry bodies close to her. Syeira was still aware of the strange buzzing, but she was comforted by the attention.

"Good morning. Did you sleep okay?" Grandmother asked as she gingerly passed through the rest of the animals that flopped on the floor.

"Make space for me," Grandmother said to the animals. Obediently, they parted a path for Grandmother to approach Syeira with her tray of grits, eggs, chamomile tea, toast, and ham. The pink pillow Syeira had given her was tucked under one of her arms. Grandmother handed it to Syeira before she balanced the tray on her hip and opened up a second window to let in fresh air.

"I tossed and turned a lot," Syeira said as she sat up, looking at the breakfast tray. She tried to ignore the wonderful smells that circled around her nose.

The animals closest to Syeira wouldn't move. They continued to sit on her, around her, and squeezed in her bed. Grandmother took a long look at Syeira. She saw the change in eye color but didn't address it.

"As you can see, I made breakfast. Eat all of it," she said as she set the tray before the girl.

"But I'm not hungry," Syeira lied, shooing a duck off her pillow. "I just want to sleep."

"It's not a request," Grandmother said sternly, as she shooed away a few cats.

Syeira looked over at a picture of Will. Grandmother noticed it too.

The memory of Will, engulfed in flames, silenced the room for a moment.

"I don't know how I can go on living. He's gone." Fresh tears streaked down Syeira's cheeks. She tried, half-heartedly, to wipe them away.

Grandmother's powerful energy kindled and overtook the room as she addressed Syeira. All the animals stopped and watched Grandmother as she spoke.

"Listen here, girl. You aren't the only one who already misses Will."

"Well, yes, but…"

"Don't interrupt me. I'm not done speaking to you. Right now, you are a stranger in my house. You are not the woman that my Will fell in love with. You are not the woman he gave his life to be with." Grandmother's anger boiled in her stomach. "We both know Will would want you to live life to its fullest."

Syeira was speechless. No one other than her father had ever dared talk to her in such a manner.

"I challenge you to push past the sadness for right now. Find the strong young woman who loves life. The woman my grandson adored. You sit there appearing to be a fool and a coward, feeling sorry for yourself. I know the truth about you. I refuse to feel sorry for you. How dare you disgrace Will! He deserved more than weakness and misery. You deserve more than that too. Last night, when you came to me for help, I saw who you really were. You had courage."

As the older woman continued her rant, Syeira looked down at her hands. She still wore the gold band Will had given her.

"Or, if I am wrong, and if you really want to give up, go on. Get out of my home. Kill yourself for all I care, just not on my land. I don't need that kind of energy here. There are already too many bodies to lay to rest this week."

Ahy nudged Grandmother. She looked at the dog and then realized she was shouting at the girl. Embarrassed at her outburst, she turned to leave. Syeira grabbed the small mirror at her bedside again and looked at her reflection. She did not recognize the puffy-faced girl who stared back at her in the mirror.

"Grandmother Zenobia," Syeira said quickly, stopping the older woman before she exited the room. "You're very wise. I'm sorry. Forgive me, please. I apologize if I offended you. You're right about Will. I want to believe that you're right about me too."

Syeira was surprised to see sadness on Grandmother's face when she turned to her.

"I accept your apology," Grandmother said softly.

"Thank you for reminding me of who I am."

"Of course. It's what my grandson would have wanted."

Syeira studied Grandmother for a moment, not daring to look directly at her, and looked around Will's room.

Syeira considered how she felt about Grandmother. She was not a nice person, but, looking back, she saw that the Voodoo woman was incredibly generous to her. She could have easily left Syeira with the tribe, which would have been horrible. Instead, Syeira, who was still a stranger, was invited to stay in her home. She was given a warm bed. The woman stayed with her when she was sick. She comforted her when she had terrible nightmares, and even now Syeira was offered a huge breakfast. She should have been grieving the death of her grandson.

"If it isn't too much trouble, may I please stay here with you? The Camlo family is dead to me. I have no place to go. This is where Will lived and it's where I want to be."

Grandmother softened as she spoke.

"Princess, you may stay here, in my home, as long as you wish."

Syeira managed to smile.

"You will respect my rules, and not question me," Grandmother warned as she pulled up a chair next to Syeira.

"Yes, ma'am."

"Don't call me ma'am. Call me Grandmother," she said as she poured Syeira a cup of steamy tea.

"Yes, Grandmother."

"I know you're sharp, and I'm sure you'll learn my rules quickly. Your father didn't raise a weak fool."

Syeira wondered how Grandmother knew anything about her father.

Grandmother's favorite white-and-tan cat left Syeira and curled in Grandmother's lap.

"Will was right to want to marry you. I can tell you have a good heart. As long as you are respectful, I know we'll get along."

Syeira watched Grandmother as she softly stroked the large cat's ears.

"You are more like a mother to me than my own mother," she said as she sipped on the tea Grandmother gave her.

Grandmother flashed a small smile and stood up with the cat in her arms.

"If you need anything, don't hesitate to ask."

"Thank you, Grandmother Zenobia. I am thankful you are in my life."

Grandmother returned the cat to Syeira's bed.

"There is one other thing I need to talk to you about. I think something is wrong with me. My eyes are green. When I woke up I noticed they changed color."

"I noticed that too. Do you have a headache? Does it hurt to blink or anything?"

"No, my head and eyes feel fine. I'm just hungry."

"Hopefully it's temporary. I'll talk with Dr. Evans later on to see what he thinks. Not to worry – consider yourself in good hands as long as you are under this roof. If you feel any pain or have issues with your vision, you let me know right away."

Syeira breathed a deep sigh.

"Enjoy your breakfast before it gets cold. The rest of you, behave while she eats," Grandmother said as she exited the room.

"I like how she talks to all of you," Syeira said to the animals around her. "I remember Will did that too."

Grandmother grabbed herself a cup of tea and sat on the back porch. She leaned back in her chair to rest, letting a small bit of peace seep into her pores with the rising humidity in the summer air. She was grateful that she wasn't alone after all.

As Syeira sipped on her tea, she tried to figure Grandmother out. She really liked the Voodoo woman. She was bossy, but she was sincere. She liked that Grandmother talked to her like an adult, not like the way her own people talked to her, like a child.

Syeira concluded that Grandmother was very peculiar. She had never met anyone who was creepy but inviting, hard and strong but elegantly formal at the same time. And magic? It was amazing what Grandmother could do. She saw why Grandmother was feared in town. Her own mother wasn't that skilled in magic. Syeira made a mental note to ask Grandmother how she wielded that kind of power and strength. It would be an honor to learn those skills from her. Real magic, not simple tricks or fancy words her mother tried to teach her. Syeira remembered how the bat flew across the room so quickly into the fireplace, and how Grandmother fed the owl. It was scary but thrilling.

Syeira scarfed down her breakfast with her new little friends at her side. The more she ate, the more she realized how hungry she really was. Her stomach spoke a foreign language, grumbling and gurgling as food filled it up. She slowed down and savored every bite. No one was there to steal food off her plate, like back home. She didn't have to share anything with anyone. This was a new situation for her.

She and her people never stayed in just one place for very long, but Grandmother Zenobia's house felt like it was where she was meant to be.

Chapter 10/Secrets

SEVERAL MONTHS HAD PASSED SINCE Grandmother Zenobia had taken Syeira into her home. Grandmother no longer gave private tarot readings, and no longer performed magic. She wanted to be a good example of an "upstanding, hardworking citizen" to Syeira. Winter finally made its way to Louisiana. Most days, everyone bundled up in the chilly sunshine, and most nights, everyone burned their fireplaces brightly.

Grandmother half knitted, half watched Syeira, as the girl absentmindedly washed a pile of dishes, pots, and pans. Syeira spent more time staring out the window than scrubbing food off the plates. Every now and then, she snuck leftovers to Ahy. He waited obediently at her feet.

"Does it snow here?" Syeira asked. A glass slipped from her grasp in the sink filled with soapy water when she struggled to pull out another dirty plate to be scrubbed. Luckily, it didn't break.

"Be careful with my dishes, young lady, and stop feeding my dog," Grandmother said.

"Sorry."

Grandmother looked at the time. Then she put down her knitting.

"It's time for me to head into town for a bit. I won't be gone too long."

Grandmother cringed when Syeira juggled another glass in the soapy water.

"Isn't there some spell we could use to do this instead?" Syeira asked.

The pile of dirty dishes, pots, and pans was never-ending. For every plate she washed, she felt there were two more waiting to be scrubbed. Syeira shifted her weight from one foot to another, bracing herself for more monotonous work. After drying her hands, she looked out the window, hoping for any kind of distraction, while she massaged her lower back. Her back and her knees reminded her that she was getting heavier every day.

"To answer your first question, yes it does snow in New Orleans. I'm surprised how summer and fall flew by so quickly." Grandmother watched Syeira taking a break from the dishes. "Looks like rain today, but it's a matter of time before the snow season starts. I can't imagine how your tribe survives in the winter."

"I don't want to talk about them," Syeira snapped.

"My apologies."

Grandmother watched Syeira look out the window again. Syeira twisted the gold band around her finger as she stared. Grandmother hadn't had the heart to take the ring back from her after Will's death.

"I miss Will too," Grandmother said as she approached Syeira. "You gotta shake off the sadness. It's not good for you or the little ones." Grandmother shook her shoulders. "It helps. Try it."

Syeira growled, and shrugged her shoulders as she grabbed another plate and scrubbed it furiously.

"To answer your second question, as I have told you several times, we no longer use magic in this house. We should be proper, God-fearing women. Quit asking me about magic."

"Yes, ma'am."

Grandmother growled to herself at being addressed as "ma'am" but didn't scold the girl.

"Shake your shoulders again. It'll give you some energy."

Syeira listened to Ahy scamper away and follow Grandmother when she left the kitchen. The dog's tail thumped on the hardwood floor while Grandmother lingered at the hallway closet, looking for something warm to wear outside. Syeira dried her hands and shrugged her shoulders. She raised them up to her ears and let them fall. As they dropped, the tension faded. Syeira drew in a deep breath. She shook her hands and wrists, jingling multicolored bracelets. Two of her favorite bracelets had dark green and onyx beads with silver bells. The bracelets weren't crafted as well as the ones she herself made. The knots around the clasps were too big. Several of the beads were already cracked and broken; some were too big and some were too small.

As the bells jingled around her wrists, Syeira was reminded of the day that she and Grandmother spent time together making jewelry. The two of them sat in the living room near the fireplace on a stormy afternoon. They huddled together and drank steamy black tea with honey and munched on burnt lemon cookies Syeira had baked. They told stories of the past that made them laugh while Syeira showed Grandmother how the women of her tribe strung up necklaces and bracelets. While picking through a large pile of beads, Grandmother complained that she wasn't skilled enough to make jewelry, or art, or anything creative. Her fingertips were sore from needle pricks and her eyes hurt at the lack of light in the room. When the projects were finished, Syeira insisted they trade at least one item from the pile of jewelry they created. It was customary, she said, that family exchange their wares. Grandmother Zenobia beamed with pride when the girl selected the bracelets she'd made. That memory broke up the monotony of doing the dishes, at least for the moment.

Syeira joined Grandmother and Ahy in the hallway. She placed a bonnet over the older woman's headscarf and tied the ribbons carefully around her neck. Grandmother wrestled with her heavy wool cloak until it settled on her broad shoulders.

"Would you mind looking for my gloves, too?" Grandmother asked. "I haven't worn them since last winter."

Syeira went back to the armoire by the door. She searched it from top to bottom, not finding them. She glanced at a wicker basket that sat next to the armoire. She noticed a pair of women's leather gloves in it, a few toys for Ahy, and one ruby-red slipper.

"Whose shoe is this? It doesn't look like something you would wear."

Grandmother chuckled.

"The shoe was from one of my first clients when I moved here. It belonged to a burlesque dancer. She came to me looking for help with love."

"Did you help her?"

"Yes but no. It's a long story. It turned out that the man she loved wanted help with love too. She didn't know how he felt about her and vice versa. Every morning, when the young lady finished dancing the night before, she came by, asking all kinds of questions. She was an amazing dancer. Every night before the young man went into town (after working in the red pepper fields), he came by, asking all kinds of questions. I will always remember that farmer's bright-red hair! Anyways, both always showed up, unannounced, on my property. As you know, I can't stand people just showing up at my home. They both bugged me every day for a week, asking for help. It took me a minute to figure out that they were meant to be together. Eventually I had each agree to have an official appointment to see me. I was tricky. I scheduled the appointments so they would have to be here at the same time, as a surprise. Love took over from there. When they left together, the young lady left her dancing shoes here. I decided that I would hang one outside, on the fence, when I was open to seeing people for advice and guidance. I haven't hung a red shoe out in a long time."

"That's some story!"

"You don't know the half of it. I'll share it with you, another day. In the meantime, I'm doing my best to be a proper role model for you. Magic can hurt as much as it can help. So I'm relying on the Lord above these days. I'm trying to be a proper God-fearing woman."

Syeira shrugged her shoulders again, with more energy, and Grandmother mirrored her.

"Proper God-fearing women sounds stuffy, doesn't it," Grandmother said.

Syeira nodded.

"Well, without magic we'll figure out the best way to live life. How does that sound?"

"I like that idea better."

"It's my job to help you keep your mind sharp and your belly fat," Grandmother joked.

Syeira laughed.

"It's my job to make you proud."

"Are you sure you don't want to come with me into town?" Grandmother cringed as she spoke. She knew the answer but wanted to ask anyway.

"No, thank you."

"When I get back from my errands, we'll do some more reading and writing if you'd like, or maybe go over some more recipes."

"That would be nice."

Syeira presented the gloves to Grandmother. They stood at the door, hesitant to open it. Syeira rubbed her shoulders for warmth.

"I prefer warmer temperatures. I'm guessing by the way you're shivering, you prefer them too. Feel free to put another log on the fire if you want," Grandmother said as she opened the front door. A cool breeze blew in, a reminder that winter was on its way.

"Don't forget these!" Syeira grabbed a plate of beignets from the kitchen counter. "I hope Charlotte and Cora will like them. This batch came out much better than the last ones I made."

"I'm sure they will love them. Your cooking is getting better all the time."

Syeira knew Grandmother didn't lie, but she had a way of bending the truth a bit, too.

Grandmother looked at Syeira and noticed dark circles under her eyes.

"They're still two different colors," Syeira said and stood back, trying to avoid the cold draft.

"Are you feeling okay?"

"I'm fine. The morning sickness is gone."

"Are you sure?"

"You are horrible at leaving the house. You should go before it gets too late."

"You look like you could use more sleep."

Syeira looked at the mountain of dishes that waited for her.

"Don't worry about the rest of today's chores. Get some rest. I'll finish up the dishes and pots later when I get back. Judging by those dark clouds, we'll do laundry another day."

"I can handle the dishes, Grandmother. I promise not to break anything. You don't have to fuss over us."

"We'll see about you and those dishes." She placed her hands on Syeira's rosy cheeks. "Princess, I'm always going to fuss over you. It is what grandmothers do."

Syeira hugged Grandmother.

"I won't be gone too long."

Grandmother stepped out on the porch and looked up at the grey sky. Her eyes searched around her property carefully before she saddled her horse.

Unbeknownst to Syeira, some of Grandmother's errands were hardly ever in town.

On this dreary afternoon, Dorian Camlo waited for Grandmother to arrive. He made every effort to not be tracked through the woods. As he leaned against a large oak tree, his fingers unconsciously tapped his favorite hunting knife that always rested securely at the right side of his waist. He liked the cold chill in the air that clung to his skin.

He closed his eyes and listened to the wind whistle through the trees overhead. When he opened his eyes, Grandmother was sitting on her horse just a few yards away from him. He didn't know how Grandmother had appeared from nowhere, but he did know that he didn't dare ask her.

"Sorry I'm late, Your Majesty."

Dorian rushed up to Grandmother and helped her dismount her horse. Once she gathered herself, he watched as she slightly nodded her head and slightly bowed. She didn't lower her eyes to the ground like his subordinates did.

"I'm the one who should bow to you." Dorian quickly stood up and removed his hat. "It's my honor to see you." He bowed until he felt her hand tap him on the shoulder.

"I brought you a goodwill offering," she said as she turned back to the horse to retrieve something from a leather saddlebag. Dorian had noticed a sweet smell when he helped her off the horse but didn't know what it was.

"Syeira made these. I thought you'd like them." She offered warm, slightly burnt beignets for her tardiness.

"Does she know you're meeting me here?" Dorian asked.

"No. She thinks I'm visiting with friends and running errands. Your daughter is still hell-bent on turning her back on her people. She doesn't know that the tribe is still around in Carrefour Parish."

Dorian shook his head and looked down at his feet.

"It's the beginning of winter. Have your people asked why you haven't moved on to a new, warmer location?"

"Lucky for me, the holidays here in Louisiana are far more festive and lucrative than we expected. We feel more welcomed here than most places we've travelled to. It doesn't seem suspicious that we've stayed so long. I'm not ready to abandon my daughter, even though she no longer claims us."

Dorian felt his body tense.

"She's a wonderful girl, Dorian. She still wears the copper ankh you gave her."

Dorian grunted.

"I can see why you don't want to leave. You raised her well. She's always respectful. Not only that, but she is smart as a fox and very skillful. I hope it doesn't offend you, but I've been helping her learn how to read. It seems that Will taught her a little. I know the women of your tribe don't read or write, but Syeira is a quick learner and I think it's important for her to grow."

Grandmother's words should have been reassuring, encouraging. The meeting caused Dorian to miss his princess more.

"Anything you teach her is a blessing. I should consider teaching some of our women in my tribe to read and write. It is against our ways, but I think it will benefit them greatly too. All of my people need to learn how to adapt a bit, not just the men, to survive these days."

Grandmother nodded in agreement.

"Dorian, you're a great leader. It's inspiring that you consider what's good for your people."

"Thank you. Being a good leader means nothing, though, if I can't be a good father to my daughter."

Dorian stood, shoulders weighed down with guilt.

"I promise you, I'll raise her as if she were my own daughter," Grandmother said to the tall, quiet man. Dorian thought more about what Grandmother had said. The earthy tone of her voice reassured him a little.

"You should know, if you didn't figure it out already, that it was your wife's curse that killed Will. It also affected Syeira. I tried to counteract it with a blessing the night Will died but it went differently than expected."

The news of the curse poisoned any assurance Dorian had felt. He already knew Patia had attempted spells often and tried to "fix things." It embarrassed him that Grandmother would have to use her genuine power and cast her own spell.

"I don't care about her or her foolish curses," he lashed out. "I'm thankful Syeira is alive and is in your hands." His words came out with an unplanned bitter edge.

"You have to find other ways to let go of your anger. Don't put your hands on that woman anymore," warned Grandmother. "God will punish her for us."

"But she is always attacking me! Always disrespecting me!" he growled. "She yells at me. She threatens me. She slaps and kicks me when we're alone!"

"You can't control her, but you can control how you react to her. You are a king! Can you send her away to another tribe? Can you somehow separate yourself from her?"

"That is not the gypsy way."

"That woman will be the death of you if you continue to raise your hand to her."

Dorian paced around, shaking his head. He didn't know what else to do or say.

"I'm at a loss," he said. "I can't control much of anything, it seems."

Grandmother cleared her throat.

"There is something I need to tell you, something that I have struggled to share with you these past few months."

"What is it? You can always talk to me about anything."

"I wanted to tell you at our last meeting, but, well, Syeira was having a very hard time. We all did, actually, on what would have been Will's birthday."

Grandmother watched Dorian cover his mouth with his muscular hand, trying to hold back any emotion that might threaten to escape.

"Will's birthday…" Dorian's words trailed off. He remembered his behavior that day, when he drank himself into a horrible rage. No one else in the tribe knew the significance of that particular date. As king, he did what he pleased, generally without question as long as no one was harmed. Patia, who could be a devoted wife when she chose to, gave him plenty of space and did not question his erratic behavior. He could not imagine what either Grandmother or Syeira felt that day.

"As you remember, it took time to get Syeira back to her right mind. She was doing well, and I was so proud of her, but then she got pretty upset."

"Why? What happened?"

"She was hysterical, practically inconsolable, on Will's birthday. She thinks I don't hear her when she cries herself to sleep some nights."

"If she's that upset, please, let me see her. I can make things right. I swear it!" Desperation leaked from his baritone voice. He was losing his struggle to hold in his emotions.

"No, Dorian, not yet." She watched him pace faster around her. The temperature around them was dropping.

"What are you hiding, Zenobia? Just tell me!"

Grandmother was about to scold him for calling her by her proper name. Instead, she chose not to speak. She tugged at her cloak, defending herself from the cold. Grandmother looked at the broken man who stood before her. She waited until the truth came to her lips freely.

"Syeira is pregnant."

"Pregnant?" Dorian's stomach spasmed as if he'd been struck by a ghostly sucker punch.

"Yes. Apparently Syeira and Will consummated their relationship after they were cursed."

Dorian clenched his jaw in anger.

"I wish with all my heart that I could predict what will happen for her. I'm too close to her to have any real insight into her future. Some days, she's strong. Some days, she's terribly weak. I don't even know if she will be able to carry the babies to term. And worse, I don't know if the babies will be okay if they do see the light of day."

"Babies?"

"Yes, babies. She is having twins."

"How is that possible?"

"I could be wrong, but I think it was Patia's curse."

Lightning crackled and thunder boomed in the distance, interrupting an uncomfortable pause between Grandmother and Dorian. Dorian was speechless, torn by conflicting emotions. He was the king of his people, but now he was weak, helpless and lost. He knew this situation wasn't Grandmother's fault. If anything, she had been a blessing to him. He had allowed things to get so far out of hand. In the few moments he could steal away from his tribe each day, he mercilessly punished himself for pushing his daughter out of his life. Now, with this unexpected turn of events, both Dorian and Grandmother were very concerned for Syeira and her babies.

"Should she need anything, don't hesitate to contact me. I am your humble servant, Grandmother. Thank you again for taking care of my princess. I wish there was more I could do to repay your generosity."

Grandmother stepped closer to the broken man and placed both her hands on his chest, directly upon his heart. As it thumped sadly, Dorian felt the warmth of her hands through his thick coat. The kind gesture broke through into his loneliness. Dorian looked at her as tears ran down his cheeks. He had been strong for so long, but now he was at the end of his rope. The hot tears opened a large space in his heart and he began to sob uncontrollably.

"I wish I could promise you that everything would be okay. I can only promise you that we will do our best to get through this."

Grandmother held him close. Dorian tried to collect himself, but the act of kindness only created more tears.

Grandmother stroked the back of his head, consoling him. The gray sky darkened more and large, cold raindrops spattered everywhere. Grandmother's embrace was warm and soft. She smelled like cinnamon.

"I'm more than happy to look after your daughter. She is a wonderful girl. I promise, I will do everything I can to keep her healthy and safe."

Dorian could only nod his head in agreement as his body shook. Rain continued to fall.

"Before we go our separate ways, promise me that you'll take care of yourself too. I know you're punishing yourself too much. I can see it in your eyes. I feel it all around you. Maybe the time will come and her heart will be open to you. Maybe, if the babies are healthy, she'll accept you back into her life. I'll try to help you as much as I can. You need to be the strong, vibrant man I know you can be. We have to let the situation run its course."

Dorian gasped for air and looked up to the clouds in the sky, trying to calm his nerves. He looked back at Grandmother, realizing she had lost a great deal in her life too. Grandmother put her hands on his face, wiping away his tears through the raindrops.

"I am amazed that, even to this day, you help me."

"You remind me of one of my husbands, when I was younger. He was a good man, and a good king."

Grandmother neglected to mention that she referred to one of her former husbands, Palmyrian leader Septimius Odaenathus. He'd taught her how to be a strong ruler, before he was assassinated. Just like Dorian, he too had a soft spot for his family.

That was another story, for another day.

"I can never thank you enough, Grandmother."

Dorian hugged Grandmother tenderly, gathered his emotions, and reminded himself that he was a mighty king. The fickle Louisiana rain stopped abruptly as they went their separate ways.

Chapter 11/The Red Moon

IT WAS A LIVELY SPRING evening in Louisiana on May 23, 1890. A full moon smiled in the dark sky, and a much-anticipated lunar eclipse, predicted by *The Old Farmer's Almanac*, was imminent. Grandmother and Syeira enjoyed frosty glasses of lemonade while relaxing on the front porch. Syeira painstakingly read *Wuthering Heights* out loud to Grandmother until the eclipse was more interesting to pay attention to.

A chorus of crickets was disrupted by Grandmother's dogs. They howled and growled at owls that played in the darkness. Syeira felt one of the babies kick and then the squeeze of a contraction. She had experienced a few throughout the day so she didn't think much of it.

"Is everything okay?" Grandmother asked.

Syeira struggled to get out of her rocking chair. Her back throbbed, so she stood up to stretch and tried to calm the agitated dogs.

"Everything is fine except for the dogs. I wonder what's gotten into them."

The babies kicked more aggressively, causing Syeira to double over in pain. A small puddle of liquid appeared between her legs on the porch. The ground slightly shook, rocking the house gently.

"Oh my Lord in heaven! It's time!" Grandmother squealed.

Syeira watched Grandmother as she clasped her hands to her chest with joy.

Warm liquid oozed down Syeira's inner thighs. Her insides cramped with pain.

"I don't know if I can do this! I'm not ready!" Syeira said.

Grandmother saw panic in the girl's eyes.

"Come inside. Everything will be fine," Grandmother assured her as she ushered Syeira quickly into the house. "How about I draw you a bath? You can get cleaned up, and it'll help you relax a bit," she said. "I'll sprinkle some lavender and rose petals to make it nice."

Syeira agreed.

"I think the big night has arrived. Your babies have decided they've waited long enough. They are ready to see their mama."

Once Syeira got into the tub, Grandmother sent word to Charlotte Weston-Evans by way of an owl. She tied a note to its leg with scarlet thread.

Word was also secretly sent, by way of a mockingbird, to Dorian. A note secured with scarlet ribbon simply read, "It is time."

After her bath, Syeira tried her best to get comfortable in her room, but the pillows were too lumpy and her blanket was scratchy. Ahy kept scampering in and out of her room as Grandmother began making preparations for the birth.

Grandmother hummed as she boiled water and collected towels and candles, but it didn't comfort Syeira. The babies kept sporadically kicking. She lifted her nightgown and rubbed her hand on her smooth, tight skin to calm them down. She noticed that a dark, two-inch-thick line ran down her pregnant belly. Up until now, it had been a small tan line. Syeira heard hooting and cawing coming from the front room.

"Grandmother?" Syeira croaked.

"I'll be right there. Remember to breathe like we talked about."

Syeira didn't want to breathe. She didn't want the cramps or the pain. She wanted to close her eyes, curl up in a ball, and pretend that none of this was happening. She wished she was racing her horse in a large field of flowers under a deep-blue sky.

"What was that noise?" she asked.

"It was just an owl. When you were getting cleaned up, I sent Miss Weston – I mean Mrs. Evans – a message. She's on her way over to help with the delivery," Grandmother said. Then the scuffling of paws and claws followed her down the hallway. "May I come in?"

"Of course."

Grandmother's excitement annoyed Syeira. She wasn't ready for any of this.

"I didn't think you'd be comfortable with Dr. Evans," Grandmother said as she rambled on excitedly. "While he did help her finish her midwife training, I believe a woman is better suited to help a young girl deliver her babies than a man."

"Yes, I would feel better with her. She's nice."

"She'll be here soon. Can I get you anything in the meantime? I have more clean sheets and a few pillows if you need them."

"No, Grandmother, I'm okay for now," Syeira said.

Ahy ran inside the room again. He ran in circles, chasing his tail a few times. He stopped to see if he had an audience, and then chased his tail again.

"Go away!" Syeira yelled.

"Wait outside like I told you," Grandmother said to her dog. Instead of leaving, Ahy sat next to Grandmother and pawed at her feet. She fussed at her dog.

"I need a minute to clear my head. Alone," Syeira snapped.

Grandmother nodded and turned to leave.

"Come, Ahy."

A sharp contraction sent waves of pain through Syeira's body.

"No, wait. I changed my mind! Please stay!" the girl said, panicked.

Being alone wasn't a good idea after all. She missed her tribe. She missed talking with Auntie Mirela. She missed playing games with her brothers. She missed the monotonous lessons with her mother Patia, although all of this was her fault. She missed her father and his laugh most of all. No matter what mood he was in, she knew she was always safe when he was near. She was about to be a mother and start her own family, and without Will. She wasn't ready for any of it. She was lost and it seemed no one could save her.

Grandmother rushed to the bedside without her dog.

"I'm here for you," she said. It was like Grandmother had heard her thoughts.

"Maybe less talk? Maybe a little more silence? I'm overwhelmed and scared and tired and I...I just need you next to me. Is that okay?"

"As you wish. I'm here for anything you need."

Syeira allowed Grandmother to sit next to her on her bed. She leaned on her shoulder and Grandmother held her hand. She hummed a song Auntie Mirela used to sing to her little ones at bedtime. When Syeira gripped her hand as the contractions passed, Zenobia never complained. She simply sat with Syeira as long as she could. Grandmother left her side to let Miss Weston in, but then came right back to comfort her as best she could.

As the eclipse set in motion, the babies officially started their journey to the outside world.

"My eyes hurt, Grandmother. Is that normal?" Syeira asked.

"Honestly, I don't know. How about I turn off the light and burn a few candles? Maybe that will help." Grandmother snapped off the loud, electric light. She left for a moment and returned with a few white candles.

The room was dim, which helped the headache fade. It didn't ease the labor pains though.

The eclipse, now at its fullest point, gave the moon a burnt red hue. Syeira's screams were heard for miles. Her bed shook and vibrated as she gasped for air in between contractions.

"Grandmother, I'm so scared!" Syeira cried.

"It'll be okay. You're doing well," Grandmother said as Syeira crushed her hand. The red moonlight filled the candlelit room.

"I don't know if I'll be a good mother."

The floorboards rattled. Charlotte's hands shook as she watched the first child's head begin to crown.

"You will be a great mother. Think of Will and how much you love him," Grandmother said. "You are having his babies. A piece of him is still with you. The babies are products of your love. They're your family."

Syeira nodded as tears streamed down her face.

"We need you to push, Syeira," Charlotte said. She looked over at Grandmother and shook her head. The baby's head slipped back in, rather than came out.

"I know that it hurts, but I need you to push again. The first one is really shy and needs a little extra effort to come out."

Syeira gritted her teeth and pushed. As the baby's head fully crowned, the bed stopped shaking.

"Don't push anymore. Just breathe," Charlotte said. "Your body will do the rest. Breathe like Grandmother showed you."

With a great deal of effort, out came a baby boy. He had dark, curly hair and skin the same olive color as his mother's. As the dogs howled and barked wildly, the baby wailed above the din with strong lungs, and everyone was relieved.

"It's a healthy baby boy!" Charlotte cheered as she cut the cord. She cleaned him up, wrapped him in a soft blanket, and placed the boy temporarily in Syeira's arms. Syeira kissed him gently.

"Look at him," Syeira said as she looked at the two women in the room. They beamed back at her and her son. Grandmother took the baby and placed him on top of more soft blankets, in a large wicker baby basket.

A second wave of contractions ripped through Syeira's body, and several dark lines ran across her belly.

Grandmother and Charlotte flinched. Syeira screamed at the top of her lungs.

"I've never seen anything like that," Charlotte said. She wiped her brow and chewed the corner of her lower lip.

"Do your best, Charlotte. We'll help Syeira get through it."

Grandmother turned to Syeira and gently patted her streaked belly.

"Your second son is ready to see you! Breathe," Grandmother said as she wiped Syeira's forehead with a cool washcloth. Charlotte frowned at the amount of blood that pooled in between Syeira's legs.

The bed shook again, stronger than the first time.

"I don't understand what's going on! I can't deliver the baby with the bed moving around." Charlotte crouched at the foot of the bed, trying to hold on.

Syeira and Charlotte looked at Grandmother.

"I'm not doing it!" Grandmother said as she shrugged her shoulders and shook her head.

Another wave of pain shot through Syeira's body. Charlotte stood a little taller, determined to deliver the second baby.

Syeira bawled, with Grandmother at her side.

The second baby slipped out easily, and the bed stopped moving. It was also a boy. He had skin the color of molasses, and black, curly hair. His cry rivaled his older brother's.

"It's another healthy boy!" cried Charlotte. She cleaned him and wrapped him up in a blanket.

Although her body throbbed from childbirth, Syeira managed to look up at the red light of the eclipse as it shone on her new sons. She noticed that the copper amulet her father had given her softly vibrated on her chest.

"Are you okay to sit up?" asked Grandmother.

Syeira nodded, although it hurt to move.

Once she was in a comfortable position, Grandmother and Charlotte presented Syeira with the babies.

"Syeira, meet your sons!"

Syeira admired them. The babies cooed and gurgled. Love had returned into her life.

The two boys were as different as night and day, just like her eyes. No matter how different they looked from each other, however, she was determined to love them both.

"I will call my first son Anton, because he is priceless," Syeira said, though her throat was raw from screaming through the pain of childbirth.

"Anton is a wonderful name," Grandmother said.

"I will call his brother David, for just as the Good Book says, he is beloved."

Grandmother couldn't have been more proud.

Syeira kissed both of her sons and smiled at them. Her love for the babies was contagious. Grandmother and Charlotte could not help but stand by and grin widely too.

Grandmother delicately said prayers over the babies and their mother. Charlotte cleaned Syeira up a bit more, and, once the new mother was somewhat presentable, she put away the soiled linens and bloody towels.

Syeira was thankful as she looked down at her sons, but then, from out of nowhere, pain and sadness crept in.

"If only Will could have been here to see our family."

Her happiness faded with her energy, and the babies cried.

The moment was interrupted by an aggressive knock on the door.

Syeira looked at Grandmother, who continued to pray silently. Charlotte was heard washing items in the bathroom.

Finally, Syeira replied, "Come in."

She looked nervously at the bedroom door as it creaked open. No one was allowed to step on Grandmother's property without permission.

In crept her father, Dorian. Once his eyes met hers, he ran to her bedside and dropped to his knees. Syeira was shocked. Grandmother stopped praying.

"Syeira!"

"Dati, what are you doing here? How did you find me?"

Syeira looked around wildly to see if anyone else was about to creep in. Grandmother motioned for to Syeira to calm down. The babies cried.

"It's okay. Your father is a friend of mine."

"What?" Syeira asked.

"I'll tell you about it later. He has my permission to be here, if it's okay with you. Charlotte, you can come back now."

Charlotte slipped back into the room and lingered by the door.

"I can't believe you're really here," Syeira said. "I missed you."

"I missed you too. Grandmother told me about you and the babies and I had to be here. You are my heart. I beg of you…whatever you want to do, I will allow it. Please, let me be in your life. All of this is my fault. All of it. I love you so much. This silence between us must stop."

The twins stopped crying at the velvet-smooth sound of Dorian's deep voice. Syeira looked at her father tearfully and revealed a weak smile. The twins gurgled and cooed. Dorian reached out and touched each of them gently.

"I agree; the silence must end between us."

Dorian kissed her lightly on her forehead, and then the babies.

Charlotte motioned for Grandmother.

"I don't like that she's lost so much blood. She's very pale," Charlotte whispered to Grandmother. "We need to get her some water or juice. I might need to get my husband. He could give her a transfusion."

"Dati, I will always love you," Syeira admitted.

Syeira considered the weight of her words as she spoke to her father. Grandmother constantly reminded her that words have power and meaning. When she looked into her father's eyes she understood why Grandmother harped upon it so much. Her father deserved to hear the truth.

"But I can't forgive what my daj has done to me, to us. You know what her spell did. You see my boys. I will never accept that the gypsy way is the only way. I can't." She knew the words were like a sharp dagger in Dorian's heart.

"My mother is a wicked woman. She is a murderer and I take that fact to my grave. I will never forgive her for what she has done to our family. I hate how she treats you. I can't trust her to be around my sons. We have to stay away from her, which means we have to stay away from you, too. I'm sorry but it's how I feel."

Dorian, Grandmother, and Charlotte noticed Syeira had trouble breathing.

"I'm sorry to interrupt you two. How are you feeling?" Grandmother said as she approached Syeira, and Charlotte disappeared into the kitchen.

"I'm lightheaded but okay."

She looked at Grandmother, who stood behind Dorian.

"Thank you, Grandmother, for all your love and the light you brought to my life. I mean it. I love you with all my heart."

Syeira broke her gaze from Grandmother and looked at the foot of her bed.

"Oh my God!" Syeira said. She clutched her chest. "Will, is that you?"

Grandmother stared hard, trying to see what Syeira saw.

"It is you! I've missed you so much," Syeira wept.

Dorian strained his eyes. He didn't see anyone at the foot of Syeira's bed either. Charlotte rushed back in with a glass of orange juice. Ahy pushed his way back into the room, sat near the foot of the bed, and stared where Syeira looked.

"Drink this. You lost a lot of blood. It'll help with the lightheaded feeling."

Syeira shook her head defiantly and frowned. The adults in the room watched the young girl cock her head, as if straining to hear something. The dog wagged his tail slowly, methodically.

"Yes, you're right, as usual. I'll do as she says," Syeira said. Then she nodded and accepted the glass of juice. "Aren't our boys sweet?" She took a few sips of the juice but never broke her attention with whatever she saw at the foot of her bed.

"She's delusional," whispered Charlotte to Grandmother. "She's too stressed from the labor."

"I'm gonna turn on the light so we can get a better look at you and the boys," Grandmother said. "Everyone, get ready." She turned on the light in the room and everyone recoiled except Syeira.

"She is just like you said she'd be. I love her. You probably know that already," Syeira said softly. "Yes, they keep telling me to breathe too. I guess they can't see you. Ahy is thrilled you're here."

She giggled and took a deep breath. When she slowly exhaled, her eyes turned back to their original deep green. Syeira continued to nod as if engaged in a conversation. She mumbled a few incoherent words and looked at Grandmother. She looked back at the corner of the room.

The foot of the bed squeaked. Grandmother, Dorian, and Charlotte watched as the corner of the bed pressed in, as if someone sat down and moved closer to Syeira. A soft gray mist appeared, having the outline of a person. Everyone but Syeira flinched.

"My Lord in heaven, it is Will!" Grandmother said.

"Will says he'll take really good care of me. Grandmother, he asks if you would take care of our little family. He knows they are in great hands."

Grandmother trembled.

"Will, we've all missed you so much."

"Dati," Syeira continued. "Thank you for being here. It means a lot to me. I love you. Will loves you too."

Those were Syeira's last words, as she breathed her last breath. Will's spirit vanished. Ahy went to Grandmother's side and lowered his head. The dogs outside howled. The babies cried again.

"No, Syeira!" Dorian cried.

"Dorian, she's gone," Grandmother said as she tried to tend to the twins while they fussed and cried.

"Let me hold them," Dorian said, rising to his feet with outstretched arms. He took each boy in an arm and slowly rocked.

"I don't understand," Charlotte said. "She was healthy the last few months. She's young. She should have been fine!"

"No one can predict matters of the heart," Grandmother said. "Worse, for reasons I can't bear to say, these boys are miracles."

Grandmother and Charlotte watched Dorian as he held the twins. The small group looked outside the window at the full moon. It was bright and white once more. As Grandmother looked over her shoulder, she saw that Syeira's body had an angelic glow in its light. She looked back outside and noticed two fireflies dance, close to the glass.

Chapter 12/A Tale of Young Love

GRANDMOTHER ZENOBIA SLOWLY MASSAGED HER temples as she sat on her large purple-and-gold velvet throne in her prayer room. Ahy slept on a matching purple-and-gold pillow at her feet. Many summers and winters had passed. Dorian and the gypsies had packed up and moved away after Syeira's death.

The twins, who were now four years old, fought each other incessantly the entire day. A few hours ago, at dinnertime, David threw a crumbly piece of cornbread at Anton, who in turn, threw a warm, dripping handful of collard greens at David. An inevitable, messy food fight erupted. Grandmother warned them repeatedly to behave, but the toddlers ignored her. Finally, when everyone was covered with food, she insisted the boys pick up after themselves. When they started hitting each other instead of cleaning up, she had given into her anger and cast a sleeping spell upon them both. For a single parent, raising two rambunctious boys was a huge challenge. Grandmother loved her little family, but she was always tired and overwhelmed. Currently, she sat alone in the quiet room, trying to shake off a headache.

She hated that she'd resorted to a spell to discipline the boys tonight.

"Mortals seem to raise their children just fine, so why am I having such a hard time?" she wondered.

Now that the boys were in bed and the kitchen was clean, she finally had a free moment all to herself. She looked around at her surroundings and enjoyed the silence. The square room (which she rarely visited anymore) was decorated with heavy red velvet curtains trimmed in gold. On shelves all along the walls were dusty religious books, a few crosses – some with and some without Jesus – a large brass pentagram, and a jade statue of a dragon. High above her left shoulder, a human skull stared down at a bouquet of fresh white roses that she placed in front of her. The bouquet rested neatly upon a small card table covered with black velvet. A stiff wooden chair with a matching black velvet pillow sat across from her throne.

Large, heavy trunks sat under a windowsill. She used to take pride in the many magical artifacts she had collected over the centuries. Once, she'd had an impressive Voodoo altar for blood sacrifices, a large collection of human bones, and a real monkey paw, among many other religious artifacts she used in ceremonies. Most, if not all, of those things were locked away and forgotten over the years. A large plant half-heartedly hid a shrunken head she'd received as a gift from a tribe in the Amazon.

Two newer trunks containing Will and Syeira's possessions had been added to her collection. They too were covered with dust and mostly forgotten.

The room was lit by handmade candles. There was a thin pink candle on her left and a chunky blue candle on her right. Both candles were anointed with a mixture of blessed oil and Jamaican rum to ensure no negative energy could creep into her spell. Grandmother leaned over, picked up the bouquet of roses before her, and drew three Xs in a row with pink chalk on the black velvet. She carefully replaced the flowers on top of the marks and laid her hands on the white roses. Carefully, she chanted in Haitian Creole.

"Mwen rele sou ou, nan parèt devan m', zanmi mwen renmen anpil. Ou se Byenveni nan kay mwen an. Mwen mande pou jis yon ti moman nan tan ou."

She repeated herself three times. Nothing stirred in her prayer room.

She chanted once more in English.

"I call upon thee to appear before me, dear friend. You are welcome in my home. I ask for a moment of your time."

The pink candle flickered once. Nothing else happened.

"Nothing is working the way I want," Grandmother said with a frown. *Raising Angelica when she was younger didn't seem as difficult as raising these boys*, she thought.

She reached her left hand out toward the closest bookshelf and a handmade scrapbook floated effortlessly to her, resting carefully in her lap. The book contained drawings, letters, and knickknacks from the past. It was a powerful book for Zenobia. It held vivid memories of both happiness and pain.

She opened the book and flipped through a few pages when a soft, feminine voice broke the silence. Both candles flickered.

"Greetings, Zenobia."

Grandmother looked up at the chair across from her but saw nothing. Her eyes dropped back to the scrapbook as she spoke.

"Marie, I didn't think you were going to show."

"I almost didn't. I thought your chant was a joke."

"A joke?"

"Zenobia, you are predictable. You usually start out with a Bible verse rather than something personal. It's not like you to summon me. We haven't talked in a very long time. When I first heard the request, I assumed it was one of those pesky tourists visiting one of my graves at the St. Louis Cemetery."

"They do make quite a spectacle at your tombstones. You should feel honored that they treasure you, Madame Laveau."

"Perhaps. So why did you summon me?" said the disembodied voice.

Grandmother looked again across from her. The petals of the roses quivered.

"I was going to visit your daughter, the other Marie, but I fear she may be joining you on the other side soon."

"True, her time on the earth is coming to an end."

A cold gray mist formed around the seat across from Grandmother Zenobia. Slowly, Marie Laveau appeared before her. First, her favorite turban, the black one with flecks of silver and gold, emerged distinctly, followed by her dark-brown eyes that glared at Grandmother in the candlelight. Grandmother admired Marie's light-brown Creole skin and high, rosy cheekbones. Marie fully materialized, wearing a soft cotton tunic, and examined the bouquet of roses carefully. Then she managed a wry smile and spoke to her fellow high priestess.

"Zenobia, thank you for the flowers. They're beautiful. But I ask again, why did you summon me? You could easily request an audience with Ogun Orisha."

"I don't need him for anything at the moment."

"Well, with those boys, you could use a bigger home. I'm sure you could ask him for a larger house."

"Marie, I will have a bigger house when I'm good and ready."

"I'm just saying. Or you could have called upon Papa Agwe. I bet with a good offering he could help you with those two ankle-biters. Nago Shango has been quiet so he'd be easy to call. I hear he hasn't been up to much lately. No one really needs a god of weather these days, I guess."

"Marie, I…"

"Anyways, you have the wrong-colored candles to call upon any of the Loa. Pink and blue won't get anyone's attention. You should have pulled out the magenta one and the silver one you have from your collection. They are more powerful that the ones you're wasting right now. You could use some extra clairvoyance. With them, you would have foreseen the food fight earlier."

"Marie, I know whom to call, and for what."

"All right, I'm just saying. The way you mix and match stuff, I'm not sure why you call yourself a Voodoo High Priestess. You're good with magic and all but…"

"I forgot how bossy you could be," Grandmother Zenobia said, interrupting.

"Well, Zenobia, what do you want? Why am I here?"

"It's just that…well, I…uh…"

"Come on, Zenobia, spit it out. I don't have all day."

"You know what, Marie, never mind. I shouldn't have bothered you. I'm sorry. You can go."

Grandmother shook her head and flipped through the pages of the scrapbook that rested in her lap.

Marie Laveau glared at Grandmother. The flames of the candles grew tall as her eyes widened.

"I didn't come all this way to be dismissed."

Grandmother continued to look at the scrapbook.

"Again, I'm sorry to have disturbed you. I will be sure to pay my respects to your daughter later this week before it's too late."

The flames shrank to small blue flickers and Marie's image began to shimmer away. Grandmother flipped over to one of Angelica's first drawings as a child. Rudimentary stick figures in different colors filled the page.

"As a little girl, Angelica loved drawing cats. She drew so many of them. I don't know why. I'm more of a dog person."

Tears rolled easily down her cheeks when she reminisced about her daughter.

Marie Laveau saw Grandmother's tears and decided not to leave. Instead she appeared again, much brighter than before, and made herself comfortable. The candles returned to their usual glow.

"Well, Zenobia, I didn't really have anything else to do. I could sit here a spell, I guess."

Grandmother tried to hide her tears.

"Your daughter Angelica was very talented."

"Yes, she was."

"And beautiful. I wish I had her beautiful, thick hair. Everyone at my hair salon was so jealous."

Grandmother flipped through more pages, admiring Angelica's progression of talent as she grew older. She stopped and stared hard at a picture Angelica had sketched with charcoal. The attention to detail was precise. It was such an excellent piece of work that had it not held such emotional meaning, Grandmother would have displayed it in the living room. It was the portrait of a young, slender man. Angelica had managed to capture a rarely seen, sly grin.

"I'm sorry she won't speak to you. I saw her once or twice on this side. She smiled at me."

"It's okay. She moved on. I understand, I guess."

"You say that you moved on, but I can't help but notice you grow a lot of angelica herb in your garden," Marie said.

"I want her to know she's always welcome here," Zenobia said with a helpless shrug.

"You know that her death wasn't your fault."

"That's not true."

"It is true! Why don't you believe it?"

Grandmother looked at the picture of the young man once more. It was Dorian Camlo, before he was pronounced King of the Gypsies.

"She loved him so much."

"The gypsy?"

"Yes. My heart was so hard back then. I said many horrible things and I kicked her out of our home because of him. I drove her away."

"Why would you turn away your own daughter?"

"I turned her away because I couldn't control her. We are descendants of Queen Cleopatra and he was a scoundrel. Back then, I didn't think he was worthy of my Angelica. I had too much pride. I wanted too many things for her. She had so much potential for greatness. I just knew that with some training, in time, people from around the world would flock to her, the way they still come to you and your daughter."

"All that attention isn't as great as you think."

"I know that now. She had such a bright future ahead of her! When I found out she was consorting with a gypsy, I was going to punish her. It would have been something wicked, too, until she revealed to me that she was pregnant. She told me they were going to get married. She showed me a ring he had made for her. It was a gold band with roses all around it."

"But instead of accepting him and their baby, you turned her away."

"I can't believe that I turned away my only family back then. I treasure family more than anything in this world. I regret my actions to this very day. Did you and your daughter ever have mean, nasty fights?"

"Of course. I think all mothers and daughters do."

"I thought eventually she'd come back, but she didn't. Angelica ran off into the bayou. I was so angry. I didn't really care until Dorian showed up telling me he couldn't find her. Apparently the gypsies didn't want them to be together either."

"Is that what helped the two of you to reunite?"

"I've been rattling on too long. You have been so generous to spend your time here with me. If you really do have to go, I'm okay."

"Zenobia, listen here. We haven't enjoyed each other's company in a very long time. I miss it. I see why you didn't call upon any of the Loa."

Grandmother paused. She leaned forward and looked at Marie.

"I still envy your relationship with your daughter. At least you didn't kill her."

"Zenobia, stop it. I know for a fact that you didn't kill your daughter. You had to have some kind of reconciliation. You did a wonderful job raising her son."

Grandmother sat back and flipped through the book until she stopped at a page with long, shiny black feathers.

"Can you believe it took divine intervention to bring Angelica and me back together?"

"What do you mean?"

"Let me tell you the story. It was a hard lesson I had to learn..."

Grandmother Zenobia reflected back to that day, years ago, when she sat on her porch in her favorite rocking chair, watching a storm brew in the distance. She was clueless that her daughter, whom she hadn't seen in months, needed her. The blue sky, speckled with a few clouds over her farm, was deceptive. Without any warning, thunder boomed loudly overhead. Lightning struck an old oak tree across the road from her home, exploding it into fiery bits and pieces. When the smoke cleared, Zenobia saw a strange man appear, standing in the ruins of the tree. He wore a black three-piece suit. Jet-black hair shone as it poked out from under his black velvet top hat. He stood at the edge of her property, staring at her.

Zenobia stood up, overcome with fear.

"Zenobia of the Jalio tribe, I presume?" the stranger asked with a smooth Southern twang. He bowed and removed his hat, revealing thick black locks. "Or do you prefer that I refer to you as Queen Zenobia of Palmyra?"

"Who are you, and what do you want?" she asked, trying to hide her fear.

"Your Highness, I mean you no harm. I am not the one that you fear. The one who causes your nightmares is nowhere near. He isn't coming for you. At least for a while."

Zenobia thought she would faint on the spot. No one knew who she really was, other than her daughter. She never uttered to a single soul anything about the nightmares that plagued her most nights.

"I am here on behalf of Cassiel. He does not usually interfere with those who walk the earth. However, he was compelled to send you a message, Your Majesty."

Zenobia, with her knowledge of creatures in the spiritual realm, knew exactly who Cassiel was. The archangel watched events unfold with very little interference. He presided over the death of kings. For him to send one of his messengers to her was a serious gesture.

"Cassiel has a message for me?"

"Yes. May I have permission to cross the threshold, onto your land?"

"Yes, of course. What name do you go by?"

"I have many names, but you may call me Wren. I am one of many who watch over the winged creatures of the air, land, and sea."

"Wren, you are welcome to come upon my land," she nervously declared.

In the blink of an eye, he appeared less than a foot away from her. She tried not to choke on the overwhelming scent of roses and tried not to stare directly into his dark eyes.

"What message do you have for me?"

"Relax your grip. You are strangling everything around you."

"What is that supposed to mean?" snapped Zenobia defensively.

Wren smiled at the sorceress, revealing sharp, pearly white teeth. It did not comfort Zenobia.

"I am only a messenger."

Zenobia took note of her disrespectful tone quickly.

"Why would such a benevolent being say such a thing to me? Is it some kind of riddle?" she asked.

"Your Highness, look around. You were once called queen, one with many followers. You fought the Romans in Egypt, yes? And now? You have no control. Nothing grows on your land anymore. You have no visitors. You have no family. Even your dog Ahy cowers in your presence when he usually sits faithfully by your side. You are blind to many things and you are losing what powers you once had. You have the stench of death about you and you do not even know it."

Zenobia looked at her hands and then looked around. The angel had a point. Her once-lavish garden was a plot of dust. Ahy rarely came in the house anymore.

"If I were to dare interpret what my master means, I would think it means open your heart. It is cold and hard and you will become just like the one you fear, unless you change your ways. Stop trying to control so much. Let things unfold. Everything around you will continue to die until you learn this."

"But I have worked so hard to be where I am today."

"Is this truly where you want to be?"

The words the angel spoke rang true again. Zenobia wasn't happy. Everywhere she went, people feared her. She was lonely.

"There have always been and always will be things you have no control over. Consider this, however: why build walls when you can dig ditches for blessings?"

"Release my grip?"

"Yes. I would imagine that for you it is not an easy task. It is probably something you will always struggle with. But I sense that you are strong enough to do what is right. Just my humble opinion, Your Highness."

Zenobia gritted her teeth. She thought messages from angels would give her more power or strength. The last thing she wanted to hear was some abstract mumbo jumbo. That was the cheap kind of advice fortune tellers sold to tarot clients.

"And now that you have received the message, I must leave you. It was an honor to meet you, Queen Zenobia."

Wren turned away from Zenobia, and as he stepped off the porch, his body transformed into a flock of blackbirds. They flew away effortlessly in the angry sky. A few black feathers collected at her feet as another reminder of the supernatural visit. As the birds flew away, Zenobia noticed the storm still brewing in the distance.

"Visits from angels are no joke. I can't say that I've ever seen a real one," Marie Laveau said. "I pray to them and I tell people about them, but I've never seen them."

"They are a sight to behold."

"Back to the day you were visited by Wren – was that the day your daughter died?"

"It was. I had still refused to open my heart to the fact that Angelica loved Dorian. My daughter eventually reconciled with her gypsy boyfriend. They made her little home in a small little shack tucked away in the bayou. He would sneak away from his people to visit her from time to time. In my own selfishness, I didn't sense that

Angelica was in danger that day. She was in labor and all alone. Back then, my powers had weakened and worked against me. My anger blinded me."

Grandmother turned to the next page in the book, which had a square of soft cotton with spackles of blood on it.

"She was all alone? What about Dorian? Where was he?"

"His father got word that Dorian snuck off to be with Angelica, and he had had enough of his behavior. So King Shandor sent his people to take Dorian back to their camp. They tried to capture him, but they got caught in the middle of a storm. Eventually he broke free, and when he got to Angelica she was in labor."

"Wait, I'm confused. How did you know Angelica needed help then, if Dorian didn't tell you?"

"I did as the angel told me, that day. I was cranky and arrogant when that angel left me. How dare anyone tell me how to behave! But I considered his visit, and I knew he was right. So I took a moment to be still. I looked up to the heavens and asked for help to 'release my grip.' Then a soft breeze blew by, whispering 'Angelica' in my ears. I got right up and went searching for her. The whispers led me to the bayou. Her little home was in the path of that wicked storm. I found her, with Dorian at her side. She had just given birth to a cocoa-colored baby boy. That young man was overjoyed to be in her presence with his newborn son. That baby had hazel-colored eyes just like his daddy. I never underestimated the power of angels after that."

"It was the whispers from heaven above that reunited you with your daughter."

"But don't you see, Marie, all of this is my fault. I was so headstrong about what I thought was best for my daughter that I wasn't there for her. She had that baby alone when I should have been there. My daughter had powers, powers that I wanted her to cultivate. Instead, she used her powers to block me out. I pushed her away, so she pushed me away. I lost so much precious time with Angelica because I was angry and spiteful. By the time I came to my senses, it was too late."

"What about the baby?"

"When I arrived to find her in that little shack in the bayou, after she had given birth, Angelica was delusional and feverish. There was too much blood. I will always remember seeing that ivory-handled knife Dorian had. I told him to use it to cut the umbilical cord."

"But she must have been happy to see you. You were her mother."

"No, she was in a horrible state. Angelica tried to fight me. She thought I wanted to steal her baby."

"What did Dorian do?"

"He was so young back then, and so scared. There was blood everywhere. Angelica was wailing, the baby was crying. The storm was horrible. She kept shouting that I'd cursed her. She said she saw shadows all around her. She insisted they wouldn't leave her alone. Eventually, Dorian took his son in his arms. He held the baby close to his heart and spoke softly to him until he stopped crying. When Angelica saw how Dorian held their son, she calmed down too."

"So that was how Will was born."

"Yes. I didn't tell anyone about his birth or about who his father was, until today."

"Well, then what happened? There must be more to your story."

"I got right on my knees and asked Angelica for forgiveness. I told her that she was my baby girl and that I loved her, very much. I told her I was so sorry that my heart was too hard. I was closed-minded. I said at first I didn't want to accept that she loved that gypsy boy, but anyone in their right mind could see it was true love. Clearly, he loved her and she loved him. Love is a powerful force and I had no business trying to shut it out of my own daughter's life. Love is a gift from God and should be treasured."

Grandmother was choked up.

"Zenobia, what aren't you telling me?"

"When I touched Angelica, a vision filled my mind. I saw what she saw. There were hundreds of angels all around, watching over Angelica and her son. I couldn't make out their specifics but heard them as they whispered and sang soft prayers over my daughter, Dorian, and the baby. They constantly whispered her name. Had my heart been open, I would have sensed the supernatural presence much sooner. When I placed my hands on her face, Angelica snapped out of her hysteria and looked at me. Hearing her call me Mama melted my heart. I explained to her that she was going to be just fine. The faces in the shadows she saw were her guardian angels. She had the most beautiful smile when I told her they watched over her and her family."

"Did she forgive you, Zenobia?"

"I thought everything was going to be okay with us. I thought everything would be fine. Dorian put the baby back in her arms. But then she said something I will never forget. She told Dorian that she would always love him. She told him she couldn't forgive him for being a coward. He should have chosen a life of love. He should have left his people and been with her, not abandoned her with their baby. She and her son deserved a real home. She declared that she was the daughter of a queen and should have been treated accordingly. Her words stabbed my heart. She said maybe Will would find it in his heart to forgive Dorian, for what could have been."

"What? But she loved him!"

"My hard-headed point of view poisoned her. Her stubbornness was tougher than my own. It was my fault for planting the seed in the first place that she deserved to live a certain way. No matter how much Dorian begged for her forgiveness, no matter how much he assured her he loved her, she wouldn't forgive him. He swore that he would do whatever it took to be a great husband to her and father to the baby. I came to his defense, but it was too late. The damage was done. She reminded me that I always said that words have power and meaning."

"What did you tell her?"

"The truth. Dorian was a man of his word. He loved her dearly. I knew it then and I know it now. To this day, he still is a man of his word. Angelica's last words to me were, 'Mother, I love you. Thank you for your love, and the light you brought into my life.' Angelica looked down at Will and told him she loved him. I watched her life force slowly fade away."

"Zenobia, that is such a sad tale."

"It was one of the saddest days of my life."

"And what happened to Dorian?"

"He's a good man. He wanted to stay and raise Will. That's when I insisted he call me Grandmother. The title rang true for me. Now I insist everyone call me Grandmother. I want to be the kind of woman my own grandmother was. She was respected, and loved by her family."

"I can't believe you are so proper, after all this time," said Marie. "Here in the South we don't use the word 'grandmother.' We say maw-maw, or paw-paw if you are a grandfather."

Grandmother shook her head. She flipped through a few more pages until it revealed a black-and-white photo of Dorian. He wore his finest clothes and stood proudly next to his father.

"Dorian stayed with us for about a month, and then I sent him away. I would have let him stay longer, but just as my daughter is a princess, he is a prince. Eventually, the gypsies would look for him if I didn't send him on his way. His father and his people needed him to carry on their traditions. Sadly, I understand the situation all too well. Dorian reluctantly dragged himself back to his people; he was the prodigal son who returned home. He kept his word about helping out with Will. When Will was little, he sent small handmade toys and trinkets. He sent money, too, not that I ever needed it. He always wrote me letters whenever he had a free moment away from the tribe. He even managed to write when he married Patia. He was miserable but agreed to the arranged marriage."

Grandmother turned the book one last page to a photo of Dorian as he stood with his tribe.

"I don't know how I missed the name of his daughter, Syeira. So many years had passed, so many letters with so many names. He would mention 'his princess' every so often. A few times, he mentioned Patia was unfaithful to him and his princess was probably his only real flesh. He wasn't sure about any of the sons they had. I guess I forgot the name of his princess."

"I see why your heart is heavy. Even the great Zenobia couldn't forecast that Will would meet and fall in love with his sister."

"I can barely think about what would have happened if he had lived."

"Well, luckily for both of them they never found out that truth. I'd hate to be in that situation. Incest is nasty. This isn't the King Tut kind of society, like you're used to."

"That's true. Still, Angelica…"

"Zenobia, stop it! None of this is your fault in the end. All you can do is try to follow your own path, and listen when heaven speaks to you."

"You're right, Marie. I keep blaming myself for many things, including Angelica. After rattling on and on to you, I guess I can see that her death wasn't my fault. But it feels like it should be. Letting go and watching life unfold is still a hard lesson for me to learn. I'm trying."

"You should try to appreciate this quiet moment before those brats wake up," joked Marie.

"Speaking of lessons, I am grateful to have those boys in my life. Anton and David seem to be okay."

"They seem like rambunctious boys to me."

"I still worry. As you pointed out, they are the product of incest. Worse, they have Camlo gypsy blood and traces of Jalio blood. They could still be susceptible to unnatural things. They were conceived when both parents had vampire-bat blood swimming in their systems."

"There you go, worrying about too much. Those rascals are fine. You try too hard to control too many things."

"You do have a point, Marie."

"Is now a good time to tell you there is a little rice stuck on your turban? I hope you're ready for more food fights."

"It's wonderful you kept your sense of humor, even in the spiritual world," she said.

Grandmother playfully rolled her eyes at Marie and noticed she was fading. She looked at the blue and pink candles as they flickered in the darkness. They had melted more than halfway down.

"All joking aside, you've been here a while and I should let you go. Do you mind if I ask you just one last question?"

"Go ahead, Zenobia – or should I call you Grandmother?" Marie chuckled.

"How did you do it? How did you raise your daughter? She always followed in your footsteps. You two were always such a sight to behold. Did you use magic?"

"That was three questions," Marie said with another chuckle. "I was lucky to have help and a rich husband. And of course I used magic. You have to use whatever you can. Raising a child is hard work. You should have more contact with spiritual people."

"That's why I summoned the legendary Marie Laveau. I want to be like you. People still call upon you for blessings, not that you answer them. I've seen them mark your grave asking you to grant their wishes. You will always be remembered in history."

"It's true, I have a legacy. It is nice to be remembered, and in some cases adored. But you? The great Zenobia? You have many more natural gifts and much more power than I ever had. You'll figure out how to raise those boys and still be yourself. Life is about balance. The best advice I can give you is to make some friends. The people of Carrefour Parish are friendlier than you expect."

Grandmother sat back in her chair and took in what Marie Laveau said.

"Marie, thank you for listening to me. I guess I needed to rattle the bones in my closet a bit. I really appreciate you."

"Good luck, old friend, and I do mean old."

"I wish more people saw your playful side, like I do," Grandmother said sarcastically.

"Thank you for sharing your stories with me. Now get yourself together. Those boys are waking up," said Marie.

Marie Laveau shimmered once more and faded away. Grandmother heard small footsteps run up and down the hallway, one set chasing another, signaling the start of another day.

Chapter 13/Hello and Goodbye

Grandmother Zenobia found herself standing absentmindedly in her kitchen. She stared at the date, June 9, 1894, on The Old Farmer's Almanac calendar. Earlier in the week, while the boys visited Charlotte, she'd done a little shopping at the French Market. There, she came across a nun from St. Ursuline's convent. After taking Marie's advice to make friends, she was open to chat with the woman, rather than avoid any type of contact. They spoke at great length about the symbolism of numbers and their meanings in Christianity. After her nice conversation, she went home and researched the mythologies of numbers from a few books in her prayer room.

Now she stood motionless as her mind reeled with many thoughts. She applied what she'd learned and added up the numbers of today's date. She broke them down, purposefully manipulating them to equal the number twenty-three. She was obsessed with the number. June was the sixth month of the year. That meant it was six, nine for the day, and one plus eight plus nine plus four representing the year. Six plus nine plus one plus eight plus nine plus four. She came up with the number thirty-seven, but it wasn't enough to satisfy Grandmother; three plus seven equaled ten. Dividing ten by two (two representing the twins) equaled five. There were five points in a pentagram. There were five wounds of Christ. Humans had five senses. From there, Grandmother broke down the number five, which was two plus three – or twenty-three. In her readings, twenty-three was a suspicious number. In a frenzy, Zenobia continued to look for forced connections and patterns to numbers.

Was it coincidence that the boys were born on the twenty-third day of the month? Was something unexpected going to happen today?

Zenobia continued with her madness.

The boys are now four years old… The number four, according to the Egyptians, was the sacred number of time. The boys were born in the month of May, the fifth month of the year. Five is two plus three. It's now June, the sixth month, six which is two times three…

Grandmother had to stop herself from holding on to strange thoughts.

Stop this nonsense! I have been on the earth for far too long. I know that people should never base their lives strictly on numbers. I had a lovely chat with that sweet nun and now I'm making mountains out of molehills. Why am I searching so hard to come up with the number twenty-three? Marie was right. I need to get out more often and talk to people. Otherwise, I am going to drive myself crazy.

She decided to grab a handful of walnuts and prepare some chamomile tea to calm her thoughts. She had a feeling of dread with no logical explanation.

What can I be thankful for today? she thought, trying to put positive energy into her day. She was grateful to have made a new friend earlier in the week. Upon hearing David yell at his brother outside, she focused her thoughts on the twins. Having family in her life made her happy. With a little help from Charlotte, Grandmother had proudly raised two healthy boys. It took lots of discipline and hard work, but Grandmother rarely used magic anymore. She considered herself to be more 'spiritual' and read her Bible daily. Just like when she raised Will, and cared for Syeira, she wanted the boys to have a somewhat normal life. The twins having parents that were half-siblings disturbed her. She couldn't share that truth with anyone, not even Charlotte. She was grateful that the boys were healthy and happy. If she had any say in the matter, she expected they'd grow up to be respected members of the community.

Anton and David were fraternal twins. However, no one would believe they were related. The fair-skinned Anton was extremely sensitive to light, while darker-toned David hated darkness. In the muggy summertime, David thrived in the sun, his laughter heard all day long. Anton was miserable and fussed until sunset. When forced outside to play, Anton was usually found in the shade of a tree or hiding under the porch, enjoying the cool earth. David would lie outstretched in the sun, basking like a butterfly. Conversely, in the winter it was Anton who bloomed. In the darker months, he was quiet but cheerful, always at Grandmother's side, trying to help her around the house. He wandered the house in darkness, after being put to bed several times. David was agitated, cranky, and miserable, usually found huddled by lanterns and candles. No matter how much he was warned, he played with fire as much as possible. No matter how different their personalities were, Zenobia was thankful to have the boys in her life. She was happy to be a part of a family again.

Zenobia sat in her breakfast nook sipping on her tea while the twins played outside with Ahy. She decided she had time to read Dorian's most recent letter. She had received it weeks ago, and this was the first moment she had to sit and read it. The twins had her undivided attention most of her days, especially when Charlotte couldn't visit. She had almost forgotten about the letter altogether. Had it not been for the boys fighting in the kitchen the night before, knocking things over, she might have forgotten the letter entirely. When she separated the boys, the letter rested on the floor at her feet. Today, after lots of scolding, the twins were momentarily well behaved. She finally had a little time to herself.

After Syeira's death, Dorian continued to write to Grandmother. Sometimes he sent toys and trinkets for the twins, too, as he had when Will was a little boy. She looked forward to whatever he wanted to share. She appreciated that no matter where the travelers roamed, Dorian made a point to write to her.

In this letter, Dorian spoke a great deal about his people and their experiences in South Carolina. Time passed very quickly to him, it seemed, but they had had more than enough of life in the Southern states. They appreciated the richness and safety of the land, but, being a nomadic people, everyone was anxious to head out to greener pastures. Some of the families in camp were restless. Many were getting into trouble with the locals. Putting the clan's needs ahead of his own, Dorian, with support from the elders, finally agreed to pack up again and head to Alabama.

He was sure that, because of past troubles in Alabama, they wouldn't stay long. He would lead their caravan to a new location. This time, it would be a big move, one they had never done before. They were going back to the motherland. They were going to Romania! Patia and the mystic women read tea leaves for a week and insisted that Romania would be the best place to have a fresh start. They sensed strong energies there. "Baxtalo! Baxtalo!" the women exclaimed to the elders often. They were lucky.

Dorian finished off his letter by saying that even though they had been away from New Orleans for years, he still didn't know how to break the news of Syeira's death to Patia.

Grandmother put the letter down.

Romania? I don't know why, but that doesn't settle well with my spirit.

She shook her head, trying to shake off the strange thoughts that bounced around in it. She finished her tea and walked to the back porch to get some fresh air, hoping the dread would melt away. She watched as thunderclouds rolled across an angry sky. The weather couldn't decide if it wanted to pour buckets of rain or scorch the earth.

The same June morning that Grandmother sipped her tea, thinking positive thoughts, Dorian's people excitedly packed up camp. They stayed in an old pasture in Louisiana for the night before heading to the Port of New Orleans. The idea of going to Romania was thrilling. Old women and young women alike buzzed about it. Dorian shared a few words of encouragement with his people and then, in grand fashion, boldly led the tribe. He sat high on his horse as they moved out. The caravan of families rumbled along with high hopes. Some of the gypsies played music. Some sang songs and some shared ideas of what to expect on their new adventures. They eventually turned south, onto a small dirt road. There was nothing for miles but tall, green grass and a few oak trees.

Inexplicable unease gripped Patia when the caravan ground to an unexpected stop. Dorian dismounted his horse right in front of a small, lonely house with a large purple door. A strange humming filled the air.

"We aren't near the Mississippi River," Patia grumbled. "You got us lost."

"Why are we here, Kralis Dorian?" asked Markos, who followed closely behind the king. In front of the tribe, Markos was always formal with Dorian. However, as he grew older, he became closer to Dorian than his own father. When they were alone, they were relaxed and casual. Dorian treated him as if he were his favorite son.

"We are here to collect one last family member," Dorian said carefully.

Patia was dumbfounded.

What family member? Who is Dorian talking about? she thought. Then it clicked. *Syeira! Dorian wants to surprise us! He must have found her and is bringing her back where she belongs.*

It had been many years since Patia had seen her daughter.

Grandmother Zenobia heard gypsy music tinkling in the distance. Her dogs barked, the usual alert that strangers were afoot. She went to the front room and looked out-side the window as Dorian and his people approached.

What on earth?

A wooden crate of Dorian's letters rattled in a shelf by the table. Grandmother walked back to the box and absentmindedly waved her hand in the air. One yellowed envelope with red trim popped out from the rest in the box. It came to rest in her open palm.

Grandmother racked her brain. When Dorian wrote, he always sent money, sometimes included handmade toys, and asked about the twins. Dorian mentioned every so often that he wanted the boys to learn about their culture. Her hands trembled as she reopened the worn letter.

The tone was different than that of most of his letters. Dorian was insistent that the twins should learn about the Camlo people and their heritage. The challenge was dark-skinned David. Both Grandmother and Dorian thought that although David's mother was Roma, he would not be accepted by the gypsy elders. It didn't matter that Dorian was king; the group would fight accepting the black child. In the South, racism always found a way.

Grandmother felt sick as she gripped the letter.

Despair cast a shadow over her home. A distinct memory flooded back like a slap in the face. She remembered her response to the letter she now clutched in her hand. She'd suggested that whenever Dorian and his clan were ready, he could take Anton with him. She agreed that culture was important. The fair-skinned Anton, having more of his mother's features, would fit in nicely with his people. The darker-skinned David, having more of his father's features, would remain with Zenobia. It was a difficult, painful decision to separate the boys, but it was probably for the best.

Could this explain my crazy mood? I've been blindly obsessing over a stupid number. She thought hard about the number twenty-three again. The Chinese I Ching said twenty-three was the number of separation.

This was the day that the boys would be separated from one another.

She dreaded this moment. Losing a family member made her so sad that she pushed the idea away. She had forgotten that this day would eventually come to pass. She had forgotten that she and Dorian had a mutual understanding. She'd promised that the day the gypsies showed up at her walkway, she wouldn't dismiss them.

She carefully smoothed out the crumpled letter and placed it back with the other letters in her collection.

The Camlo tribe had arrived.

Patia, believing she would be reunited with her Syeira, called out from her highly decorated wooden caravan, "Syeira! We're here!" She clasped her hands together and smiled brightly as she anticipated seeing her daughter. "We found you!"

There was no immediate response. Grandmother cringed. Patia's voice grated on her nerves.

"Syeira, come out. I demand it!" Patia shouted. The others watched as things unfolded. The trip was instantly much more interesting to them than counting cattle and trees along boring pastures. Patia struggled, as usual, to get out of her wagon until Markos helped her to stand on the ground. The sun hurt her eyes, so he pulled out an umbrella to provide her with a little shade.

"Syeira!" she screeched again.

Dorian approached Patia carefully. "Syeira is not here."

"What? Then why are we here?" Patia asked.

Dorian stepped back from Patia and addressed the crowd.

"My family, my friends, I am sorry. I did not know how to tell you, but my princess, our princess, is gone forever. She's dead. She died years ago, months after she left our camp."

Gloom struck the crowd as clouds passed over the summer sun.

As Dorian made his announcement to Patia and his people, Grandmother opened her front door to look at the caravan. Ahy ran to her side. She surveyed the group carefully and reluctantly lowered the protective shield around her home.

Many members of the caravan cried. Some recoiled when they saw the Voodoo High Priestess, the woman who took away their princess in the darkness. A few of the women noticed that the strange hum went away.

"She's dead? Why didn't you tell us sooner? How could you keep this from me? I am her mother!" Patia screamed.

A horrible weight pressed upon Patia's heart, and her eyes stung with tears.

Are we here for her body? she wondered.

Ahy yodeled and wagged his tail when he saw Dorian. Patia brushed away her tears when she glanced up the Voodoo woman.

Grandmother stared hard at Patia. Patia tried to look back but couldn't muster any courage. Grandmother continued to look down at Patia – and through her.

Patia looked at her feet for a moment, trying to settle her emotions. As she refocused her sight through her tears, she noticed a fair-skinned boy rolling around in dirt under the porch. Anger flashed across her mind, crushing any sadness she felt. The moment the little boy peeked out to look at the entourage, sunlight revealed green eyes that were unmistakably the same color as Syeira's. Rage quickly replaced her anger.

"We are here for him, aren't we?" Patia pointed her crooked finger at the dirty little boy.

Dorian nodded in agreement.

Little David ran out from the side of the house. He paused behind Grandmother and then stooped by the stairs that led down to the porch. He carefully climbed down the stairs and crouched to look at Anton.

"Anton, come play with me!" he shouted at his brother.

Anton scuttled back under the darkness of the porch. He then threw a small rock at his brother. David picked up the rock that missed him and threw it back at Anton, hitting him in the forehead. It caused no real harm but startled Anton, who began to cry for attention. David climbed back up the stairs and hid behind Grandmother's skirt.

"David, be nice to your brother," Grandmother said.

Patia tried to put all the pieces together. Syeira had two boys? Dorian had kept much information from her. She was incredibly bitter about losing her daughter. She blamed Dorian, the Voodoo woman, and anyone else who could possibly be involved.

Patia watched the Voodoo woman as she stood still on the porch.

"Anton, come out and let me see you," said Grandmother, not taking her eyes off her visitors. "Come, I said!"

I will not stand for this! thought Patia. Fury unleashed itself. She wanted to attack the woman who'd robbed her of her precious daughter. *Dorian will pay dearly for this too.*

Anton stopped crying and threw another rock, but he stayed under porch.

"How dare you treat our boy as if he were a dog! Hand him over, Negro woman, and be quick about it!" Patia yelled.

"Don't you speak to me like that, on my land," Grandmother Zenobia said. She'd promised Dorian she would not refuse to give him the child, but she would not tolerate being disrespected. Patia took a few steps forward so that she could get a good look at her rival.

Calm down, she reminded herself. Grandmother wanted to gather her will and strike down the horrid gypsy woman. She considered that she should have killed the woman when she had the chance, back in the bayou. Grandmother's fingers twitched.

Relax your grip, she thought, shaking her hands to get them to relax. She didn't want to use her magic in front of the boys. They were her family. Dorian was here for his family too. She sensed fear emanating from the whole group that stared at her from outside of her property. Grandmother held her stance, but took deep breaths to calm down. She looked at her hands again and noticed they were balled up in angry fists. She released her hands, exposing her palms. She then stared back at Patia.

"AAAAHHHHHHYYYYEEEEEEEEEE!"

Patia screamed like a ghoul, at the top of her lungs. She frightened the twins and other small children in the caravan. Ahy growled.

"Foolish woman." Grandmother smirked and continued to stare at Patia.

Anton remained under the porch, hiding in the shade. The humid June afternoon was too much for him. David clung to Grandmother's dress. Dorian saw the beginning of a stand-off.

"You have no business with Anton," Patia hissed. "He belongs to his people. No porch monkey deserves to raise him as one of their own."

"Who are you calling a porch monkey? Continue to disrespect me and you will regret it, Patia Camlo," Grandmother said. The sun was brighter and there were no clouds close enough to offer shade.

Patia recoiled.

"The Voodoo woman knows my name?"

That didn't sit well with her or the other women of the tribe. In the world of magic, many things could be done to a person just by uttering their full name.

Patia looked back at the women who continued to cower behind her.

"Sisters, help me!"

Instead, they stepped back and looked away from her.

"Fine, this is my battle anyway." Believing herself to be cunning and clever, Patia decided to hurl a curse at Grandmother Zenobia. She held up her right hand and uttered a few sinister words. "Potestatibus invoco..."

"Enough!" Dorian shouted. "This has got to stop before things get out of control."

Dorian lost his patience. He looked over at his wife with regret. Patia growled where she stood but didn't challenge him.

"I will handle this."

Dorian noted that the woman's face had turned different shades of color, from an ashen pale to a rosy blush to a sickening green and back to pale. He quickly looked away.

"You will 'handle this' the same way you 'handled' her stealing away my daughter?" Patia said.

Fear, heartbreak, and embarrassment ran through Patia. Each emotion had its own color upon her skin. She clenched her fists and tightened her jaw. She was frustrated that she couldn't do more damage to anyone.

"Go back to the wagon. You are lucky that Grandmother hasn't lost her temper."

Dorian stepped without hesitation across a white powdery line, onto Grandmother's walkway, and casually walked up to the house. His people murmured as they watched their king.

"Grandmother," Dorian said respectfully as he bowed and removed his hat in her presence.

"Dorian." Grandmother proudly nodded back.

Ahy ran down the steps and excitedly greeted Dorian with dog kisses.

Many of the gypsies, including Markos, flinched at his boldness. Markos knew, as all the gypsies did, that no one casually stepped on the spooky woman's land. The people in town murmured that it was impossible to even be invited.

Patia didn't like the easy exchange between Dorian and the Voodoo woman.

Why does he address her so casually? she wondered as she chewed her lips. She didn't notice the blood as it spotted the corners of her mouth.

"Come here, Anton. Come to me, son," Dorian said warmly as he bent down, trying to seem less intimidating. Ahy backed off and sat next to him.

Anton slowly crawled out, looking up helplessly at Grandmother and David for approval. He winced in the sunlight. Grandmother didn't want to show that her heart was breaking. She simply nodded at him with her consent. Ahy circled the little boy a few times before running back to Grandmother.

Anton wandered over reluctantly to Dorian, who continued to kneel down to the little boy's level. Dorian placed his large felt hat upon the little boy's head, blocking out the Southern sunshine. He gently picked Anton up in his arms and stood up. At first Anton was afraid, and looked at Grandmother and his brother again.

"Go on, Anton. It's okay," Grandmother said. She put her arm around David, who started to cry.

Everyone watched as Dorian carefully held the little boy in his arms. He spoke softly and privately to him. Both he and Anton exchanged a few nods. They turned to Grandmother and David with big smiles. They whispered again to each other and then Anton blew a kiss to Grandmother and to his brother.

"Bye bye," Anton said as he waved his pale little hand in the sun.

David stopped crying when he saw his brother smile. He returned a smile and blew a kiss back. Dorian chuckled and kissed the little boy on the cheek before walking over to the caravan. Grandmother noticed a blue spark when Dorian kissed the boy. When travelling folk gave heartfelt kisses, there was always a magical spark.

As if holding precious cargo, he carefully handed Anton over to his sister, Mirela. She was his favorite sibling, always great with children. Mirela tried to comfort the little boy, holding him in her arms. Grandmother looked to the heavens and said a prayer while Dorian's back was turned.

"Lord above, please show mercy upon these boys, as their paths are separated. Bless them as they walk the earth," Grandmother said.

Patia had had enough of feeling helpless. Emotions erupted in her stomach.

Someone needs to pay for my daughter's death, she believed from the depths of her bitterness. Patia figured the only way for her to really hurt Dorian and the Voodoo woman was to hurt the innocent boys. Her own mother had done the same thing, hurt her when she was younger, to get revenge on her father many years ago. It was an unfair but effective emotional tool.

They will pay!

Patia pushed Markos, who still held an umbrella, away from her. She spun around twice and angry words came easily to mind. She spat a curse upon the twin boys, shouting loudly, clearly, in English for Grandmother to hear.

"I, Patia, queen of this tribe, command those boys be doomed!" Patia threatened. "In full spirit, I declare that when they grow up to be men, this woman's so-called innocent blessing will cause horrible fate, agony, and despair to fall upon their heads. I declare that they will be condemned as they walk the earth! True light and love of a woman will be stripped from them mercilessly. In return, they can only be saved by the true light and love of a woman. Take that, you old tar baby!" she cackled.

Everyone stared at Patia as the boys started to cry loudly, simultaneously.

Markos wondered, *How could someone be cursed by having love taken from them and in return be saved by love?* He wondered why Patia was always so angry. He remembered the night the black man died. It was never spoken about openly, but he knew that Patia had conjured a spell that killed the man. He would never forget how the body rose from the flames. Markos still had occasional nightmares about dead Will and his mournful cries in the night.

Many of the women felt sorry for Patia. She looked foolish as she said her crazy words. She had always had a flair for being dramatic, but once again she had gone too far. Certainly, Patia could conjure a few potions and small spells here and there, but to them, she had no real power. Her card tricks were entertaining at best. Had she not been married to Dorian, she would just be some lonely, crazy lady.

Grandmother pushed David protectively behind her. She stared hard at the gypsy woman. Ahy's ears lay back on his head and he bared his teeth. Grandmother nervously patted him on the head, encouraging him to calm down.

Dorian understood Patia's pathetic threat. He understood many of his wife's outbursts all too well. He felt it was his fault because he hadn't shared the truth about Syeira sooner.

"Stop this nonsense, woman. We'll discuss this later in private," he said.

"We will do no such thing, Dorian! You are a selfish fool. That porch monkey probably cast some spell on you. You call yourself king. You are weak. I will do as I please, and dare you to cross me!" Patia spat the venomous words at her husband. She then spun around to seal her strange curse with a jerky dance move.

Dorian had a hard time containing his anger as he approached his wife.

"Not once were you grateful that I saved you from death, years ago," Dorian said in a low voice to Patia. "You and I know that it was your curse that killed that woman's grandson. It also killed our daughter. This is your fault, not mine. And yet you still insist on disrespecting me. I have had enough! Get back in the wagon."

Dorian spoke to Patia as if she were a child having a temper tantrum. Rather than obey, she screamed and spit in his face. She lunged at him, trying to scratch his face.

Dorian's anger boiled over. He slapped his wife hard across her face, leaving her speechless. She fell like a rag doll and rolled around on the ground, in direct view of Grandmother Zenobia. Had Dorian not smacked her down, Grandmother could easily have called up a horrible spell to attack Patia; both women knew she was tempted to do it.

Dorian stepped over the bitter woman and motioned for some of the women to help her up. Casually, he strolled back onto Grandmother's land. He approached Grandmother as she and David watched from the porch.

"I am so sorry," he said to Grandmother as he stood near the steps leading up to the porch.

"I understand your struggle. We all see it, but you have to find another way to deal with her abuse," Grandmother said. "Don't put your hands on that woman."

Dorian nodded in agreement.

"May I talk to David?" he asked.

"Of course," Grandmother said as she twisted around, looking for the small boy who hid behind her. "David, this is my friend."

David let go of her dress and held her hand. He took a few steps forward in the sunlight. Ahy sat next to him.

Grandmother was surprised that Dorian looked almost eye to eye with the little boy at her side. Approaching David slowly, Dorian reached up and softly touched David's cheeks, wiping away his tears with a soft red handkerchief.

"Young man, my name is Dorian. It is a pleasure to see you," he said softly.

David stared at the man before him. He stared at his curly black hair and his hazel-colored eyes. His nervousness slowly faded as he listened to the velvet, soothing tones of Dorian's voice.

"Your brother is going away with me and my family. He's going to learn about our culture. I promise to take good care of Anton, if that is okay with you."

David shook his head no.

"Are you sure? Grandmother gave me her permission."

David looked back at Grandmother and then to Dorian. He lowered his head but nodded.

Dorian wiped away more of David's tears before gently tucking the red handkerchief in the little boy's pocket. David smiled shyly. Dorian smiled back at the little boy.

"May I ask a favor of you, young man?"

David nodded quickly.

"Would you please take care of Grandmother and Ahy for me? They will need someone strong to help around the house. I know that Grandmother has a very big heart and needs lots of love. You seem to be perfect for the job. Do you think you could do that? Take care of Grandmother and her dog for me?"

"Yes, sir," replied the little boy shyly.

"I would be forever grateful to you, David."

Dorian reached out, offering his large hand to the little boy. David extended his little hand slowly and they shook hands, man to man. To Dorian's surprise, David leaned over and hugged Dorian around his neck. He hugged the boy back.

Dorian stepped back to leave. He paused and ran up the stairs to the porch. Grandmother was impressed with his agility. Inspired by little David, he stepped closely to Grandmother and gave her a big bear hug, slightly lifting her off her feet. The audience continued to stare at their king as he embraced her.

"Grandmother, please believe me when I say that Anton will be safe, and in good hands," Dorian said earnestly. "I will teach him as much as I can about our people and our culture."

"Be mindful of that wife of yours," Grandmother warned again. "Anger and pain can be very powerful. Negative emotions are dangerous if not handled properly. When she gets out of hand, make sure someone else is around. Don't isolate yourself."

"Grandmother, I'm king…"

"And I'm telling you, surround yourself with your people. That boy Markos is great to keep at your side. If you need to talk to an adult, try talking to your sister. She has a good spirit."

"I will consider it."

"I know it's not easy, but try. Controlling your anger is a hard lesson to learn. It's a lesson I constantly face too."

"I will try. I'm sorry our arrival turned out this way."

"I know. Take care of my Anton."

"Thank you for all you have done for me. I know you showed my wife mercy. I am, as always, forever in your debt."

They both looked back at Patia, who was still on the ground refusing help. Grandmother shook her head and looked back to Dorian.

"You're like a son to me. You don't have to apologize. Just always do your best, and control your anger."

"Yes, Grandmother."

"While on your travels, will you continue to write?" She was almost afraid to ask.

"Of course! You will hear from me soon."

Grandmother already missed Anton and Dorian, even though they were both in front of her.

What can I do to help their voyage? she wondered. Too often in the past, she'd judged people and exacted vengeance upon them. She wasn't used to sending positive energies.

She considered the idea that if she had asked permission to say a blessing upon the twins first, Patia might not have been so aggressive toward her. Grandmother quickly dismissed the thought. Patia's spell had killed Will. That woman would never earn her respect. Grandmother would do as she pleased.

"Let us part ways on a positive note."

Grandmother looked behind him at the caravan. Their reaction to her saddened her. The travelers cringed as they watched her speak to their leader. The last time she was this feared by so many people, there was too much bloodshed. She wasn't that wicked person anymore.

Dorian read a strange look on Grandmother's face. He looked back over his shoulder at his people. Young and old, they watched their king. Patia continued to wallow in the dust.

"Thank you. I…we will need all the help we can get," he joked.

Grandmother winked at Dorian and whispered, "I believe I can get you started off on a good foot. Do I have your permission, to bless you and your people?"

"I accept anything you can do for me."

She took a few steps back. She grounded herself and closed her eyes. As she drew a deep breath she opened her heart. She sensed the presence of every soul in Dorian's caravan. Their auras spiraled in the air and blended with sparks of energies. The surge of energy was overwhelming, but Grandmother continued to breathe. *Bless them…bless them.* Slowly she opened her eyes and waved her arms gracefully in the air around her.

"Almighty King Dorian Camlo, powerful ruler of these people!" Grandmother spoke loudly for his people to hear. Little David watched Grandmother in awe, and copied her movements.

Dorian regally stood back, arms folded, head held high.

"Thank you, ever so much, for gracing us with your presence. It was an immense honor," she announced, ceremoniously. "I wish that the sun continues to shine brightly upon you and your people."

Grandmother outstretched her right arm toward the caravan. A soft, cool breeze swirled around the caravan. The older women flinched, until they noticed a soft, sweet scent fill the air. Immediately, they outstretched their hands to receive the energy that flowed to them. Other members followed suit. Faithful followers of Dorian, including Markos, stood taller, also believing the blessings to be true. Patia grumbled as dust blew in her face.

"I wish that your pockets be full and your bellies fat, by the powers that be from the Lord above," she said and bowed slightly. David also bowed.

Dorian grinned. The pomp and circumstance wasn't necessary, but he knew it would help appease his people. He slightly waved his hand in her direction as he did occasionally to his own people who addressed him.

"As you were, Grandmother Zenobia of Louisiana." The calm breeze disappeared as quickly as it came.

"Godspeed, Dorian," Grandmother whispered. "It's time for you and your people to go on your new adventure. I wish you much success, son."

He turned to his people and shouted, "Let us leave this place! On to the motherland!"

Grandmother was pleased when the people cheered for their king. Grandmother, still aware of the audience, collected young David, motioned at Ahy, and went inside. Patia, who continued to kneel in the dirt, made mental note of the black woman's first name. Markos slowly approached her, offering her his hand for assistance. She roughly accepted and eventually climbed, awkwardly as usual, into her covered carriage. Dorian whistled for his horse, quickly climbed upon his steed, and led the caravan away. He looked back once more at the vibrant purple door and tried to make peace with where he had been.

Part Two: Voodoo Wishes

Chapter 14/Happy Birthday

"HE WILL PAY," GRUMBLED PATIA to herself as she gingerly touched her face. She knew that in a few hours, her eye would be black and blue and swollen shut. She placed ice on her sore, patchy skin. *I am eighty years old. I still hate him after all these years. I hate this place. I hate how my life has ended up.*

It was now the year 1936. April in Romania was very bitter and very cold, like Patia's heart.

Dorian had not laid a hand on Patia in many, many years. As they grew older, bitterness and resentment continued to grow, but physical violence lessened. At least until tonight. It was she, as usual, who'd sparked tonight's fight. Patia came across a letter from that wretched Negro woman from Louisiana addressed to Dorian.

"How is that woman still alive? I still don't understand how she found Dorian here, across the sea, in Romania? Our wagon is small, and in the middle of nowhere."

The thought of Dorian being friends with Grandmother made her angry. The Voodoo woman seemed to have a magical reach out to him. When the tribe had left the United States forty years ago, Dorian admitted to Patia that he wrote to the Voodoo woman, but she believed there had to be more than just letters between them.

"There is something to be said about Voodoo wishes," she mumbled to herself. She wondered how Grandmother Zenobia conjured her magic. Quite a few travelers were publically Christians. But outside church doors, spells were cast, fortunes were told. Patia knew magic was very real, even if she had to work hard at it.

Through the years, Patia had continued to work her makeshift spells. They had few results and created lots of mistakes. Once, Patia predicted that a woman who came to her complaining about stomach pains was barren because of her sins in the past. Her victim needed to pay Patia a hefty "donation" to cleanse her spirit and alleviate her pain. It turned out, however, that the woman was unknowingly several months pregnant. She almost lost the baby, thanks to a concoction Patia insisted she drink. However, luck was on the woman's side, and she delivered a beautiful baby boy. Patia was forced to return the money to the new mother and give an additional amount as a gift for the child.

Several times, Patia did card tricks in town, and rather than trick onlookers to gain money, she got confused and was tricked herself. She lost more money than she started out with.

The worst mistake she made, magical or not, was encouraging Dorian and the tribe to relocate to Romania. The more the tribe moved from town to town in Europe, the worse things were for them. It seemed, to Patia, that the world hated gypsies. Many of the younger children learned to steal rather than learn an honest craft. Many of the tribe's men were arrested for crimes they committed. Some were arrested for crimes they did not commit. A handful of tribal members, including Anton, denied their heritage altogether, and ran off as far as they could manage.

Eventually, the remnants of the tribe did settle in Romania. However, Germans, usually with large guns, showed up frequently and asked too many questions. The "Renaissance" Patia and a group of the older women believed in all those years ago was a curse, not a blessing. Europe was a dead end, not a new beginning. Her people were fading away and she couldn't stop any of it.

This evening, Patia had not expected the eighty-six-year-old Dorian to be so aggressive with her. Caught off guard, she'd found out the hard way that the old man still had some physical strength left in him.

"He will pay," Patia muttered again. Patia had found the letter for Dorian from the Voodoo woman. In the letter, she reminded Dorian that the twins (who both were supposedly still alive and well) were coming up on another birthday.

She had forgotten how much she loathed the black woman. She wondered how she could harm her. She remembered the day they'd collected Anton. Patia had spat a curse, right before Dorian smacked her to the ground. She was embarrassed as she wallowed in the dirt in front of everyone.

Ah yes, my curse. The idea of revenge made her a bit less miserable.

Zenobia the Voodoo woman asked Dorian's permission to send them both gifts. She wished to protect and bless them. In doing so, she warned, she would have to reveal the truth about who they were, who their parents really were. They might or might not want to reconnect with him, and Grandmother was not sure how Dorian felt about it.

Bless them? Again, with her so-called blessings? Why would they care about their grandfather? Patia wondered what Zenobia's intentions really were. *There must be more that Dorian has not shared with me.* Patia had accidentally come across Dorian's letter while he was out drunk somewhere. The date on the letter was from a week ago. Just the thought of the letter, tucked away in his personal stash of clutter, infuriated her.

Patia reminisced about cursing the boys when they were four years old. It was more than forty years ago! Now that the Voodoo woman reached out to Dorian, she intended to activate the curse.

If I could just get the spell to start, the curse would easily run its course.

Patia would see to it that the boys, now men, would pay dearly. They were the black woman's weakness. She thought back to when Syeira left with the woman instead of returning to her people. She wanted to make sure Zenobia would suffer the consequences of taking her child. Hurting the twins would serve as a great way to seek revenge against Dorian too.

She wondered how she was going to deal with Dorian. Earlier that day, when Patia had accused Dorian (who was usually drunk and useless) of corresponding with the Voodoo woman, it was as if he was transformed into a completely different person. No, not a person – a beast. The old man erupted with hateful energy and pounced on her. She assumed he'd yell, as usual, but instead he unleashed a powerful beating. Patia was caught off guard. It was as if he were a fierce lion attacking a hyena.

He will pay, she thought again, and this time an exquisite plan crossed her mind. It hurt her face to express happiness, but it was worth it.

They all will pay…

The next morning, Dorian loudly snored in his usual spot, on a thick brown velvet chaise longue in their cramped wagon. Patia crept out, doing her best not to disturb him. The couple had silently agreed years ago that it was better that they slept separately. Patia turned back and looked at the snuffling, grunting beast before she softly closed the door. She wished she had run away from Dorian and her family long ago, rather than marrying him "until death do us part."

Patia stepped outside into the cold, unforgiving weather. The air was thick and her clothes felt heavy. No matter how much she bundled up, she felt cold deep in her bones. Her ears and nose burned with pain as freezing wind gusted around her. Nevertheless, she was hell-bent on vengeance. It would take more than some ice or wind to stop her. She simply needed to find a safe, secluded spot to incite her magic.

After trying to hide her bruised face with a scarf, she had purchased a lamb from a young boy who guarded the livestock. She insured his silence about the purchase with a few extra gold coins and serious threat to his life. "If anyone knows of this transaction," she warned him, "my husband will find you. You will beg to escape his rage." It wasn't until the boy accidentally saw her puffy face that he took her warning seriously. He knew not to speak to anyone, believing he'd suffer Dorian's wrath as well.

Once she collected the animal, her old book of spells, and a bag of tools needed for black magic, she slowly stomped through the darkness, deep into the forest.

Though hindered by snow, she was at least half a mile away from the sleeping gypsy camp before the sun began to rise. Even as light gradually brightened the sky, the air was frigid. Snow-covered trees were hard as stones. They grew closely together, barely allowing the sun's rays through their icy branches. The ground was frozen solid. Everything around her was white, shiny, and covered with ice. Now in her eighties, Patia moved stiffly but deliberately. The calculating old woman was careful not to slip and fall. The last thing she needed was to break a hip and die out in the wilderness, all alone. The wind blew harder, burning her face and ears. It hurt to breathe. Her face throbbed, her hands and feet ached. Part of her missed her small but soft, warm bed.

Do I have your permission to send my blessings? I wish to protect and bless them popped into her mind again. Patia visualized Zenobia's letter to Dorian. Her handwriting was beautiful and artistic, unlike Patia's own chicken scratch.

It is her fault Dorian raised his hand to me, Patia thought as she slowed down. Her knees creaked with each step. She was tired and considered turning around and going home. She touched her cheek and searing pain shot through her face, a souvenir from the last beating Dorian gave her. Her resolve was renewed and she moved faster.

I will have my victory or die trying. The thoughts kept her moving as she tugged at the rope of the sacrificial lamb that followed reluctantly behind her.

After the sun hung at a decent place in the gray sky, the perfect area in the forest revealed itself. The scent of fresh pine filled the air. She stopped where she stood and looked at her surroundings. She found herself in an area secluded enough to create a spell and sacrifice the lamb without any interruptions. Patia propped her book of spells on a tree stump. She laid out a rusty but sharp knife she'd stolen from one of her sons, several dusty old candles, and (after several attempts) tied the lamb to another tree. Before she initiated her ritual, she removed her gloves. She took out stone runes that were held in a black silk bag she'd stolen from another woman in the tribe. She clutched the stones in her bare hands for a few moments, and then, with hands closed, shook them gently. She opened her hands and stared at the shiny brown rocks. The small white slashes and dots should have represented a message of some kind for her. The runes and her eyesight betrayed her. No matter how much she demanded for future advice, they always appeared face down, revealing nothing. She put the runes back in her pocket, thrust her hands back into her worn-out fingerless gloves, and began her ritual.

She squinted at an old sacrificial spell from her book. After a few awkward attempts, she slaughtered the innocent animal with a rusty, crooked blade, all while shouting incantations as loud as her lungs would bear.

When she was a young girl, Patia had learned how to read the spells in Latin, but she had always had a hard time casting them with the same ferocious intensity as her mother could. She questioned the effectiveness of the spell that she cast against Syeira's lover, so long ago. Was any of it worth her agony? She stood alone in the cold, with a black eye from her husband, when she should be somewhere else, anywhere else, safe and warm. She should have run away when she was younger. Maybe she should have encouraged Syeira to run away instead of threatening to marry her off. At least the girl would still be alive.

Patia struggled, doubting herself. She began to remember her mother. She was beautiful and crafty, and at times, Patia had hated her. Patia was not nearly as skilled as her mother had been. She reminded herself to keep going with her curse. Somehow it would be worth it.

Grabbing the lamb carcass, Patia skinned it with skill and precision. Its bright red flesh steamed in the cold air as the knife separated meat from hide. She carelessly wiped away blood as it spattered on her face. The warmth soothed her dry skin. She chanted until the animal's body was completely skinned. After storing some of the blood in a jar and preparing the rest of the meat in a separate jar, she placed its skin on the ice at her feet. The thick, metallic smell of the lamb's blood stained her hands, smothering the fresh pine scent all around her. As she took a moment to catch her breath, thoughts of her mother resurfaced. She remembered that she had thought of her mother the day she cursed the Negro boy too.

Considered very beautiful by many men, Mrs. Jaelle Karela had been a lonely and troubled woman. She was an expert at casting small spells and reading palms but had very little patience with people and a horrible temper.

This particular branch of the Karela family tree was not the most honorable clan of travelers. They lived up to every stereotype there was about gypsies. Harmon Karela, her husband, was a cheat, a liar, and a womanizer. When he was a younger man, his parents arranged his marriage to Jaelle. Restlessness kicked in and within six months of their wedding, he was back to his old ways, sleeping with other women in the area. He didn't care in the least that gypsies frowned upon promiscuity. As time dragged on, Jaelle was miserable. She became more and more aggressive, picking fistfights with her husband to get attention. No matter how much she slapped him or beat upon him, Harmon just laughed at her, deepening her loneliness. He mocked her for being an unfit wife. She was ridiculed for not bearing him a child to carry on his name. Two different women from nearby tribes proudly revealed they had sons by him. Daily, Jaelle's self-esteem plummeted.

Eventually, after a few fertility spells and love potions, Patia was born. Patia was not a son who would carry on the family name, but Jaelle was happy to finally be a mother. She foolishly thought her husband, now a legitimate father, would change his ways. As Patia grew up, she was taught fortune-telling tricks and introduced to her mother's big book of spells. Unfortunately, as Patia grew into a healthy, beautiful young woman, she was also very much like her scoundrel father. She was promiscuous at a young age. She looked for love from too many people, rather than finding it within herself, following her parents' example.

For some time, the only way the mother and daughter could get along was through lessons of learning the dark arts. By the age of twelve, Patia had lost all interest in magic, disregarded her relationship with her mother, and gained lots of interest in men. The more men Patia slept with, the more she drove her mother away.

In desperation, on the night of Patia's sixteenth birthday, Jaelle cursed Patia with a spell that she believed would "save" what little was left of her daughter's honor. It caused her to appear ugly to anyone around her.

"Find the cure to your ugliness and you will find great power to do as you want in life, with magic at your side." This was Jaelle's challenge to young Patia.

Patia cried and cried as she stood before a mirror, seeing the new, horrible reflection stare back at her. Within days, Harmon was ridiculed for having the ugliest daughter the tribe had ever seen. The elders mocked him for having a daughter that would need an exceptional dowry, if he ever managed to marry her off. Everyone knew Patia wasn't a virgin. The women whispered that her own mother had cursed her. None of the women who claimed they could do magic offered to help Patia. No one wanted to cross Jaelle. Her spells were few, but legendary. The constant shifting and changing of the girl's face, the way her flesh would slither on her skull, was proof of Jaelle's abilities.

The impetuous young Patia looked for shortcuts and temporary fixes. Makeup didn't help. She tried small, simple cosmetic potions, rather than researching, studying, and conjuring the real cure for the horror that distorted her face and body. Coming across a spell that she barely understood, Patia called upon herself a spell that would reveal her inner essence. She sat impatiently on the floor of the family tent, cross-legged in front of a mirror. The spell created a purple cloud that hung over her head. In its mist she saw a black-and-orange caterpillar writhe and pulse. In frustration, she destroyed her potions and dismissed her vision.

Sadly, if only the young girl had been more patient, she would have seen the caterpillar transform into a beautiful butterfly. The vision was symbolic of who she was.

Unbeknownst to Patia, her heart held many layers she would have to work through. Selfishness, arrogance, and a false sense of entitlement ran easily within her. Beyond those were pain, loneliness, and fear. These elements did not contain any aspect of beauty. But deeper still, beauty and peace of mind waited to be revealed. Patia, looking for instant gratification, thought she would be ugly forever.

Jaelle knew that if Patia had taken the time to dig deep within her heart and soul, she would have found happiness and genuine love. Patia needed to take time to meditate. With patience, she would find out who she really was and learn to love herself. Then she would understand how to love others. She would find happiness. Her inner beauty would shine and the curse would lift easily.

Ironically, Jaelle had the same lesson to learn as her daughter, but refused to deal with it. She continually tried to force Patia and her own husband Harmon to love her. At best, sporadic moments of happiness and love came and went for both women.

Soon after Patia left the Karela tribe and married Dorian, her mother was overcome with severe depression. She hung herself from a nearby tree.

As an icicle fell from a nearby tree, yards from where she stood, Patia snapped out of the stale memories of her mother.

Painstakingly, she took the steps to make the sheepskin into luxurious vellum.

Every morning for two weeks, regardless of weather, Patia snuck away from the clan. She read the incantations religiously from her book and treated the sheepskin, meat, and blood. She washed the skin in lime juice and fresh water to get rid of any flesh still stuck to it. After the skin was clean, she washed it again, sprinkled powder on it, and stretched it out on wooden sticks. Handling it with great care, she faithfully went over the routine again and again. Memorizing spells in the book, she imprinted the skin with swirling magical symbols. Once the sheepskin finally turned into soft, beautiful vellum, she could set her plan into action.

On a fresh April morning, Patia no longer snuck away into the forest. Instead, she carefully approached the unsuspecting Dorian, as if he were a tiger lying in wait.

"My husband, may I speak with you?" she asked fearfully as she approached him inside their wagon.

He sat hunched over in his favorite chair, reading a book. In his old age, he had more books around him than friends and family members. Nowadays, Dorian was a mean old man and Patia was a mean old woman. The family showed the couple respect when they had to, but the negative energy the couple generated was unbearable. The younger Camlo men were recognized as elders in their community, but none of them were dynamic enough to be crowned King of the Gypsies like their father. That honor eventually passed to Markos, who was more of a son to Dorian than his own flesh and blood. King Markos ensured that a new book or two was delivered to the old king every month. He understood that Dorian was more comfortable with books than he was with people; he enjoyed his solitude away from the other gypsies. Dorian barely noticed that members of the tribe had snuck away to safer lands, or gone missing. He was aware, however, that outsiders, especially the Germans, marched closer to their location every day.

"What do you want, old hag? Leave me alone," Dorian growled at her. His eyes never left the pages of his book.

She dared to take a small step forward anyway and revealed to him a basket of small treasures as an offering.

"I humbly ask you for forgiveness. I was wrong to question you about your dealing with the Negro woman a few weeks ago."

Dorian carefully closed his book and watched Patia more carefully, calculating. His sharp focus frightened Patia more than she expected.

"Go on." He was suspicious of her formal behavior toward him.

"Please, accept my gifts for atonement," the crooked old woman said as she did her best to bow before him, lowering her eyes. "A wife should never question her husband, at any age. It was not my place to read your letter."

She revealed the contents of the basket. There were two bottles of red wine, shiny fresh fruit, chocolates, fresh bread, sausage, and cheese. Dorian stood up nimbly and approached her. He snatched one of the bottles of wine. He squinted as he examined the label.

"Where did this come from?"

"I bought it from one of the boys. He stole a case from a fancy restaurant. He said the wine was very expensive." Patia didn't dare look at Dorian directly.

"He was right, this is good wine." He smelled the bread and his stomach growled.

"Fine, I accept your apology," he grunted. He rifled through his side of the wagon, searching for a glass and something to open one of the bottles of wine with.

Patia considered criticizing him for drinking so early in the day; it would be so easy to do. Her mind filled with insults to spit at him, but it was more important to keep focused on the task at hand. Remembering her most recent beating and the black eye that had finally faded away, she knew to choose her battles with him carefully. She held out a corkscrew, which he snatched from her.

"If I may add, I would like to be of service to you. I'm sorry if I'm talking too much, but maybe you want to write to the twins yourself, about their birthday. I'm old. I said many angry things, a long time ago."

Dorian paused, sizing up his wife.

"I forgot all about the curse I threatened back then, until I read your letter, which, again, was none of my business. You should wish them many blessings. People like to hear nice words on their birthday. I made ink and vellum in hope of making things right with you."

Patia reached her clawed hand deeper into the basket and presented several pages of fine vellum, a pen made with eagle feathers, and a bottle of ink.

Something about the situation seemed wrong, but Dorian couldn't put his finger on it. He was still slightly drunk from cheap wine from the night before. Against his better judgment, he accepted her gifts. It was beautiful vellum, he admitted, very soft to touch.

"Go away. I said I accept your apology, you elephant of a woman."

"Anything you say, husband."

Patia exited their wagon awkwardly. To many people's surprise, she joined a few women working on quilts in the nearby sewing wagon. She nodded politely to her counterparts and sat quietly. She sewed earnestly and appeared unusually content in their midst.

Dorian set off with his wine and other treasures stuffed carefully in a burlap bag. He wasn't sure if there was enough vellum, so he also grabbed a few pieces of his favorite paper when he stormed out of the wagon.

Spring had barely begun and the ice melted slowly at the base of the Carpathian Mountains. The winter had been brutal and Dorian was thankful it was starting to pass. Today had turned out to be a bright day, and he made his way to his favorite quiet meadow. A few patches of grass had already sprouted up through the cold earth. He got settled on an old, worn quilt. He had a few sips of wine, which warmed him up right away. It took a moment or two to get comfortable on the hard, cold ground, but he cherished the quiet moment. Excitement and nervousness came back to his spirit as he thought about what to write to Anton and David, the boys from so long ago. He didn't trust Patia; she was so angry when she found Zenobia's letter. He wanted to warn them that a curse was cast so long ago, but it sounded silly. He also wanted to send them blessings, like Grandmother suggested. It was the least he could do, especially for Anton. They'd parted ways when Anton was in his twenties. It hurt Dorian deeply when he thought about their last encounter. Both men had said very ugly things to each other, and fought fiercely.

He had no idea what to write to David. All he knew about Anton's twin brother was whatever Zenobia wrote to him, which was minimal. The last thing she'd mentioned about David was her disappointment at him running off to college, up north, and marrying some woman she didn't approve of. He didn't know what David liked or disliked. He didn't know if David even remembered him. At best, the blessings would be a way to strike up a conversation with his long-lost family members.

Dorian raised his head toward the sun, feeling the rays melt the cold air off his tired face. He shook off his sad thoughts the best he could. He remembered that

Grandmother encouraged him to think of things to be grateful for. It helped calm his upset mind.

Dorian decided he was grateful for the fresh air that filled his lungs. He took his time considering what he wanted to share with the men. Time was no longer on his side, and he wanted to make sure he was very clear and meaningful. It might be his only chance to communicate with them, so the letters had to be perfect. After writing, reading, drinking wine, rereading, and writing more, he was satisfied with the words from his heart. Still, he wished there was more he could do for David and Anton.

He shifted his weight, trying to get more comfortable. When he leaned in, his large ankh medallion poked out from his shirt and glittered in the sun. He touched the pendant softly. It had a long history. Angelica had said it was a family heirloom, and had given it to him when he was a teenager. He was honored to receive a beautiful gift, a token of love that was passed down to her from her mother. After Angelica died, Grandmother Zenobia let him keep it. He always remembered that painful day; barely fifteen years old, Dorian was a new father and had no means of taking care of himself or an infant. Grandmother had promised to look after his son Will. She insisted Dorian go back to his tribe. Family and culture were important, which she respected. Years later, Dorian gave the ankh to his daughter Syeira when she was ten years old. He loved looking at it glitter in the sunlight when she danced with the other girls of the tribe. It was painful when Grandmother handed it back to him, in the moments after Syeira bore the twins and passed away. Still, it was a piece of him. It represented family and the bonds of love that were formed.

"When I'm done with the letters, I'll melt this down into two pendants for my grandsons. Then everything will be perfect."

Dorian took a break, noticing a few wildflowers poking out from soil that had been frozen solid just a few weeks ago. As he reached out to stroke the soft petals, he noticed ink all over his large, meaty fingers. He realized he only had enough vellum for the letters he'd written to the boys. Using his regular stationary, he also wrote to Grandmother Zenobia. He always enjoyed corresponding with the woman who never seemed to age.

Satisfied with his work, he ate the bread, sausage, and cheese in the basket. The sausage seemed a little spicy but the creamy cheese and soft bread made it all a fine meal. After finishing off the first bottle of wine, he decided to head into town. Sitting on the hard ground for most of the morning had taken its toll on his legs. He got up slowly, and as he stood, the world spun around him. He'd expected the usual tingling in his old legs, but the wine hit him harder than anticipated. He shook his head, stiffly climbed upon his horse, and rode into town. He stopped by the blacksmith's shop and painstakingly melted down the copper ankh into two smaller ones. He etched small markings, including roses, like the ones he'd etched on a wedding ring for Angelica. Once they had cooled, he made his way to the small postal office. He held his head high when he entered. He hummed to himself when he mailed the letters to the twins and a special note to Zenobia, granting her permission to deliver the birthday messages along with any gifts she wanted to include.

I miss the savory smells of Grandmother's cooking. I miss that basenji following me all over the house, Dorian thought.

Grandmother Zenobia's home was the only place in the world that had felt like a real home to him. Even now, after living in countless places around the world, Louisiana had a special place in his heart. Dorian swore to himself that every now and then it haunted his dreams, like the sweet kiss from a long-lost lover. He longed to escape Romania, escape his wicked wife, escape his old age with its aches and pains, and visit the resting place of his princess Syeira, his son Will, and his true love, Angelica.

When he arrived back at his wagon, early in the afternoon, Dorian was relieved that Patia was nowhere to be found. He reflected upon his day and how wonderful it was to write and share his feelings with his grandsons.

But then, strangely, he was embarrassed at how he'd treated Patia. On the other hand, he knew in his heart that she was a horrid, fiendish witch, like in the old stories they used to tell small children that misbehaved. He wished he'd had more courage when he was a younger man. His life would have been so different. Today, he was a sad old man, tired of fighting so many things, so many people, in his life.

After taking a nap to try to sleep off the warm buzz from the wine, Dorian walked into the woods. A stroll in the woods at sunset was unusual, but after writing to the boys, he felt different – rejuvenated. He was a new man. His head was still foggy, but he didn't mind that he couldn't seem to shake it off. He liked the buzz. Venturing out farther than he had planned, he noticed a secluded area, deep in the woods. The trees were thick and the remaining bit of sunlight could not sneak its way in. Residual snow and ice still covered the ground. Curiosity beckoned him to move in closer. He drew a big breath, expecting to take in the scent of pine, but the air had a stale, metallic scent to it. As his eyes focused on his surroundings, Dorian realized he stood right where an animal appeared to have been slaughtered in a strange ritual. Blood, bits of bone, fur, and ashes were in the middle of a pentagram with strange markings surrounding its perimeter. Dorian didn't like the looks of the scene at all. Something felt wrong. He didn't like that he still couldn't clear his head. He decided it was best to go home.

Dorian arrived back at camp just as the last bits of sunlight faded away. In their wagon, he found Patia, who had dinner waiting for him. She was humming softly to herself, something he hadn't heard her do in many years.

"You're home," she said warmly and ushered him to sit at the kitchen table, offering him a glass of wine.

Dorian sat quietly, resting in a large hand-crafted wooden chair. His head continued to buzz. He looked around and noticed there were no other family members for dinner. No grandchildren, no old men to play cards with, no old women for the hag to gossip with.

"Where is everyone?" he asked.

"I told Markos and your friends I prepared a special dinner for you and hoped for you to enjoy your quiet time. You always seem happier when you have some solitude. Markos said he would be back later to play cards. Or I can find him and your friends and invite them over if you wish. I guess I could try to make something for them, unless you want to share what you have."

"No, no. This is fine. I look forward to whatever it is you have made for me," he said as he watched Patia. For a moment, he thought he saw her smile, but it came and went so fast that he disregarded it.

Dorian continued to watch Patia as she moved around in the small kitchen and wondered if things would ever change between him and his wife. They'd had a handful of good times and he had a few good memories, especially when they'd raised their children. She wasn't perfect, but neither was he. Maybe he shouldn't have hidden his heart away for so long; there was always so much pain when he opened it.

Could she change? Could I change? He sat, considering future possibilities.

Patia placed a large bowl of hot stew before him and topped off his glass of wine.

"What is this?" he asked, looking at the food placed before him. He began stuffing his face with the steamy, warm food without waiting for her response.

"Lamb stew. I marinated it," Patia said as she watched him devour his food like a ravenous dog.

Dorian guzzled the wine Patia had offered him as if it were water.

"Do you like it?" she said cautiously.

"Yes. It's spicy, like the sausage earlier. Thank you for such a delicious dinner," he replied, smiling as he smacked his lips.

The simple words of gratitude surprised her. Patia couldn't remember the last time she'd heard Dorian say anything kind to her. She remembered every fist he made, every slap he dealt, every kick to the ribs, and every gasp for air beneath his grip.

His gratitude caused her to feel something different toward him. Patia looked at her old husband's hazel eyes. Although surrounded by wrinkles, his eyes still had fire behind them. She used to love looking up into his handsome face when she was a much younger woman. Momentarily, she regretted some of the fights she had started with him.

Patia noticed the ink stain on his hands and she shook off any warm feelings she had for Dorian. She watched him as he devoured his food and added more to his large bowl before he could finish what he had.

As Dorian enjoyed his meal, he mulled over the idea of being nicer to the woman. They were both in the twilight of their lives. They were too old to fight the way they used to. He looked at her, noticing that her black eye was just about gone as she sat quietly across from him at the table. Patia had never been attractive to him. Their marriage, like most marriages in their culture, was arranged by their parents. He considered that maybe he'd misjudged her heart. Should he dare rekindle something with her later? He hadn't kissed a woman in a long time. Dorian shook his head again, trying to ignore the erection that threatened between his legs. It was difficult for him to be with a woman he couldn't trust. Doubt often crept into his mind about who'd fathered some of their sons. Although he'd always known that the oldest was not his, he also had his doubts about at least two of the others. Nevertheless, the thought of a woman's touch aroused him.

Maybe I'm being paranoid. Maybe not. These thoughts made his head hurt a little.

"You should know I sent the letters today on the vellum you gave me. I used most of the ink and the pen was very sturdy," he said to Patia, believing himself to be complimentary.

Patia's lips curled, like a red ribbon across her face. At first, he thought it was a beautiful smile, and he smiled back. However, something disturbed him. He couldn't remember the last time he'd seen his wife genuinely smile.

"So you did send letters to that Negro bitch. Good!" she said snidely.

Dorian knew something was very, very wrong. Looking around, he noticed for the first time that she'd never taken a bite of the dinner she'd prepared for him. He felt a low, painful thud starting in the back of his skull, which radiated outward and forward to his eyeballs.

"What?" he asked in shock.

"You heard me. That black whore has been nothing but trouble. I'm trusting that she'll send the letters to the dirty offspring. I will be rid of all of them. And you too!" she said.

Dorian was hot and sweaty. His stomach cramped.

"What have you done?"

He attempted to stand, but his knees were week. His back twitched spasmodically. Trying to secure his legs underneath him, he knocked over the table, spilling food and wine on the floor. He barely stood, feeling the small space of the wagon spin around him.

"What have I done?" the old woman cackled in delight. "Nothing that can be undone, you horrible son of a bitch! You were always such a fool for food and wine. I hope you enjoyed every bite. The love potion didn't work as much as I wanted, but it doesn't matter. The poison will finish the job."

She laughed louder and louder. Dorian was the world's worst fool. How had he let himself think that this evil woman would ever change?

"I should have known you gave me some vulgar potion!"

Dorian grabbed a dictionary, traded to him years ago, from his pile of belongings and hurled it at his wife. She laughed louder and her cheeks were red when the book fell flat at her feet. He lunged at Patia, but she stepped to the side, out of his grasp. He fell to the floor. His stomach cramped more. Random muscles throughout his body constricted violently and his eyesight blurred.

"Look at you now, King of the Gypsies," she mocked, and spat on Dorian as he fumbled around on his hands and knees. "Why didn't I think to kill you sooner? This is almost too easy!"

Dorian felt the room spin faster and tried in desperation to shake it off. His stomach could no longer hold tight and he retched all over himself and their worn Persian rug.

"Help me!" he moaned.

Patia stood back, laughing hysterically.

"No one can hear you, idiot! I'm going to sit back and enjoy watching you die."

Dorian grew weaker and weaker by the moment. He grabbed his stomach in pain. As he clutched his belly, he found the answer to one of his last prayers. His fingers brushed against the hard handle of his ivory hunting knife. Dorian had always kept it close after Will was born. Patia would never know everything there was to know about the man she married.

"I'll watch you die first!" he managed to yell back.

With every ounce of energy he had left, Dorian managed to climb up on his feet and charge Patia like a wounded bull. He plunged the sharp knife into her throat. Her flesh opened easily, spewing blood. Dorian slashed her throat a second time and then plunged the ivory blade deeply into her chest. Patia uttered a choking, gurgling sound as the dark blood oozed and spurted from her throat. After the initial shock of meeting Dorian's treasured blade, she struggled, gasping for air. As her body sank to the floor, Dorian never let up stabbing her. He knelt on achy knees and pounded the knife into her body, anywhere and everywhere he could. If he did nothing else in life, he had to make sure she would die.

Blood was splattered everywhere. After a few body twitches and gurgling noises from Patia's lifeless face, Dorian was certain she no longer moved.

"Finally, I am free from the witch. Grandmother was right; she said Patia would be the death of me."

Dorian's time was short. Knowing he was poisoned, with barely a moment to spare, he wrote a short message with Patia's blood on the table that rested on its side.

"Send to Zenobia."

Breathing was difficult and his head throbbed painfully. His body seized up and he flopped around, banging his head on the hard floor, like a fish out of water. He managed one last deep breath after his body relaxed.

"Forgive me for my sins," he prayed. Then Dorian Camlo genuinely smiled the biggest smile his face would allow, for the first time in many years. He knew he'd visit Grandmother Zenobia, Syeira, Will, and Angelica soon, and he could hardly wait.

Chapter 15/Zenobia's Nightmare

ONE FINE SPRING AFTERNOON IN 1936, Grandmother Zenobia, who rarely slept in general, tried desperately to stay awake. She was tired as she rocked in her favorite rocking chair on the back porch. The sun was too bright and her eyes burned with every blink, but she refused to lie down. Her head was heavy but she wouldn't even consider a catnap. Her excuse was that she was waiting for the mail to arrive, in hopes that Dorian had a response for her. Truthfully, she was afraid to go to sleep. Her dreams were more vivid than usual. Horrible nightmares had plagued her after she wrote to Dorian about the twins and their birthday. Before, her dreams were just memories and feelings from the past. Now the dreams were dark, and disturbing.

Once again, Zenobia found herself thinking about the number twenty-three. It had been and always would be a dangerous number to some people. She remembered that even the Chinese, who put trust in numerology, avoided twenty-three at all costs. Two plus three was five. The twins were born on the twenty-third day of the fifth month, which was extremely inauspicious to those who believed in its power. It took a while to admit, but after much consideration, she confessed that she too thought it was unlucky.

Zenobia worried herself sick. The twins were turning forty-six, which was twenty-three times two. The seemingly infamous birthday would arrive in just a few weeks. She hated to admit it, but every year she always worried about Patia Camlo around the twins' birthday. She was never very good with her magic, but she had great potential to cause mischief. Zenobia mentally listed all of the elements the twins faced: they were cursed by crude, rudimentary black magic, had a tragic birth date, were born under a lunar eclipse during an earthquake, and were conceived right after a vicious attack by vampire bats. To make matters worse, their parents were actually half-siblings. Dorian's son and daughter had somehow found each other and fallen in love. There were too many circumstances that could empower the curse and affect the twins. She was thankful that, at the very least, they were born physically healthy. By now, they were adult men living their lives. She wished Dorian would let her know whether or not she could contact the twins, and send them her blessings.

Grandmother heard the screen door slam. Her visitor had arrived, on time.

"Hello there, Grandmother Zenobia!"

"Elly, you are a sight for sore eyes," she said as Elidi St. George greeted Grandmother Zenobia. "It's nice to have some company."

"I'm glad I had a chance to stop by and check up on you," Elly said.

Grandmother had now been in Louisiana for over a hundred years. Because she (and her dog Ahy) aged at such a slow rate, her appearances around town were limited. She didn't want people to notice that time practically stood still for her. Good friends, like Charlotte Evans, eventually died, while Grandmother appeared barely months older. Most of the people who had seen her real powers were dead. She couldn't remember the last time she'd performed a good séance, although she did still offer tarot readings from time to time.

"I appreciate you."

With each day, Grandmother grew lonelier. There was only so much she could do around the farm to entertain herself. She could only have so many conversations with her dog. She realized, as she spoke with Elly, that most of her friends and family were dead and gone. She still attended church from time to time, and shopped in the French Market once in a while, but she continued to believe that it was hard for her to make friends. She knew quite a few people around town, but she didn't speak to them regularly. Seeing Elly, the granddaughter of Charlotte Evans, daughter of Cora Milton Harrell, cheered her up.

"Grandmother, my mother said to thank you for the praline cookies."

"How is Cora feeling these days?"

"Much better, thanks to your cookies I think."

"You're so kind to say that. Tell her that she doesn't have to thank me for them. I know how much Cora likes pralines. She's always loved them, even when she was a baby."

"The other day, she was talking about how close you and Maw Maw Olivia were, you know, before she passed. She said you spoke of her a lot when my mother was growing up."

"Your grandmother Olivia Milton and your grandmother Charlotte were some of the sweetest women I ever met, once I got to know them. I remember the day Charlotte adopted Cora as her own. It was a marvelous day."

The memories of Olivia, Charlotte, and Cora were sad, but nice distractions from the horrible visions that kept Grandmother edgy. Nowadays, she did her best to remember the better qualities in people and dismiss the negative, without serving any judgments or punishments.

"My mother misses Charlotte a lot too. Before I came here, she was going on and on about the fun times the two of them had picking flowers in your garden."

Grandmother nodded. "Feel free to bring your mother some flowers. A lot of wildflowers popped up this spring."

"I'm going to take Mother to visit Charlotte's grave later tomorrow. Do you mind if I bring some flowers for her grave also?"

"Not at all, Elly. You are welcome to help yourself to as many as you like. By the size of your pockets and the crumbs on your face, I'm guessing you already helped yourself to some of my sugar cookies."

Elly blushed as she quickly wiped her face. When she was a teenager, Elly had had to return many borrowed things to many people, including Grandmother. Cora had warned Grandmother that Elly had what the family called "itchy fingers." As an adult, she still battled with stealing things.

"Elly, you're a kind woman, just like your mother. You are always welcome to any food in my kitchen and anything that grows in my garden. I appreciate your friendship, more than you know."

"Thank you, Grandmother."

"Have a seat. I sense that you're worried about something. I can see it in your face."

Elly plopped down in a chair next to Grandmother. "Grandmother, my oldest sister became a grandmother a few days ago." Elly gritted her teeth, trying to fight a few tears.

"I see."

"I'm already twenty-five. I haven't had one baby and the rest of my brothers and sisters are having lots of babies. Some of their babies are now having babies!"

"You have more additions to your family. It's a blessing."

"I guess so. But I worry. Peter is a good husband. I know he loves me, but I'm afraid he'll…"

Grandmother held up her hand, interrupting her.

"Elly, please don't worry yourself about that. You and your husband are good people. Peter is a hardworking man and a faithful husband. Our time isn't necessarily the same as God's time. You keep taking those herbs I set aside for you. You'll have a baby soon. It takes a little faith and a lot of patience."

"I wish I could see the world like you do."

"Honey, it's a blessing and a curse."

Elly watched as Grandmother's smile faded away.

"You look exhausted. Have you slept at all since I saw you the other day?"

"I can't say that I have…"

Last night's nightmares, foreboding as expected, had specific images. Grandmother saw fires that raced across the land and the hearts of howling, vicious wolves. She got up in the middle of the night and paced the porch to shake off the dreams. When she eventually went back to bed, she had scary feelings of being smothered in thick, cold darkness. After she got up a second time and drank some water, the dreams came back, ruining any chance of rest. She saw a pair of evil, twisted demons, resembling a man and a woman with piercing red eyes, who walked the earth, stalking victims, killing anyone who crossed their paths. They seemed familiar, but she could not make out their faces. Their evilness fed into her fears. Even as Grandmother was awake, sitting on the porch, it seemed nothing could comfort her for too long.

Elly interrupted Grandmother's dark thoughts.

"I'm going to make you some tea."

"No, I'm fine."

"It doesn't take an expert to see that you need some rest."

Elly dashed into the kitchen before Grandmother could continue her protest. Ahy followed her.

A few minutes later Elly returned holding a silver tray with a plate of sugar cookies and a steaming cup of tea. Ahy returned to her side.

"Grandmother, I know it's warm out, but drink this. It'll help you to relax, maybe get a little sleep."

"I'm waiting for…"

"With all due respect, I mean it! Drink the tea. Snack on your cookies. Then lie down!" Elly insisted.

"You're right, I need some rest," Grandmother sighed.

"I was waiting for you to mention that letter you're expecting. You've talked about it all week."

"It's just that…"

"When it arrives I will wake you up."

Grandmother ate a cookie and stared at Elly for a moment.

"You're right, I do need a little sleep. If it comes today and I'm knocked out, you can open it. I'm hoping that my friend Dorian will let me send some presents out."

"The ones on the kitchen table, yes, I remember. You've talked about it for over a week."

"Don't get uppity with me," Grandmother warned.

"When was the last time you talked to your grandson David?"

"I haven't talked to him in about twenty years. After he graduated college up north, he married some girl and didn't invite me to the wedding. It really hurt that he didn't want to share that part of his life with me."

"What about the other twin?"

"Oh, Anton? I haven't seen him since the day he was taken away with Dorian's people. Dorian would mention him in his letters to me, but I probably wouldn't know who Anton was if he walked right up on me in the market."

"Why do you care so much about people you hardly know?"

"I'm not sure, I just do. Family will always be family to me."

Elly nodded in approval.

"If you like, I would be happy to take those boxes to the post office, obviously depending on what the letter says. I'm happy to run a few errands for you. Honestly, it would be an honor to help you in any way that I can."

Grandmother stared hard at the tea. She really wanted to curl up in her bed.

"Thank you."

Elly stood proudly, hands on her wide hips. "You give me chamomile tea all the time and tell me to relax. Now it's your turn to take your own advice. Drink and rest. I'm in no hurry to go home." Elly sat in a chair next to her host. "I'll be here when you wake up." Grandmother sipped her tea and the two women sat in silence, enjoying the spring afternoon. Ahy rested at Grandmother's feet.

Elly noticed that finally Grandmother's ceramic teacup was empty. Grandmother kept fighting to keep her eyes open.

"Enough. Time for your nap," said Elly. When Grandmother stood, several ducks, a few dogs, and a baby goat got up and followed her. Ahy followed Elly.

Elly shooed Grandmother, with her animal menagerie, into the house and escorted her into her bedroom. As Elly closed the bedroom door behind her, Ahy and a large bloodhound obediently took a watchful post on the floor.

Grandmother knew that Elly was right. She yawned deeply. It was funny how small, basic things in life could change a person's perspective. A cup of tea to calm her nerves was probably what she needed. A little sleep should be safe. Ahy was right outside her door. The sun should still be out when she woke up. Grandmother closed her eyes and drifted off, hoping for just a moment of rest.

What seemed like mere seconds later, Grandmother was startled awake by a horrible, putrid smell that burned her nose.

"Good Lord! What is that?"

Zenobia leapt from her bed and followed the scent into the front living room. Elly lazily rocked back and forth in an old rocking chair while knitting a soft, cream-colored blanket. Surprised to see Grandmother, she looked at her quizzically.

"Well, don't you look rested! How do you feel?"

"What time is it?" Zenobia snapped as she looked around, disoriented.

Elly didn't know what to make of her demeanor.

"It's six o'clock."

"Well, I guess a three-hour nap is better than nothing," Grandmother muttered as she continued to search for the terrible smell.

"Three-hour nap? It's six o'clock…and it's Friday," said Elly carefully.

"Friday?" Grandmother gasped. "I closed my eyes Wednesday afternoon! I've been asleep for three days?"

"Yes, and I guess you really needed it. You didn't stir once when the letters arrived. I swear I tried to wake you."

Grandmother, still feeling groggy, searched frantically for the source of the sour odor.

"What the hell is that smell?" she demanded again. "Where's Ahy?"

She moved about randomly, following her nose until she stopped before Elly. She roughly grabbed Elly's hands, realizing the putrid scent came from her.

"Letters came?" Grandmother questioned. "What happened while I was asleep? Tell me everything."

Elly twisted away in pain from Zenobia's grasp. She pushed Zenobia's powerful hands away, defending herself. She was more emotionally hurt than physically damaged.

"A box came early Thursday morning. There were three letters and two smaller boxes. One letter said David, one said Anton, and one said Grandmother Zenobia. I took the arrival of the items as a sign of approval. I figured if the answer was no, there wouldn't be gifts or letters. Then I took the two letters, which were very soft I might add, the two small boxes, and the gifts you wrapped to the post office right away. I got the addresses you left on the table with the gifts. I thought we were very clear about what you wanted me to do. The letter for you is still sitting on the table."

Grandmother rushed to the table, where Elly had left the letter.

"Where's Ahy?" Grandmother demanded again.

"I swear I tried to wake you, but it was impossible." Elly thought it was unfair that she had to defend herself for following strict orders. "When the letters came, he ran out back. He's out there now. He's been acting strange since the stuff came in."

Grandmother's fingertips burned. She examined her hand, seeing tiny red bumps and streaks where Elly touched her wrists. Grandmother tried to put all of the pieces together. The stench that reeked in her home was the stench of an evil spell. Grandmother closed her eyes and breathed deeply. Even though they were no longer present, she sensed that the letters were marked. Cursed, dark items always had some kind of indicator or fingerprint. Sometimes they smelled awful, sometimes they started to rot, sometimes they exploded. Evil objects were unpredictable. Because Grandmother Zenobia was sensitive to such things, items like those could be extremely dangerous. Who knows what would have happened if she had had direct contact with the letters? She was sure it was why Ahy stayed away. She remembered a time when she ordered a statue of Anubis, and the wrapping burst into flames. It took a whole day to clean up the mess and another day to conjure a retaliation spell. She thanked all the powers above she had enough Florida water for a deep spiritual cleaning after that.

She looked down at her swollen, itchy hands.

Maybe I'm not out of danger. There is still a note waiting for me, she thought.

Elly, who was oblivious to any supernatural affects, didn't know that she had touched cursed objects.

"After I mailed the boxes, Ahy came back inside and slept by your bedroom door, like he always does. He refuses to come in the kitchen. He won't eat. I'm worried that maybe he's sick?"

"Elly, this note addressed to me. You said it was different from the others?"

"Yes, ma'am."

Grandmother rushed into her prayer room. She frantically searched until she found a large bottle of Florida water. She snatched it off a shelf and furiously rubbed the liquid all over her hands, while saying the Lord's prayer. She never removed her black and gold fleur de lis ring.

"Elly," Grandmother said gravely, as she came back into the living room. "Wash your hands with a spot of lye soap and lots of holy water."

"Holy water? Did I do something wrong?"

"Not at all. You'll see a glass bottle with crosses on it, to the right of the sink. Do it now."

Elly didn't understand why Grandmother was behaving strangely, but she did what she was told. She knew it was foolish to question Grandmother, especially when the Voodoo woman was serious. They were friends, but Elly knew when to give her some space. When she was younger, Cora had warned Elly not to cross Grandmother. Her family was the only one left around who knew Grandmother was a true, powerful sorceress.

Grandmother handed Elly a small bottle of oil, blessed by a Catholic pope.

"Add just three drops on each hand, just for good measure, and massage the oil in," Grandmother said.

Elly watched Zenobia flinch as if she saw something when she rubbed Elly's hands.

Grandmother, who rarely showed any kind of weakness in front of anyone, then covered her face and cried.

"What's wrong, Grandmother?" asked Elly.

"The last of my family…the twins…the letters were cursed…they are doomed. All I ever wanted was the best for them. And now there's nothing I can do. What was started must be finished, like it or not," said Grandmother through her tears.

She approached Elly and held her hands softly.

"I'm sorry I was cross with you, Elly."

Elly dismissed the handshake and gave Grandmother a big bear hug. Grandmother gratefully embraced Elly back.

"You're still a part of my family, Grandmother. You'll figure something out. You always do."

"I'm not so sure this time."

Elly stepped back and offered Grandmother a handmade handkerchief to dry her tears.

"Well, do something that makes you happy. You're always telling other people to do that. Maybe go and visit your garden. You always seem at peace out there. Plus, you still have that note addressed to you."

Grandmother turned to look back at the ominous letter on the kitchen table.

"I thought it was personal, so I didn't open it. Is it cursed too? Could you bless it or something? Maybe read it outside in the fresh air?"

"Elly, you're right!"

Grandmother rushed out to the back porch, where she saw Ahy lying by her empty rocking chair.

"Are you okay?" she asked the dog. He wagged his tail slowly.

"I'm getting rid of the cursed things. Hopefully we'll all be safe soon."

She grabbed her gardening gloves. They were an old, heavy leather pair that Will used to wear. When she slipped her irritated hands into the worn-out, soft leather, she missed her grandson. She always cherished the day he'd flashed his bright smile right before he dashed off to propose to Syeira. The memory was comforting. Feeling more secure, Grandmother charged back into the living room and carefully picked up the note. The stench from the envelope made her eyes water. She stopped in the kitchen and grabbed her saltshaker. Holding the letter away from her body, she carefully walked back outside, past the garden. She turned and went to the side of the house where there were bald spots in the grass. Elly followed her, noticing that all Grandmother's pets refused to follow. Wearing the heavy gloves, Grandmother examined the note carefully in the sunshine.

"I recognize the handwriting," she explained to Elly. "And I see that it's Dorian's usual stationary."

"That is not the same paper as the other letters that came. I am sure of it," Elly said confidently. "Same handwriting though. They were delicate and very soft to touch. This paper is plain."

Damn that wicked gypsy woman, Grandmother thought. She slowly sprinkled salt over the letter. Small swirls of black smoke rose from the ink. She sprinkled more salt and gingerly opened the envelope. A faint, sweet odor rose from the letter, and a dried-up wildflower fell to the ground. Both women sighed with relief.

"Do you think everything is okay?" Elly asked.

"I think so."

Grandmother kept the gloves on, and sprinkled more salt. More swirls of gray and black smoke rose from the contaminated ink. She shook the letter, and the air cleared. The writing was faint, but still present.

"I've never seen anything like it!" Elly said.

"That old gypsy really hates me, almost as much as I hate her," Grandmother grumbled.

"Is the letter still dangerous? Should I get more holy water?"

Grandmother sniffed the letter. The rotten smell was gone.

"No, I think we're okay now. The salt cleared any negative energy locked into the letter."

"Well then, I'm going to leave you to your business, and get back to my knitting. I love the sunshine, but it's a little too bright for me today."

Grandmother nodded at Elly as she went back inside. She heard Elly rocking slowly in her chair.

"Your blessing is coming, my friend," Grandmother whispered. She looked over at Ahy, who seemed a bit sluggish.

"The bad items are gone, boy. Let's get you some food."

Once comfortably seated on the porch, with Ahy safely at her side, Grandmother turned her attention back to the letter she held in her hands. Dorian hadn't sent any letters in a while, but Grandmother always enjoyed reading whatever he wanted to share. For someone who never studied at a university, he was well read and smart as a whip.

April 20, 1936

Grandmother Zenobia,

It's a nice spring day in Romania. My old bones are sitting on the ground, enjoying a good bottle of wine. I wish I could draw like Angelica did and send you a picture of what today looks like. There are wildflowers popping up here and there, in between snowy patches. The best I can do I guess is put a flower in the letter for you to see.

My letter to you today is different than my usual complaints about life. Today, I need to give you my deepest thanks.

Thank you for everything you have done for me and continue to do for me. I know I don't say it enough to you. It's my fault I have no contact with the twins. It's my fault that I am weak. I never should have left Will when he was a baby. You told me to go back to my family, but I should have been a man and raised my son. Thank you for raising him, as well as David and Anton as long as you did. It takes a special kind of woman to raise children alone.

Thank you for not turning your back on me in my dark days. Thank you for all of your letters of encouragement throughout the years. My heart grows heavier every day that I didn't choose to follow the path of love. I regret not being a stronger person in the past. As an old man, I see now that I should have done everything I could have for love.

Please, do whatever you can to protect David and Anton on their birthday. I wrote letters to the twins telling them the truth about the curse, their parents, and asked them for forgiveness. It was hard to write them. I wasn't sure what to say, especially to David, whom I don't know at all. Anton hates me, with good reason, but I hope he accepts my apology.

Maybe, if it is okay with you and them, we could be reunited at your home? I have so much respect for you, and for what you have done for our family. I am never at peace except when I am at your house. I miss you and I miss Syeira. I miss not ever getting to know Will. I miss our Angelica most of all. To this day, my heart still cries out for her. Maybe even if the twins don't accept me, I will still come see you myself. I would very much like to come home. You have always been my real family, even though we started out as enemies. I will say it again: words cannot say how grateful I am for all you have done and continue to do for me.

Respectfully yours,

Dorian Camlo

Grandmother held the letter to her heart. She missed Dorian too, and would love to welcome him and the twins home. Dorian had been like a son to her, and she would be overjoyed to spend time with family.

April 21, 1936

Dear Grandmother Zenobia of Louisiana,

King Dorian and Queen Patia have passed. His last word was to send him to you. I don't know if this letter will even get to you, but we need help. The Germans make Romania a bad place to be for me and my people. We are not safe, and have nowhere to go. Dorian often said you helped him. Can you help us?

King Markos Shaw

The day the letter arrived, Elly happened to be at Grandmother's home, pestering Zenobia for the secret to her sugar cookies. If she hadn't been at Grandmother's side in the kitchen, Zenobia surely would have fainted onto the black-and-white tiled floor. The plain letter, with rudimentary handwriting, spoke volumes to her. Grandmother knew that the day would come eventually. She just wasn't ready for it. No one was ready, really, to hear about the death of a loved one. Grandmother had hoped and wished to make a big dinner for Dorian and the twins when they finally came to her home in Carrefour Parish, not make funeral preparations.

"Are you okay?" asked Elly as she helped Grandmother to a chair. "Do I need to call the doctor?"

"No, no. I need a minute to collect myself."

"What is it?"

"It's a letter about my friend Dorian. He's….he's… he passed away." Zenobia tried to fight the tears but sadness gripped her chest and choked her throat.

"But the letter you got on Wednesday was from him. I don't understand."

Zenobia shook her head and closed her eyes. She held the note out for Elly to read for herself.

"Oh, I see. It's dated the day right after his letter he wrote to you. I guess something happened. I'm so sorry."

"Me too."

"What now?" Elly asked.

"Now I have to figure out how to get Dorian and his people back here, for a proper burial. I hate to cut our time short, but I'm sending you home. There's a lot I have to do."

"What about the sugar cookies? We barely started the dough."

Grandmother went to the kitchen. She rummaged through the cabinet until she found a shiny black bottle. She sprinkled a few drops of a light-brown liquid in the batter, added a few pinches of cinnamon, and covered the bowl.

"Take the batter home with you and stir it real good. Bake the cookies for no more than ten minutes. Bring me my bowl back, along with those other dishes I let you borrow last week."

"But you were going to share with me your secret to the recipe! Your cookies always come out better than mine."

"The secret is simple. Bake, cook, create your meals with love. That's the secret. Love. And sometimes a little almond extract, instead of vanilla."

Once Elly left, Grandmother sat quietly in her prayer room, trying to figure out how to help Markos and the gypsies return to New Orleans. Not a single idea popped into her head. She went to the back porch and looked up at the blue sky. Still, nothing came to mind. She wasn't hungry and she didn't want to sleep, so the kitchen and her bedroom were invisible to her. She walked around aimlessly in her garden with her mostly canine entourage. All she had left of Dorian were his letters and her memories of him. The last time she had laid eyes on him was when he took Anton away.

Grandmother walked around to the front side of the house by the front porch and looked around. Memories of the twins popped into her head. Anton loved hiding under the porch. David sat on the steps until he was too hot. She remembered the day they were separated; Dorian casually strode up to her and the boys. She pictured how his people cowered before her and yet he smiled widely. She could almost hear his voice when he talked to the twins so sweetly.

"That's it! Memories!" she yelled out loud. Her entourage dispersed, except for Ahy. She and her sidekick ran back into the house and stormed into her prayer room.

Grandmother searched through several large books while her dog lay at her feet. She sifted through a few scrolls but couldn't find what she was looking for. Ahy jumped to his feet and sprinted into her bedroom. He yodeled and jumped, causing a commotion.

"Ahy, can't you see I'm busy?" she said.

The dog yodeled again at the corner of her bedroom.

Grandmother went into her room, ready to throw the dog outside, when something caught her eye. Suspended with string, high in the corner of her room was a black-and-silver ring. It was a snake in the form of a large oval, eating its tail. Two small pieces had been broken off from the circle. In the middle of the oval was a tarnished face of a man, a bull, and a lion. Thick dust clung to it.

"The pendant of Chronos! I almost forgot I had it. Ahy, I will make sure you get a special treat for bringing this to my attention. "

Grandmother reached out her hand and summoned the pendant. It flew effortlessly to her. It was a gift, given to her by Pirate Scarlette Black. Zenobia had learned many lessons from many men and women in the past, but it was Scarlette, daughter of Black Caesar the pirate, who taught her to be fierce, a force to be reckoned with.

Giving up wasn't an option for pirates, and it wasn't an option for Zenobia either.

The pendant itself no longer held any magic. It was a representation of Chronos, the Greek god of time. The broken piece of jewelry reminded Zenobia of what she was capable of doing on a supernatural level. She could go back in time, or at least back to a feeling or memory of a specific time, and experience it, like looking at an old photograph. It took an enormous amount of focus and energy, but it could be done. At best, she could sustain it for a few minutes, and that was all she needed. She wanted to go back to the moment the gypsies were at her home. She didn't want to alter anything (not that she could), but she would be able to recognize the auras of the gypsies that day. Then, with a little luck, she would reach out spiritually to find them in the present.

"Magic this deep has a price," she reminded herself. "I would do anything for family. Dorian was family, in a sense, and his body should come home. I'll deal with whatever happens."

Grandmother Zenobia went back to the front porch and stood in front of her large purple door. After sprinkling powdered eggshells on the ground, she closed her eyes and felt the sunshine on her face. It was a typical, humid Southern day. She thought back to the day Anton and David were separated. She recalled hearing the gypsies singing when they approached her land. Dorian's aura clearly came to mind. Everyone else was shrouded in a cloud of fear. The cloud was gray and dusty. It had a peculiar smell.

"I have to be closer to them," she thought. "To where they were that day."

She opened her eyes and strode down the porch to the path that led to her home. After surveying the landscape, making sure she was safe from any negative spirits, she walked up to the threshold from her property. She sprinkled more powdered eggshells on the ground to protect her home from negative spirits. As she gingerly crossed over the line and stepped onto the small dirt road, she was exposed. No one was around for miles, but she felt as if she were being watched. She was weak and unprotected. Her dogs, ducks, goat, and an armadillo refused to follow. Ahy waited for her at the open gate.

It's now or never, Zenobia. You know you have to help those gypsies. You can't ignore the evil forces growing in Europe. Many people are in grave danger.

She took five more paces into tall green grass, turned, and faced her house. It seemed so small from where she stood. The front door, painted in Tyrian purple, was as bold as ever. The white cat with orange spots watched Grandmother from the porch where she had just been standing. She closed her eyes again and focused on that day. The cloud of fear from the travelers was still present, but she sensed a few auras around.

"If you're going to do this, really do it," Zenobia grumbled to herself.

She removed her turban, exposing her thick Ethiopian hair. She massaged her scalp, feeling the sun on her skin. She removed her house slippers and felt the earth underneath her bare feet.

She focused again and remembered her moment with Dorian. She remembered asking to give him and his people a blessing, which he agreed to. She remembered speaking loudly for everyone to hear and raising her arms. She remembered the gypsies, raising their hands to receive the blessings.

The murky cloud of fear dissipated. Zenobia sensed the spirits of the Camlo tribe. Earthy-colored auras of an earthy people hung like shadows. Some had streaks of yellow and baby blue. Some had pink and lavender auras. She took in the spiritual fingerprints of people around her, young and old. They were excited about their new beginnings. They were curious about Anton and David. They were upset with Dorian, at first, but respected him. They were in awe of how he talked to the sorceress before them. They were saddened at Syeira's death.

Zenobia liked that she'd captured their attention. Zenobia loved how they all felt united and strong as a clan. She understood why they felt the gypsy way was the only way.

And then there was Patia. Murky green with streaks of dark gray swirled where she stood and spat hideous words of hatred. Insecurity, anger, fear, and sadness tumbled around one another.

To Patia's right was Markos. He was still a scrawny boy then, but had an aura like Dorian's, when Dorian was a teenager. Majestic blues and deep greens swirled around him. They were bold, pure colors for a bold, pure heart.

Zenobia remembered her blessing again. Little David's aura was pink mixed with lavender, colors representing loving and sensitive attributes as well as imagination and vision. He was always such a daydreamer. She was certain he would be a visionary when he grew up. Little Anton's aura was also pink, with streams of orange and yellow, which represented intellect, someone detail-oriented and scientific. Grandmother knew how Anton liked order and neatness, unlike David, who was quick to start a food fight and slow to clean up afterward. Anton would be successful at whatever he wanted to do with his life.

Ahy the basenji had an array of colors in his aura. There were lots of blues and greens, but many other colors swirled around him. His loyalty and love for Zenobia was boundless. Back when she was just a girl, Zenobia and other females of her tribe had been kidnapped by marauders. Ahy tracked her, over hundreds of miles, in the hot sands of the Sahara desert to be at her side. The dog was barely alive when he found her. Zenobia would always remember the day she stood in the Temple of Set trying to hide Ahy from her captors. The Egyptian deity Set majestically appeared before everyone. He was so moved by the dog's love for Zenobia, he healed the dog and granted it immortality. Ahy's revival was the beginning of Zenobia and Set's treacherous romance. She would always love Set, but she knew that no one was more loyal to Zenobia than her dog, then or now.

"Do I dare look at my own aura?" she wondered. "Should a person look at themselves in the past, as an outsider? Would there be consequences?"

Grandmother had come this far, relishing the brief moment in the past. She decided to view herself; she wanted to see as others saw her. She dared to look for her aura. She glanced at the travelers once more and then looked at herself as she stood on the porch.

Zenobia of the past stood tall, with her head held high. Her arms were raised over her head, and David shadowed her. Ahy stood at her side. Her blessing appeared like small, soft flurries, scattered in the wind. Grandmother hadn't really taken the time to consider how she appeared nowadays. She wore whatever was comfortable, and relatively clean. Younger Zenobia was a sight to behold on the porch. Although she wore a simple housedress and apron, Zenobia still took time to be presentable. She wore a touch of lipstick and always some perfume. Grandmother noted that she needed to take care of and love herself as she did back then.

Grandmother stared harder at her past self, squinting her eyes. She wanted a small glimpse of her aura back then.

Would it be wrong to see your own soul? she wondered.

She felt a tingling in her fingertips. She ignored the sensation. She expected a cloud of color to burst over Zenobia's head any moment. But within the blink of an eye, all auras, all images, faded away.

Grandmother was flooded with nausea. She felt a wave of energy push her. Her knees were weak. She fought to get her feet back into her worn-out house slippers. She struggled to put her turban back on as her head pounded. The sunshine was too bright. Muscles in her back throbbed. There was a high-pitched ringing in her ears. Her body felt heavy, as if she moved in quicksand. She dragged herself slowly, step by step, to her property. When she crossed the threshold, her ailments barely faded. Ahy whined as he licked her face. He nudged her to try to get back in the house. Several dogs and a raccoon rushed to her side. All she could do was sit in the grass in her front yard with her furry entourage until she could muster enough strength to get back inside.

She had much work to do in order to get Dorian and his people to Louisiana, but the hardest part was accomplished.

Chapter 16/Social Graces

MARKOS SHAW WAS EXHAUSTED AS he stood on the busy dock in New Orleans. He fiddled with his brochure, dated May 19, 1936. He couldn't believe the group had made it from Romania. He shoved the brochure in his pocket, next to the letter Grandmother Zenobia had sent him, and looked at his surroundings. Many locals passed by, greeting other passengers and loved ones. Some people lugged heavy suitcases. Some pushed large crates that were offloaded from huge ships.

A black horse-drawn carriage slowly crept up and nervous energy gripped his stomach. He did his best to muster his strength as the Voodoo High Priestess climbed out of the carriage and slowly approached. Her blue dress and large blue hat almost matched the deep-blue sky. Her escort, who wore a deep-blue suit, carried a black umbrella, shielding her from the bright sunshine that danced with ominous thunderclouds. Milosh, his eldest son, stood behind Markos, arms crossed. Markos knew his son was just as frightened as he was, but they were men. They refused to show any signs of fear before the tribe. Before they disembarked, they had agreed to face the Voodoo woman together.

Only the older people of the tribe remembered the Voodoo woman, and those who had never met her had heard the stories about her. The group cowered at the edge of the wharf, watching Markos and Milosh. The contrast of the hot, humid Louisiana weather versus the cold, crisp weather in Europe took its toll on them. They were all overdressed, clinging to as many earthly possessions as they had. Most were dehydrated and starved from the long voyage. The sun was glaring and the humidity was stifling. They were tired of smelling their own body odor and hearing the squeals of seagulls.

The large group of gypsies had come to America to bury King Dorian along with Queen Patia. Dorian's request, written in blood, had to be honored. To disobey a dead man's wish would bring certain doom to their tribe, even if they were scattered to the ends of the earth. Gypsies honored family, even if the family was dysfunctional. Without question, Patia would be laid to rest next to Dorian.

As the mysterious woman and her dog grew nearer, Markos could hear his people gasp in fear. Milosh barked for their silence. When she was less than six feet away, Markos couldn't believe his eyes. She looked just as she had years and years ago, when King Dorian collected

Anton. Markos was barely eleven then, and now he was an old man in his fifties.

"King Markos!" Grandmother exclaimed. "Happy Tuesday."

Before he could respond, she stepped closely to him and wrapped her arms around him. The huge welcoming hug caught him off guard. As she briefly held him in her arms, energy surged through him, rejuvenating his spirit. Her attendant, a middle-aged Native American man, made sure she was always protected from the bright July sun.

"Dorian was always so proud of you," she whispered in his ear. "I don't know if he ever told you himself."

Tears burned his tired eyes and his knees softened as she held him softly in her arms. The smell of cinnamon around her was unmistakable. Quickly, he dried his tears before his people could see.

"Mrs…" Markos's son interrupted.

"Ah, yes, Milosh."

Grandmother turned her attention away from Markos.

"Please, call me Grandmother or Grandmother Zenobia. I insist upon it." She extended her right hand to Milosh, who immediately shook it. Markos watched his son's eyes grow large with surprise.

"It's my pleasure to meet you, Grandmother Zenobia," Milosh said as his knees shook, although the woman before him appeared harmless. He looked over at his father, who nodded at him in approval. "If you will

315

excuse me, I will leave you and my father to talk. I need to attend to our people."

"Of course," Grandmother said.

Milosh bowed and briskly walked back to the crowd. Immediately, whispers bounced around them as he reassured them everything would be all right.

Grandmother looked over at the group as if counting them. Once she was satisfied with the number, she turned back to Markos.

Markos felt Grandmother look at him, almost through him. Part of him wanted to run away screaming, but he couldn't explain why. She appeared harmless enough before him.

"Markos, I thank the Lord above that you all made it safely." Her words were soothing and Markos tried harder to relax.

"Truthfully, Grandmother, I don't how it is possible that we all stand here before you. It's a miracle any of us survived."

"Never underestimate the power of prayer," she said.

"Grandmother, Romania...the Germans...the way our people are treated. It is unspeakable."

Markos saw Grandmother shiver although it was still very hot and humid.

"I am aware of the darkness out there. We won't speak of it unless it burdens your soul too much and you need to release it." Grandmother frowned as she spoke.

"The darkness in that land only grows more twisted and evil as time passes. It breaks my heart to think about it. Many people are suffering there and there's nothing I can do to stop it."

Grandmother's attendant cleared his throat. Grandmother looked at him and nodded as if they had a private discussion between them.

"Let's talk of brighter things, starting with your people being here. I bet they're hungry and tired. We have several different options for you…"

Fifika, Markos's wife, left the fearful crowd. She quickly approached, interrupting the discussion between her husband and Grandmother.

"It's because of you and your power that we are here," she said and quickly fell to her knees before Grandmother. "You saved us from hell."

"What are you doing?" Markos was embarrassed. "Go back with the others! I insist!"

"With all due respect, my husband, I must show her our gratitude!"

An unseasonal cool breeze swirled across the dock. Grandmother shifted her weight and looked down at the scrawny woman who cried at her feet. Her face was too thin and her skin was too pale. Passersby continued to shuffle along, minding their own business.

"What's her name again?" Grandmother asked.

"Fifika. She is my wife. Her name is Fifika," Markos said as he urged his wife to get up.

"Ah, yes, how could I forget," Grandmother mumbled. Fifika swatted her husband and remained on her knees.

"I, and the women…we all had visions of our tribe's return here, our return to stand before you."

Markos panicked. He didn't want to offend Grandmother.

"Grandmother, my wife…she is clearly hysterical from the trip." He tried harder to get her to go back to the other women, but she wouldn't budge.

"I can see that the trip was hard on all of you. Still, let her speak her heart," Grandmother said.

"It's because of you and your blessing so many years ago that we are here now. Markos remembers the day of your blessing upon him with King Dorian. He won't admit it in front of everyone, but he remembers every word you said. He remembers how it felt. It's true."

Markos glared at his wife, but she ignored him.

"I'm sure you know that many of our people are gone. Some passed away, some were murdered. Lots of us hid in forests like wild animals. Many of us were scattered across the sea and across foreign lands, yet somehow most of us came together…"

Everyone but my Anton and my David. May God have mercy upon them, Grandmother thought.

"...family members we hadn't seen in a long time, from everywhere, all ended up at a port, in England, on the same day. No one could explain it. Once we were there, people who had been stranded, waiting weeks for their turn to board ships warned us we would get stuck like they did. There was something about the quota of people on the ships."

"That is true, Grandmother, about the quota," admitted Markos. "I didn't think we all would be allowed on the ship. But we're family and we stay together. When the ship came in, I showed the harbor master the letter with the strange papers you sent me. I don't know what all of it said, but once he looked over them, he let every single one of us board the ship, without question."

"We can never thank you enough for what you have done..." Fifika cried harder and kissed Grandmother's shoes.

"Queen Fifika, please. Stand up. Let me look at you," Grandmother said. She reached into her breast pocket of her jacket and pulled out a lace handkerchief. "Your Majesty, dry your eyes."

Fifika allowed Markos to help her to her feet.

"Grandmother, please forgive her outburst. The voyage was..."

"No need to apologize, King Markos," Grandmother said. "It is an honor to meet the queen of your people.

She is lovelier than I could have imagined. You are a lucky man to have her at your side."

Grandmother placed her hands on Fifika's cheeks.

"I have always had a soft spot in my heart for your tribe," Grandmother said.

Fifika cried harder. Grandmother stepped close to her and hugged her. She privately reassured her, woman to woman, that everything would be okay. Fifika stifled sobs a few times before she stepped back.

"Let's address your people, shall we?" Grandmother said. She and her attendant walked closer to the group. Markos watched Grandmother adjust her hat.

"Your Highness?" she said to Markos. He came to her side. Grandmother reached out to Fifika to join her husband, and then spoke loudly for everyone to hear her.

"Ladies and gentleman, as we say in New Orleans, happy Tuesday. I am Grandmother Zenobia. Some of you may remember me from your last trip to Louisiana. To most of you, I am probably a stranger. Let me be the first to officially welcome you to New Orleans. I was good friends with King Dorian, and it is my privilege to celebrate his passing with you and your family."

The group was restless. The older women didn't like seeing their queen on her knees before the Voodoo woman. The younger children grew increasingly cranky in the heat. The men leaned on each other for support, or sat on the ground, grateful to be off the ship. Ahy left

Grandmother's side and ran up to the group of children. The children played with the dog while Grandmother continued to address the crowd.

"Your group is led by wonderful people. I remember King Markos when he was just a boy. He always honored his elders and learned much from Dorian. I didn't have the pleasure of meeting his beautiful wife before today, but I can see she is passionate about her husband and her tribe. Queen Fifika is an enlightened woman, as many of the women in your group are. She expressed how blessed she was to be here. Truth be told, I'm the one who's grateful for you all. Blessings last as long as you believe in them. I cherish that you and your people held on to my blessing over your tribe for so long. It's wonderful that you passed it on to other generations! Take a moment, everyone. Look around at your family. Those who believed in my blessing are here now, safe and sound. Thank you, for honoring me with your belief."

Markos stepped closer to his wife and took her hand.

"Grandmother, we are all safe, but not all sound. We have a problem," Markos said carefully.

"What is it?" she asked. As Grandmother frowned, the Louisiana sun seemed to grow hotter.

"The departed are restless."

"Restless?" Grandmother asked.

"Yes. From the moment we put Queen Patia into her coffin..." Markos grimaced as he remembered the horrific scene of her death. Blood was splattered from the floor to the roof. The carpet was black from soaking up so much liquid. Not many of the deceased's personal possessions were saved. He collected a few of Dorian's books (including a thick, old-looking leather-bound book with pictures), a small box of letters and drawings, and Dorian's favorite hat. He managed to bring a few scarves, a dress, and a small jewelry box to bring to Grandmother Zenobia. It was hard, but he also packed the murder weapon, all at her request.

"I found a book that I believe belonged to Patia. It had strange small pictures and many words. We found it near her body, so burned it," Fifika said. "Patia's ways were of the old world. No one in our tribe practices the dark arts the way she tried. I think it angered her."

"Her coffin rattles and shakes, especially at night," Markos said. "It frightens the horses. Several of the men had to hand-carry it. We didn't think we'd get through the inspections and customs."

"Mr. Charles, our undertaker, will be here soon to collect the coffins… Let me ask you this: does she…it…do you hear three distinct knocks, in the early morning hours?"

A chill ran down Markos's back. He thought the situation was strange with the noisy coffin. What was unsettling was that Grandmother wasn't the least bit surprised.

"Yes, we do hear the knocks."

"Does Dorian make any noise?"

"No, just Patia."

Grandmother chuckled. He thought her laugh should make him laugh too, but it wasn't the least bit reassuring. Grandmother turned to her attendant and quietly whispered to him. He nodded, handed the umbrella to her, and slowly walked off to her carriage.

"Where are they now, the deceased?"

In unison, every member of the tribe pointed at a pile of trunks, luggage, and sacks at the edge of the dock. A large wooden crate had many items stacked upon it. A second large wooden crate sat alone, wrapped in heavy chains and locks.

"We should address this now, well before the ceremony."

"What now?" asked Markos. "You're going to do what?"

"The people of New Orleans see strange things all the time."

The tribe mumbled amongst themselves as Grandmother continued.

"Don't misunderstand me. I can't cure why Patia is disturbed, but I can make sure she rests a little easier. There has always been, and always will be, bad blood between us. Your people know that."

It was Markos this time who shivered when there was no cool breeze around.

"Are there two brave men who can assist my attendant removing a few items from my carriage?" Grandmother asked Markos. Before Markos could respond to her request, two young boys sprinted from the crowd toward the Native American man. Ahy ran behind them.

"No! You boys go back to the group. Stand by your older brother," Markos demanded.

"What handsome sons you have, King Markos. You must be proud of them. I can see that they will make you proud when they grow older."

A peculiar thought struck Markos. *How did Grandmother really know everyone? I gave her a list of names, but I know I missed a few. How did she get everyone on the ship? I haven't formally introduced Grandmother to the tribe, let alone my family yet. Dorian barely knew their names. How did she know they are my sons?* Markos felt lightheaded trying to figure out Grandmother's mysteries.

"We'll find someone else to help with the larger items," Grandmother reassured Markos.

Grandmother turned and nodded to her attendant. He stood by as the two boys pulled out huge bouquets of white lilies and a large pink pillow with hand-stitched flowers from her carriage. An additional, smaller boy rushed from the group and joined them. The attendant nodded at the small newcomer with approval. He handed him a single red rose to carry.

A dusty brown Studebaker rolled up.

"Well, look who it is!" Grandmother said.

Gunari, Markos's older brother, parked the car in front of Grandmother's wagon. Boldly, he hopped out and dashed over to the group.

"Grandmother, you did it! Thank you for bringing them home," Gunari said. Markos's heart fluttered at the sight of his older brother. He was heavier than Markos, and his thick hair was straightened. He wore a brown linen three-piece suit.

"Gunari! You're here! We thought you and your family were gone forever!"

"Markos!" Gunari hugged his brother, lifting him off of his feet. "Look at you, look at you all!"

"I have so many questions for you!"

"And I bet I have many answers for you."

"How did you get here?"

"My family and I have been in Georgia for a few months. Grandmother Zenobia found us! Those of us who were already in the United States arrived in Louisiana yesterday. We've all been waiting for your arrival! Grandmother assured us you would be here."

Grandmother cleared her throat at Gunari. Obediently, he came to her side and hugged her. She smiled and then waved him off to see his clan. All of the members were thrilled to see him. Many could barely contain their excitement. After many hugs and kisses from his clan, Gunari stood by Grandmother and held her umbrella.

"Everyone, may I have your attention please? We have the business of Patia to deal with before your reunion can continue," Grandmother said.

They all froze where they stood. Only a handful dared to look at Grandmother.

"Again, I want to thank you all for making such a treacherous journey with your loved ones. Your family, each and every one of you, is precious to me. It is my hope to help honor your traditions. The people of Carrefour Parish look forward to joining your funeral procession Friday. Here, we call it a second line. The people of New Orleans certainly know how to send off their loved ones in grand style too."

The locals will be joining us? wondered Markos. *Dorian will be pleased, God rest his soul. I can see why King Dorian thought New Orleans was such a special place.*

"I have a favor to ask of you, before King Markos and Gunari talk to you about the arrangements for your stay. Patia is not at rest. I cannot cure her, but I can ease her transition. When I say the word, I will need each of you to close your eyes, and to say your own private prayer or blessing for her. I warn you, blessings only, no curses."

"Why should we?" questioned Gunari. "She was a horrible, scary woman." Many of the tribe members agreed. "Why shouldn't we just send her body back to Romania, or dump the casket in the ocean? Burn her and all of her things and be done with it!"

"No one would deny that she was a miserable person, but she was still your queen. Trust me when I say this. You want to bury her in a proper fashion or she will grow stronger and cause serious harm. For the sake of your people, and your traditions, it's still important to respect the old ways. She should be at peace. When your culture is stripped away, or you lose your tribe, you lose an important part of what makes you who you are. I think it's a fate worse than death," Grandmother said. "Your people have a saying that the gypsy way is the only way. For this situation, it's true. Am I right?"

"Fine," Gunari grumbled.

"Do we all agree that we should bury her, along with your king, in peace?"

Markos took a deep breath and stood taller before his people. "Grandmother, we will do this." He took the umbrella from Gunari, and they wordlessly traded places. Gunari joined the crowd.

"We will wait for you to signal us, Grandmother," said Fifika.

Grandmother walked over to her attendant and the boys, with Markos obediently behind her. They all stared at the large box, still yards away. Something inside of it thumped the sides of the large wooden crate sporadically. Ahy yodeled defensively.

"We have to open her coffin and place blessed items in it, adding them to the other items you already have for her," Grandmother explained softly to Markos and her attendant. "There is no guarantee what might happen. I don't know how strong her spirit is, so it's imperative that everyone do as I say."

Her attendant nodded silently. Markos watched as the Native American man eyed the young boys before him and then said something to Grandmother in his native language. His words were aggressive and passionate. Although Markos didn't understand what was said, he knew the man was troubled about something. Grandmother responded to him in his own language, but her words were softer. She looked at the boys and then back at the whole gypsy tribe.

"Chief Qaletaqa is right."

He's right about what? Qaletaqa? What kind of name is that? Markos wondered to himself. Qaletaqa looked at Markos and rolled his eyes.

Wait, does this man hear my thoughts? Markos wondered again. Chief Qaletaqa stared at Markos without saying a word. Markos stared back at the man's dark eyes. Thunderclouds formed in the distance.

"Boys, thank you for help," Grandmother said, ignoring the exchange between the two men. Markos fully turned his attention back to Grandmother. Her smile was still present, but he noticed for the first time that she was nervous. She clenched and unclenched her hands.

"We need your inner strength today. I'm sure there will be more heavy lifting for you to do tomorrow. Ahy, please escort them back to their mother." The boys immediately looked over to Fifika, who beckoned them. Ahy jumped, as hyperactive dogs did, and playfully chased the boys away. Grandmother and her entourage proceeded to the large wooden boxes.

"We need a hammer," shouted Markos to Gunari. Gunari left the tribe and jogged over to his car. After a moment, he returned to Markos with a dusty claw-footed hammer.

"You're serious about opening the box?" Gunari said. "Yes."

"What did the chief say to you?" Markos asked.

"My friend reminded me that young boys shouldn't see such things. It would be good to have someone of pure heart nearby when we open the coffin, but he said we should have everything we really need. I know that you two have already seen more in your younger days than many men have seen in their entire lifetimes. Chief Qaletaqa says they have strong warrior hearts, like their father. I thought it best to spare them the same nightmares you and your brother have."

Markos never spoke to anyone about the nightmares he had. As much as he tried, he could never forget the memory of seeing Will's bloated body in the bayou. He

329

never forgave himself for sneaking to watch when Will's burnt body rose from the flames, calling out to Syeira.

"We should get started. A storm is brewing," Grandmother said as she looked out over the dark Mississippi River. Markos saw there were more clouds in the sky than when they'd first arrived. The air was thicker and his suit felt heavier. Chief Qaletaqa said a few more words that sounded softer than before. Grandmother didn't smile. She still seemed worried.

Grandmother waved at Fifika and the tribe.

"If you would, please, take a moment to bless Patia's and Dorian's souls."

The crowd mumbled their individual blessings and prayers for forgiveness, not minding anyone who passed by. Some of the women raised their tired hands to the sky. Gunari and Markos slowly unlocked the chains around the wooden crate that held Patia's coffin. He wished his hands would stop shaking. They fought to lift the lid of the crate. When they managed to remove the wooden lid, the men watched in horror as Patia's coffin shook violently. It knocked a side panel over, exposing the mahogany coffin to the sunlight. Shrieks and screams filled the air around them, emanating from the coffin. Markos fought the instinct to run away.

"Queen Patia of the Camlo tribe, please accept these flowers as a token of my friendship. I apologize for my harsh words against you," Grandmother said.

Chief Qaletaqa scattered the large bouquet of white lilies on top of the restless coffin. The earpiercing screams stopped.

"And now, the coffin, please. Opening it a few inches should work," Grandmother whispered.

Slowly, Markos and Gunari opened the coffin, just a few inches as instructed. The stench of decay and dried flowers filled the air.

"Patia, this is a pillow made by your daughter, Syeira. She slept on it every day until she died. It is one of my most treasured possessions, and now I give it to you. I hope it will aid in your eternal rest."

Grandmother motioned for the coffin to be opened further.

"Turn around or look away. You shouldn't see this," Grandmother said as she stared at Markos.

Quickly, he looked up at the sky. There was hardly any blue sky at all, just angry-looking clouds. He listened as Chief Qaletaqa hummed softly. Grandmother placed the pillow in Patia's coffin. Grandmother kissed the single red rose and tossed it in too.

Before she could order the lid to be closed, the corpse shrieked. The top of the coffin bounced violently, tearing away at its hinges. The lid flew off, landing yards away. The large pink pillow and the dried flowers, gold coins, and jewels left by mourners were tossed several feet in the air. Grandmother Zenobia and Chief Qaletaqa were knocked to the ground. Markos watched as the white lilies, part of the offering, shriveled and turned black. Patia's corpse sat up. She waved her arms overhead. The teeth in her skull chattered as if trying to tell Markos something.

Grandmother got up quickly and dusted herself off. Gunari and the chief chased down the lid of the coffin. The gypsies cried out in fear. Howling and screams filled the air. A strong wind picked up. Passersby ran away. Some took cover and watched from a safe distance.

Marko watched as Grandmother extended her left hand. Markos could only see her lips moving. The chief joined her, also extending his left hand toward the coffin. Gunari struggled but managed to get the damaged lid back on top of the coffin. Markos grabbed the cover of the wooden crate and, together with Gunari, managed to close it. Markos pounded the lid shut with its original nails. The shrieks faded. The violent winds and the box stopped thrashing around.

Grandmother and the chief slowly lowered their hands.

"Did we do it? Did the blessings work?" Gunari asked.

Grandmother conferred with Chief Qaletaqa in his own language.

"Grandmother Zenobia! I apologize for my tardiness," interrupted a man with a rich Creole accent.

Mr. Charles, the undertaker, shouted from his horse-drawn hearse. His presence captured everyone's attention. Behind his wagon were three large school buses.

He climbed off the carriage and slowly approached Grandmother. He was painfully gaunt in his black suit but had a welcoming, toothy grin. He ceremoniously removed his hat, exposing his shiny bald head, and bowed before Grandmother. Markos found himself standing protectively next to Grandmother, obediently holding her umbrella.

"Happy Tuesday," he said with a bright smile. "I would have been here sooner, but I needed to have a few choice words with Mr. Ewell. He said I only reserved two buses for the afternoon, when I insisted that it was four. We had to agree upon three. I am terribly sorry for any inconveniences it might cause you and your group."

Markos watched Grandmother carefully. He didn't like that her smile faltered.

"It is fine, Mr. Charles. Your timing was perfect, actually."

Mr. Charles eyed the large wooden crates carefully and then turned toward Grandmother. "I will have my men move the deceased to my hearse once everyone is safe and sound on the buses."

Markos didn't like the feeling in the air around them. The clouds were much darker. He noticed for the first time that there weren't any other souls to be found on the docks. Everyone dispersed. Not even the pesky seagulls squawked.

"Everyone, thank you. Thank you all for your prayers and blessings," Grandmother said earnestly as she addressed the group. "Your words were much more effective than I imagined. Now, if you would gather your belongings, please head on over to the buses. I have arranged for you all to stay at a hotel at the edge of the French Quarter. It used to be a plantation, but the owner renovated it. It's not close to the grounds that your people used to stay on, but you can choose whatever will make your stay comfortable here. Gunari and the others are already checked in. When you arrive, there will be soft beds, and warm food waiting for you."

"Thank you, Grandmother, for everything," Gunari said.

"You're welcome."

Markos noticed Chief Qaletaqa talking to Mr. Charles. They kept pointing at the caskets and the hearse. He swore he heard them speaking in French.

"Markos, as I told Gunari earlier, the kitchen in the hotel is open twenty-four hours. If the women of your tribe want to prepare your own food instead of eating what's on the menu, tell the head chef."

"Everyone loves the food there," said Gunari and rubbed his belly. "Especially my wife."

Grandmother barely smirked at Gunari's joke.

"If there is something you need that the kitchen doesn't have, they will fetch it for you," she continued.

"You have to get your own alcohol. If your people want to stay outside, in their tents, which I do not recommend in this weather, the hotel has extra blankets should they need them."

"I cannot guarantee that items my people find in the hotel will be there when we leave," Markos said quietly into Grandmother's ear.

"King Markos, whatever your people want or need, they can have. I want you and all of your family to be happy. You and your wife have the master suite, next door to Gunari and his wife."

"Markos, you won't believe it when you see it! It's so large."

"I hope it's fitting for a king," Grandmother said. Rain began to fall softly from the angry sky. The umbrella that shaded her from the sun now protected her from the rain.

"The owner of the hotel owes me a favor. The hotel staff will be compensated handsomely for the month. Stay as long as you wish. Don't you worry about a thing while you're here, understand me? The buses will come for you in a few days for the ceremony. That's customary for you people, right, Gunari?"

"That's right, Grandmother. After the third day of mourning, we bury our dead."

The more Grandmother spoke, the more Markos sensed her energy slowly fading from her. She frowned as she spoke and her shoulders drooped a bit.

"Well, most of the day is gone. I insist that you make yourselves at home. Once you are rested and fed, mourn your losses. I will see you folks at high noon, at the church this Saturday. I hope that will be enough time for you. We will have a traditional service, Catholic style, and then we will go to the cemetery on my property in Carrefour Parish. Here in New Orleans, we don't actually bury the dead. We are below sea level. I have special places for them in my personal mausoleum, close to where Syeira was laid to rest. The funeral will include a good old-fashioned New Orleans second line procession parade with dancers and a brass band. If you need anything before then, don't hesitate to ask."

Markos was overwhelmed. In his wildest dreams, he'd never imagined that his people would be treated so nicely by outsiders. He was shocked that the Voodoo woman had her own cemetery, too.

"Everyone, make your way carefully to the buses. We have come too far for anyone to get hurt now. Milosh, make sure the boys behave." Markos pointed at his youngest son, who splashed in the large puddles that quickly formed around them.

"Of course, Father," Milosh said as he picked up the little boy and headed off to the first bus.

"Everyone, I will see you shortly at the hotel."

Markos waved at everyone before turning back to Grandmother. She seemed vulnerable to him as she watched everyone climb into the buses.

"Grandmother, you didn't have to do all of this for us," he said, looking directly at her.

"Yes, I did. It's what Dorian would have wanted." This time it was Markos who hugged Grandmother. Thunder boomed overhead and larger raindrops fell.

"Thank you, Markos, for bringing him home," she whispered.

After the last family member squeezed into the last bus, Markos and his wife climbed into Gunari's Studebaker. Markos watched Grandmother as Gunari drove away from the curb. She frowned and shook her head while Mr. Charles and Chief Qaletaqa talked to her. Her dog sat rigidly at her feet. Markos noted that Grandmother never answered when asked if the blessings had worked. Judging by her frown, they hadn't.

Chapter 17/Old Faces, New Friends

May 20, 1936

Dear Grandmother Zenobia Jalio,

It is an honor to fill your request to host funeral services for the Camlo family. It's my understanding from your letter to me that we're expecting a larger, more "interesting" crowd than usual. We will be happy to accommodate as many people as we can. Should it rain, we will move the service indoors and have a tent set up outside for anyone who cannot fit inside the sanctuary. Should your guest speaker need anything, please have him or his people contact me directly.

Thank you for being such a loyal member of the church over the years. The congregation welcomes you and your colorful visitors with open arms. Speaking also as a member of Carrefour Parish, we are sorry for your loss. It is a pleasure to serve you and your needs. I wanted to share this passage with you:

"Peace I leave with you; my peace I give to you. Not as the world gives do I give to you. Let not your hearts be troubled, neither let them be afraid."
John 14:27.

By his grace,

Reverend Eugene Milton III

GRANDMOTHER RE-READ THE LETTER SHE'D received from St. Augustus Church. It was hard for her to grasp that so many years had passed since she had last held a letter in her hand from St. Augustus. Of all the places she expected to be, standing in freshly cut green grass in front of this church, on this day, was the last. It was honorable that the great-grandson of the late Reverend Milton took over the church. She watched the sun slowly sink behind the rolling hills that protected the lush valley. She glanced at the newly painted steeple and closed her eyes. Olivia's death still hurt, even though it was so long ago. Memories of Will, all dressed up, and his laughter while serving the children cookies hurt even more deeply.

Chief Qaletaqa softly patted her back, to console her.

"There is nothing more you could have done," he said.

"How is that possible? There is always more than can be done, isn't there?" she asked.

"May I speak freely?"

"I always expect you to be honest with me, my friend."

"You are too fickle with your power. You struggle with it too much. Even then, with that woman's death. You only use it or hide it when it suits your needs. Let go. It needs to ebb and flow naturally like the moon. Many do not understand, but I know how powerful you are. You were with me when I was trapped in the form of a wolf, far away from my clan. I would have died if you hadn't released me, and nursed me back to health. You were there with me when I found out most of my people were destroyed. Years later, we danced together in your garden under a new moon, to heal our boys. You danced with such grace then. This land is graced with your presence."

Grandmother wiped tears from her face and looked up to the stars.

"When was the last time you just sat and let your energy, your soul, stir within you?" he asked.

Grandmother shook her head. Once again, she was disappointed with herself. She couldn't remember the last time she'd sat quietly on her porch to listen to her own heartbeat. She had sat on her porch many times, but always trying to figure out how to fix or teach something. She always had to be in control.

"Yesterday could have been a very bad day without the travelers' blessings. If they weren't there, that gypsy queen's anger would have been very destructive," he said.

"She can't kill me, Chief."

"No, but your soul could have been in jeopardy."

Grandmother considered his words carefully. "I know. I'm grateful that you were there. I'm grateful that you are here now."

"You saved my life, Zenobia. It is the very least I could do."

"So what happens now?" Grandmother asked, changing the subject. She wished Ahy was at her side, but she knew he'd be safer at home, away from Patia's anger.

"I wish I had Patia's book. I wouldn't feel so blind trying to deal with her spells."

She heard something stirring in the darkness overhead in a nearby tree. A firefly with a red hue buzzed around Zenobia's horses. The chief nodded as another horse-drawn carriage pulled up from the side of the church. Headlights from a limousine bounced down the road just moments later.

"The legends are arriving."

Chief Qaletaqa and Grandmother Zenobia discussed options of how to handle Patia, after the dead woman's outburst on the docks. Together they agreed upon a list of local people who could help lay Patia to rest, once and for all. Each person they selected possessed supernatural abilities or traits. Many of them had stories told about them. Some stories about these people were fictional, created by locals to frighten children and anyone who listened to them. Some stories were fact. For each person selected for help, Grandmother Zenobia had an offering for them in exchange for their time and service.

Some of these people were old friends, and some could possibly be new friends to Grandmother Zenobia. They all stood together near the front door of the church.

"Thank you all for coming tonight, and on such short notice," Grandmother said as she stood before her guests. Father Moretti, a small man with dark hair and pale skin, along with his associate, Sister Mary, who was equally pale, had appeared from inside the sanctuary and closed the doors behind them to join the others outside.

"Allow me to take a moment and formally introduce everyone," said the Native American man.

"I present to you all Queen Zenobia of Palmyra, last living member of the ancient Jalio tribe. She prefers to be called 'Grandmother Zenobia.' It's her way of honoring family and family traditions."

Grandmother bowed slightly and lowered her eyes before the group.

"Representing fire and metal, we have Father Moretti from the Saint Gaston Monastery and Sister Mary from the Ursuline Convent. The Gaston Monastery is a sanctuary for lost boys and broken men. Father Moretti and the members of his priesthood provide a certain level of guidance that only the supernatural can give, to help poor tormented souls heal. The Ursuline convent provides similar services to women of all ages. The convent is the only building in the French Quarter that has withstood every major fire to plague New Orleans. They bring nails, blessed by the pope. They will seal Patia's coffin."

The pair nodded in unison.

"As a token of my gratitude, I offer you a troubled young girl named Agnes," said Grandmother. "She is a handful, a restless child. No one can control her. She hurts anyone who gets in her way of what she wants, including her parents. She will be at your doorstep tomorrow evening and is in need of, shall we say, 'guidance' that only your convent can provide. Her blood is pure, untainted."

Sister Mary smiled widely, revealing long fangs, which she bashfully shielded with her right hand.

"We brought an empty trousseau box as well," Father Moretti said quickly. "It was used by one of the sisters when the ladies came over from France. We thought it might be useful, in case Patia's coffin was too damaged."

"Thank you."

The two bowed slightly before Grandmother Zenobia.

"Representing water, we have Monsieur Letiche, the Alligator Boy of the Bayou," the chief said.

"Lately, I go by the name of Johnny," Letiche said. "Less formal, easier to remember." He appeared to be a young Cajun boy around twelve years old. He wore a straw hat, cotton shirt, and overalls. His red eyes glowed in the darkness when he looked up at Grandmother. His head and shoulders looked like those of an average Caucasian male. His extremities, however, were those of an alligator. In one scaly green claw, he held a bucket of water and mud from the Mississippi River. At the bottom of that bucket thrashed half a dozen juvenile water moccasins. In the other scaly green claw he held a bucket with a cluster of white and purple walking irises.

"Treasures from the Mississippi River."

Grandmother eyed his long, horned tail as it flitted about in the darkness.

"Pleasure to meet you, Johnny. I must apologize. I didn't know that you'd be here tonight. I will have an offering for you in the next few days."

"Don't you worry about that none, cher. I owe Chiefie here a favor or two and he said he needed some extra help."

Johnny removed his hat, revealing dirty-blond hair. He bowed before Grandmother and stepped back.

"Representing air, we have Madame Virginia Dupuis, handmaiden to Madame and Mademoiselle Laveau." Everyone looked at the young Caribbean woman. Her angry eyes darted around as she summed everyone up, from head to toe. Jewels on her green, yellow, and purple turban sparkled in the light from the church.

"It's always a pleasure to see you, Miss Virginia," Grandmother said.

"Zenobia, Madame sends her regards. I brings de baklava, from a recipe by de Laveaus. De honey comes from de precious honey bees from dis sweet land and I makes de flour myself."

Grandmother heard soft clucking in the darkness.

"Did you bring the chicken? I refuse to be a part of an animal sacrifice," she growled.

"Calm yourself, Zenobia," Miss Virginia said. "It ain't for no sacrificing. It be here to represent air, is all."

Grandmother eyed the Caribbean woman carefully. Virginia had always been a tense person. She was quick to start a fight and cause mischief. Grandmother didn't care much for her but knew the Laveau women trusted her. Chief Qaletaqa cleared his throat.

Why is this so hard? Grandmother thought as she cut her eyes toward the chief.

"I'm sorry, Miss Virginia," Grandmother said. "To honor my daughter, Angelica, I can't bear killing animals. I will not stand for it. Sadly, I couldn't care less about people sometimes. Until the day I die, I will always have a soft spot for animals."

Virginia relaxed her stance a little and nodded. "Mademoiselle Laveau did mention dat when last we spoke."

"Thank you for your understanding. We should have tea sometime after all of this is done."

"In de meantime, what can ya offer me that I dwon already have?"

"How about more business? It would be my pleasure to send you a list of potential clients for card readings and such."

Grandmother sensed Virginia relax at her offer. She uncrossed her arms and offered up the palms of her hands.

"That be fair to me, High Priestess Zenobia."

Virginia bowed before Zenobia and stepped back.

"For extra reinforcement, we also have Seraphina of Avery Island, representing fire and air."

A bright red firefly glided in from the darkness. When it entered the light of the church, it transformed into a young woman with shocking red hair. Her skin was speckled head to toe with freckles. She wore a skimpy green summer dress and smelled of Tabasco.

"Hello everyone," she said, waving fire-engine-red nails, flashing a devilish red grin to match.

"Seraphina, thank you for coming. I didn't know if you were able to get permission to leave Avery Island," Grandmother said.

"One of my sisters promised to tend the Pepper fields tonight while I'm gone. We all take turns. A handful of us usually come over for Mardi Gras. The revelers love our fire dance."

"I reckon it is a spectacular dance," Johnny said. Everyone nodded in agreement.

"When Chief Qaletaqa mentioned you needed help, I didn't hesitate. My sisters and I fought about who would be the one lucky enough to spend time with you."

"Thank you again, sweetheart. I'm speechless. What can I offer you for your help today?"

"Take care of my cousins in the bayou. Plant more flowers in your garden. Lightning bugs love them."

"I'll be sure to get right on that once this business is done. Please give my regards to your grandparents. I still have your grandmother's red shoe. I put it out when I am open to giving readings."

"I'll be sure to tell her. She and Paw Paw will get a kick out of that for sure."

Seraphina bowed before Grandmother and took a step back. Grandmother noticed that even her toenails were bright red. The fairy had inherited her bright-red hair from her grandfather, the farmer who pestered Zenobia looking for help with love years ago.

Chief Qaletaqa stepped forward.

"Lastly, may I officially introduce myself to you all as well. I am Chief Qaletaqa, of the lost Chapitoulas tribe. I will be representing the earth element. I am a skin walker; I can change into any animal I wish. I will do a sacred dance of my people."

The chief turned to Grandmother and bowed deeply before her.

"Chief, I don't know what to…"

"It is my privilege to be here for you. You understand the plight of my people. You saved me from certain death when you could have turned your back. You're my friend. It is with much pride that I honor you and your spirit tonight."

"I can't thank you enough for your friendship."

Father Moretti frowned and Sister Mary nudged him until he spoke.

"I have to say, before we start, that the gypsy woman isn't truly evil, but she's in a great deal of pain," said Father Moretti. "…and she blames you for many things."

"I understand that, but…" Grandmother said. She clenched her hands into tight fists.

"Please allow him to finish," the chief said softly.

"Of course," she said, remembering to open her palms.

"When she was alive, she told many lies and played with the dark arts," Father Moretti continued. "Now, in death, her spirit clings to the false words. If you all take a moment, you can see and hear her bitterness. If that bitterness isn't dealt with, darkness will feed what's left of her soul, and she will be dangerous. She will infect or attack others. The darkness will grow and kill everyone and everything in its path."

Grandmother Zenobia growled.

"Grandmother Zenobia, make no mistake, you were on track with what you offered to appease her yesterday."

"Because she views you as an enemy, and because you view her as an enemy, you shouldn't fight this battle. You're too close to the situation, too involved. That's why we are here to help you," explained Sister Mary, almost whispering. Grandmother was surprised by the pale woman's voice. It was soft and melodious.

"I don't think I'm too close that I can't use sound judgment," Grandmother said. She felt heat rise around her neck and her cheeks flush.

"Who is David? Who is Anton?" questioned Father Moretti. "The gypsy keeps…"

"Dear Lord in Heaven above. Are they all right? What did she do to them? What can I do?"

Chief Qaletaqa placed his hand on Grandmother's shoulder. "You are too close. Now do you understand why you need help?"

Grandmother clenched her fists.

"All of this commotion is because the gypsy woman hasn't acknowledged one of her life lessons. We all have something to learn as we walk our path of life," Grandmother said.

"We ain't here to teach dat gypsy to change her ways, we be here to silence her," snapped the young Caribbean woman.

"Yes, Miss Virginia, you are correct," Father Moretti said.

Zenobia didn't like the tone of the conversation, but she knew Virginia was right.

"Zenobia, we're here to silence this woman. We all have brought offerings representing the elements," Chief Qaletaqa said. "This will only work because Patia has come to rest on Louisiana territory. If this were somewhere else, you'd need a new set of legendary allies."

"I understand. Thank you all again for coming to help me."

"Are there any last words anyone wants to share before we start?" Father Moretti asked.

"I could say a few things, but there are ladies present," Johnny said. His lips squished when he revealed his alligator smile, and the line of his mouth ran back farther than it should have, as if it might go all the way around his head.

"Then I suggest we begin."

Father Moretti and Sister Mary opened the heavy wooden doors of the sanctuary. Grandmother slowly walked in, noticing that the sanctuary hadn't changed much over the years. The same stained-glass saints were still imparting their wisdom to anyone who cared. She looked over at the hard wooden pews she'd once sat on, trying to console Olivia Milton. She looked up at the giant statue of a savior many people prayed to. He didn't stare down at her with the judgmental stare she remembered. He seemed to look down at her in empathy. Behind the pulpit rested two large coffins. A large circle along with small pentagrams were drawn in ash on the polished wooden altar floor. They created a larger pentagram around the coffins.

"All that ash will be gone once this is done, correct? I don't want to upset the reverend. He wouldn't understand."

"Grandmother, everything will be fine," Chief Qaletaqa said. "Please, allow us to make this offering for you."

"Places, everyone," Father Moretti said.

Sister Mary handed out white candles and Seraphina blew on them, causing them to light. Sister Mary handed Grandmother a blue candle. Seraphina winked at Grandmother. Her candle lit up with a blue flame.

"These are for protection," Sister Mary said.

"I don't need protection," snapped Grandmother. Her response was harsher than she intended it to be.

"Everyone, take your places, please," ordered Father Moretti. He stood in the center of the pentagram.

Grandmother looked around, realizing she was number six of the group. There were only five small pentagrams in the big circle. Father Moretti was in charge of the ceremony so he stood center stage, in front of the two coffins.

There are only five elements. Five is two plus three, she thought to herself and chuckled. She still wouldn't let go of the number twenty-three.

"What am I supposed to do? Where am I supposed to be?" Grandmother asked.

Father Moretti ushered Grandmother over to a stiff wooden chair that sat below the stage and pulpit. It was away from the large pentagram. It was in its own circle of ash.

"This is where you sit."

"And do what?"

"You sit and you observe.

Very reluctantly, Grandmother sat on the wooden chair. Not only was she hot around the collar, but her hands started to sweat. The chief handed her a paper fan he'd found stuffed in one of the pews. Sister Mary approached Grandmother and knelt before her. She offered Grandmother a small gold-trimmed ceramic plate with a single slice of baklava, a small white lily, and a crystal goblet of water.

"Places, everyone!" Father Moretti said again. "I'm looking right at you, Johnny. Leave Seraphina alone and get to your spot."

Then the light in the sanctuary turned off with a sharp click. Grandmother watched as everyone took a defensive stance on their own pentagram around the caskets. Their offerings were laid at their feet in the circle. Grandmother watched their faces in the candlelight as Father Moretti began his prayer.

"De nos coeurs, nous désirons vous reposer la reine Patia. En ce jour, vous pouvez dormir en paix. Nous vous honorons avec des éléments de ce monde."

Grandmother spoke a little French, but didn't understand the prayer.

"Puissent vos soucis fondre dans la chaleur de l'incendie; que votre cœur soit aussi léger que l'air. Que l'eau laver votre douleur. Comme votre corps est mis dans la terre molle puissiez-vous être relié à la terre. Puissent les fleurs révéler votre beauté, et la nourriture nourrir votre âme. Que le métal et les bijoux autour de vous ouvrir les portes vers les cieux au-dessus. Que votre esprit soit léger, peut-être vous sentez l'amour de votre Créateur."

Grandmother was irritated. All she was supposed do was sit obediently, like someone's pet? She wondered why they weren't saying the Hail Mary prayer. It was more powerful and more suited for the gypsy. The small plate on her lap annoyed Grandmother. She stuffed the baklava in her mouth. The sweet honey and crunchy pistachios surprised her. Her daughter, Angelica, had tried to make it for her once. Grandmother wondered why that memory popped into her head. She looked at the empty plate and saw an etching of a blue-and-green peacock, with its tailfeathers spread wide.

"Reste, très cher, le repos."

Grandmother grew more agitated as she shifted in the uncomfortable chair.

"I don't think this is working…" Grandmother complained, until she saw a white mist slowly creep up from the large pentagram on the stage before her. The temperature in the sanctuary dropped quickly.

"What is wrong with me?" she mumbled to herself. "Relax."

Grandmother drank the water Sister Mary had given her. It was cool and soothing as it ran down her throat. She hadn't realized she was so thirsty. She closed her eyes and listened carefully when Father Moretti repeated his prayer. This time, although he continued to speak in French, she easily understood what he said.

"From our hearts, we wish you rest, Queen Patia. On this day may you sleep in peace. We honor you with elements of this world. May your troubles melt away in the heat of the fire, may your heart be as light as air. May the water wash away your pain. As your body is laid into the soft earth, may you be grounded. May the flowers reveal your beauty, and the food nourish your soul. May the metal and jewels around you open the gates to the heavens above. May your spirit be light, may you feel the love of your creator. Rest, dear one, rest."

Grandmother was touched by the prayer. The personal ones always resonated with her soul. The words were sweet and endearing. As the prayer echoed off the walls, Grandmother's attitude soured. Patia didn't deserve such a heartfelt prayer. Her body and soul should plunge to the depths of hell for killing Will. The gypsy should burn from a thousand suns, gnawed upon by a thousand demons.

As Grandmother stewed in her anger, Patia's coffin began to shake. Three heavy knocks pounded from within the wooden box. The mist grew thicker, drifting over the entire stage. Moans wafted up from the pulpit.

Father Moretti continued his prayer, but muffled screams were heard from the coffin. They grew louder and louder.

"This is ridiculous! I was right. It's not working," Grandmother said.

Patia's coffin flew open, startling everyone in the circle, but they refused to leave their spots.

Grandmother stood, looking at everyone's faces in the candlelight and mist. Father Moretti continued his prayer. Sister Mary stood completely motionless. Her eyes had turned solid black and thick dark ooze leaked down her face. Her thin lips and pointy teeth were also black. Johnny, the legendary Cajun gator boy, cackled and did a jig. He clapped his claws furiously. His movements jerked in the mist. In contrast, Seraphina danced slowly in the mist. Fire bounced from hand to hand, arm to arm. Her red hair caught on fire and ran down her back. Chief Qaletaqa shape-shifted from man to bird, back to man, then to black bear. His transformations were erratic and deformed, not holding one form for very long. Then

Grandmother looked over at Miss Virginia. She was in her tribal Voodoo trance, something that Grandmother recognized instantly. As Miss Virginia thrashed about, she grabbed her live chicken in one hand and brandished a sharp metal blade in the other. She raised the blade overhead and held out the squawking bird. Patia's corpse rose, sitting up in the coffin and reached out toward Grandmother.

"No! Enough of this nonsense!" Grandmother bellowed in anger.

The entire church shook. The rafters creaked. Stained-glass windows in the church shattered. The stage rocked as she pointed her left hand toward Patia. The blue candle Zenobia clenched in her right hand burst into a fireball. She tossed it to the floor with disgust. A nearby pew easily caught on fire. The earth beneath them sank. Wind howled outside, rattling the walls. Zenobia physically grew larger before everyone. Her dress ripped and her shoes split. Her black-and-gold fleur de lis ring she wore on her left hand bent out of shape. She twisted it off her fat fingers before it broke. She clutched it as she continued to grow. The legendary creatures of Louisiana who gathered on the stage looked up at Zenobia, cowering in fear. She towered over them and roared in anger. Her head bumped against the roof of the church. Her left elbow punched a hole in the side of the sanctuary.

"Um, Grandmother Zenobia?" said Markos as he innocently opened the sanctuary door. Ahy was making his way through the man's steps. Markos held a large mirror with a handcrafted gold-and-bronze frame. Grandmother fiercely looked over her shoulder to see the thin gypsy struggle to make his way in with her dog at his side. "My wife insisted that I…"

Zenobia saw her reflection in the mirror Markos awkwardly held.

"Dear God, what am I doing? What have I become?" Zenobia thought.

Time stopped. Everything froze. Zenobia looked around at the destruction she had caused. She realized the people on the altar meant no harm. They were trying to help, even though she wanted to control everything. Because of her anger, the church was swallowed by the earth, sinking into a pit. The roof had broken into pieces and was dropping to the floor, revealing sparkling, cold stars. She saw through the holes that the steeple leaned at an angle, ready to topple to the ground. Behind her, several pews were split down the middle and swallowed by a newly formed hole in the wooden floor. Small fires glowed around her. She looked over at the statue of Jesus that barely hung over the altar. Holy, bloody tears slowly trickled down its face. She looked at her ring that she still clung to. It held a sliver of her husband's heart. Her husband was a god of destruction. She'd left Set because of his anger and his disrespect for life; now she stood on holy ground, doing exactly what he used to do.

Zenobia looked back to Markos, who was frozen in time. His mirror caught not only Zenobia's reflection, but also the reflection of Patia's corpse. Zenobia saw Patia's ethereal body. She was younger, with thick black hair. She stood straight, with an athletic build. She had soft, creamy skin. She was in agony and pain. A large bloody hole gaped where her heart should have been. Patia held her own heart, but kept insisting someone had stolen it from her.

Ahy looked directly at Grandmother.

The fight with Patia isn't really about me. That woman is in pain. They were right, she needs peace. I need peace. I need to make this right. Grandmother closed her eyes.

"Dear Lord above, forgive me. I ask for forgiveness from the universe for being so selfish, so self-absorbed. To this day, I continue to do too much. I am overbearing and controlling. Vengeance is yours, not mine. Please help that creature find her peace. Please help me find peace, even if I have no family to call my own. I refuse to walk the path of the one who cursed me so long ago."

Grandmother took a pin from her hat, which precariously sat on her head, and pricked her finger. She shook a few drops of blood around herself on the circle of ash. She raised both hands overhead and chanted as loudly as she could. Slowly, she danced in a circle, moving counter-clockwise. Pieces of the roof fell to the floor and the ground shook as she moved.

"I command the sands of time to do my bidding. Iubeo iubere facere arena tempus. I command the sands of time to do my bidding. Je commande les sables du temps pour faire mon appel d'offres."

The earth shook again. Cold, sharp pain burst in Zenobia's chest. She stumbled onto the floor, sharply twisting her back as time rewound itself. As the church readjusted, seemingly healing itself, coldness ran deeply through her bones. Her body shrank to its original form. The dress she wore appeared as it had just moments before. She put her ring back on her hand and kissed it softly. Her teeth hurt, her ears pounded. The stained-glass windows around the church gleamed as they reassembled. Freezing pain pierced her skull and ran through her veins.

Once she managed to get back to her chair, she slowly raised her right hand and whispered, "Enough."

Grandmother watched again the faces of the creatures on the stage. They all blinked simultaneously and then Father Moretti continued his prayer. Patia's coffin was closed again, and continued to shake as it had moments before, but the screams were less. Miss Virginia raised her sharp blade in the air and chanted loudly.

Instead of becoming angry, Grandmother cried. She was sad for Patia. It must have been awful for her to live a long life of pain and suffering. Grandmother would forgive her for killing her son, but she wouldn't forget. Patia would stand in heaven and reap her own judgment.

As she wiped her tears, something shiny caught her eye. It was the gold trim from the dessert plate. Grandmother picked up the small plate and placed it carefully on her lap.

"This was an offering for me, and I was too headstrong to realize it. I can't remember the last time I was honored in any way. The peacock, a bird of land and air, is for protection. It represents nobility and true inner beauty. They gave me holy water and dessert befitting a queen. White lilies, from the earth, used to be offered to the goddess Juno, back in Roman times. They are honoring my powers. The light-blue candle with its flame is to give me peace and tranquility. It protects those who stand before me. All five elements, in simple form."

Father Moretti's prayer was for Patia and for Zenobia.

Grandmother looked down at her hands and noticed they were older. There were more creases. She saw a small gray hair on one of her knuckles. Her skin was ashen. She reached over for the crystal goblet when her back screamed out in pain.

It didn't have to be this way. Serves me right, trying to control too much.

Grandmother obediently watched her allies through the mist and candlelight. Patia's corpse screamed as it reached out for her.

Miss Virginia spun a few times, brandishing the blade, but then put the live chicken gently in the middle of the pentagram. She put the blade away, back in her turban, before she continued to thrash about. Johnny danced with a few water moccasins in his hands. Seraphina's phoenix fire dance was sultry and bright. Her body caught fire and burned down to a statue of ash. She shook her hair and returned to her original state. She never stopped her dance as the flames grew and died. Grandmother glanced over at the representative from the Ursuline convent. Sister Mary stopped baring her black fangs. Her face relaxed. Black ooze continued to flow but slowly diluted into fresh clear tears as she stood in place, repeating the chant Father Moretti spoke. Chief Qaletaqa shape-shifted from a large black thunderbird back into his human form. He danced his tribal dance, waving his arms gently in the mist. Grandmother silently counted to three, and, like clockwork, Markos entered the sanctuary.

"Um…Grandmother Zenobia?" Markos asked as he managed to open the sanctuary door. He held a large mirror with a gold-and-bronze frame. The glass was dirty and smudged. It seemed very heavy for him to carry, but Grandmother thought it might have also been his nerves.

Father Moretti stopped his prayer and everyone looked at the innocent intruder. Patia continued to howl, and Ahy bolted to his mistress.

"My wife, Fifika, insisted I bring this last gift for our queen. It was handmade by our people and has been blessed with kisses. She insisted every single member of our tribe kiss it." Markos looked at the scene and tried his best to seem calm. "Your dog showed up and refused to leave me." Grandmother knew he was shocked.

"Ladies and gentleman, may I introduce to you King Markos. Dorian and Patia were members of his tribe."

Everyone nodded in Markos's direction.

"This is my dog, Ahy."

Chief Qaletaqa bowed to the dog.

"King Markos, dear, bring the mirror up to the stage to Father Moretti. Don't be afraid. Patia can't do anything to harm you."

As Markos approached, Grandmother saw his expression when he looked at her.

"Are you all right? You look so, so…" he whispered.

"I'm okay. I'll explain this later."

"Grandmother, who are these strange people?"

Seraphina, engulfed in flames, waved at him.

"They are here as a favor to me. They are here to help. Don't worry that they look strange. It's makeup and theatrics, I assure you. They are my friends."

Markos continued to frown at Grandmother.

"Is there anything I can do for you?"

"For now, just give Father Moretti…"

Patia stepped out of her coffin. Her shrieks grew louder, and echoed off the walls of the sanctuary. Markos stood before Grandmother and instinctively pointed the mirror at Patia. Patia stopped in her tracks.

"Beautiful….so beautiful," Patia moaned. She saw her reflection, just as Zenobia had. Everyone stood motionless.

"Sister, help me up the stairs, please."

Grandmother leaned heavily on the young woman as she was escorted up the wooden stairs to Patia. Grandmother was now frail, and each step took effort. She could tell that by morning she'd have large bruises on her arms and legs from her large, abnormal stretching in the small church.

"Markos, continue to show Patia her reflection in your mirror."

The Voodoo woman reached out and grabbed the gypsy woman's bloody, throbbing black heart with both hands.

"Patia Camlo," yelled Grandmother.

Patia's corpse eyed Grandmother, who stood in view of the mirror.

"I am Zenobia of the ancient Jalio tribe, Queen of Palmyra. I am not your enemy. I stand before you, woman to woman. I am here to tell you that you are beautiful, and you are loved." Zenobia shoved the bloody heart into Patia's chest. Zenobia stepped in closer and embraced Patia. She hugged her with all the strength she could muster.

Patia stopped screaming. Her rotted corpse wrapped its flesh around Zenobia, and hugged her in return.

"Markos, bring the mirror to us, please," Grandmother said. Father Moretti and the others stood aside as Markos nervously approached. Patia released Zenobia when she saw her reflection and the kisses that covered it. Her skin was radiant. Her hair was thick and curly. Her smile was small but graceful. The kisses whispered sweet compliments and words of love to their former queen. She slowly backed up into her coffin. Markos laid the mirror on top of her.

Quickly, burial offerings were picked up off the floor and also placed into her coffin. Father Moretti and Markos nailed the coffin shut with the blessed nails. Chief Qaletaqa ran to Grandmother and held her in his arms.

"Your Majesty, are you all right?" he asked. By the concerned look on his face, she knew she was in bad shape. Ahy whined and pawed at her. Grandmother looked over at the statue of Jesus, who had returned to its original pious-looking state. She noticed that tears slowly rolled down its cheeks.

"Chief, you were right. I still have much to learn. Please take me home."

Epilogue

"There was sugar everywhere!" shouted Gunari. "And then King Dorian looked down at me. I thought I was in serious trouble for sure, but then I swear to you, he laughed! He laughed at me!" Gunari tried to catch his breath in between his own hysterics. "Remember his rich voice? Our king laughed so hard he had tears in his eyes, and then he said to me, 'Quick, boy, bring me a few more before they are all gone!'"

The tent erupted in laughter. Grandmother Zenobia laughed until her cheeks hurt. King Markos sat the head of the table, his wife to his left and Grandmother to his right. The travelers had provided an honorary black-and-gold throne decorated with Mardi Gras beads for her to sit upon. At her request, Chief Qaletaqa sat next to her, on her right. Grandmother looked around at the large tables before her, shaped in a U. There was more food and drink than the eye could see. Everyone sat crammed elbow to elbow, stuffing themselves and socializing after the funeral procession. Grandmother loved that the travelers and locals from Carrefour Parish had all come together. They laughed, sang, and shared stories about

365

King Dorian and Queen Patia. Little children fed Ahy bits and pieces of food. The guests who didn't know the deceased enjoyed the stories and paid their respects. The band, a mixed group of local jazz musicians and gypsies, played lively music in the corner. Grandmother marveled that everyone enjoyed each other's company on the sunny afternoon.

"No, little one, I can't eat any more, but thank you," Grandmother said as she held one of Markos's very messy granddaughters on her lap. The little girl ate a handful of dried berries, then offered some to Grandmother. She tried to press the food through the black lace veil that Grandmother wore. The veil was an attempt to hide her tears for the deceased, as well as a way to hide how much she had aged overnight. The little girl offered some to Qaletaqa, who accepted a few berries and gave her a smile.

"Grandmother, I'm so sorry to burden you with her," Fifika said, leaning over her husband. Markos barley noticed.

"Milosh," she yelled, "have your wife come get your daughter. She's terrorizing Grandmother!"

"She's not a burden at all," Grandmother said with a smile that came through her veil.

"She always likes to share her food," Fifika said. "I'm sorry her mother is taking too long to fetch her. She's always kissing Milosh. They are still in love, after having many children. Anyway, let me take her from you. Lala seems to have calmed down. She should be with the other little ones."

Miss Virginia Dupuis made her way up through people who socialized and ate from the opposite side of the tables. She grinned as she approached the head of the table.

"Grandmother, I have come to pay my respects to you and your friends. It was an honor to spend time with you."

"I'm the one who's grateful for all you've done for me," Grandmother said.

Miss Virginia leaned in closer.

"I never forget what you did for dat woman last night. I never seen nothing like it in all my days."

Miss Virginia touched Zenobia's hand.

"Keep your list of clients. People need you. You should show your face around town more often."

Grandmother noticed that her skin buzzed from the Voodoo woman's touch. The gypsy baby in her lap giggled and clapped her hands.

"May many blessings come your way."

"Blessing to you too, Miss Virginia. We'll have a nice sit-down soon."

As Miss Virginia left, Grandmother noticed a small line of visitors in front of her. Some people she knew from around town, some she didn't. They all came to pay their respects and speak to the legendary Grandmother

Zenobia. As each approached and offered a small blessing, Grandmother's skin tingled.

Fifika eventually took the two-year-old girl from Grandmother. At first the baby threatened to cry, but Grandmother waved her gloved hand at the little girl. "I will see you later, Lala. You be a good girl now."

"You have a way with the little ones. You have a way with everyone, actually. I see why everyone calls you Grandmother," Markos said. "It seems you and Chief Qaletaqa are the only ones Lala listens to today."

As Fifika worked her way through the boisterous crowd in the stuffy tent, Lala blew Grandmother a kiss. Grandmother pretended to catch it and put it away. She watched as Fifika exited the tent, revealing a flash of sunlight.

"Markos, if you will excuse me for just a moment, I need a little fresh air. I'll be right back."

"Of course! Everyone, make way for Grandmother Zenobia," he announced. "Our guest of honor needs some fresh air. Should you want to leave her a donation for all she's done today, there's a box by the punch bowl."

"No, no, it's not necessary. I'm happy you all could celebrate the passing of my dear friend and his wife," Grandmother said.

King Markos stood and helped Grandmother off her throne, seated next to him. He leaned in closely and spoke to her.

"Grandmother, I had to say something. Many people have blessed us and wanted to make sure you had something too. Your people insist on leaving offerings. Gunari said that is the third box he put out for you. You should see our family chest by the door. Such generous people."

He pointed to a wooden box by the punch bowl. Paper money, flowers, and jewelry already peeked out from the top edges. Markos handed her a hand-polished wooden cane.

"I am so honored by all of this. It wasn't my intention at all."

Chief Qaletaqa stood up next Grandmother as well, making sure she was steady on her feet.

"I'm fine, I'll be right back." He nodded and returned to his seat. Ahy left the children he played with and sat at the chief's side.

The partygoers quickly cleared an exit path for Grandmother, and in no time, she was outside of the multicolored tent. She lifted her veil and removed her gloves. She drew in a deep breath, enjoying the fresh air, and looked around the camp. The sun was a treat when it warmed her wrinkled face. Her back throbbed. She reached her hand up to the blue sky and whispered, "Thank you, thank you, thank you." The stretch was good for her back. To her delight, there weren't as many wrinkles or liver spots on her hands as there had been when she woke up and began her day. A small flock of little brown birds with tiny white dotted feathers flew in front of her, landing a few feet away from where she stood.

"Hello, little ones. I'm sorry I have no breadcrumbs for you right now."

The little wrens peeped and searched around in the grass before her.

If God watches over them, I know he's watching over me, she thought quietly.

"Yes, Your Highness, he does watch over you," interrupted a familiar voice. Grandmother slowly turned to see Wren, the angel. He removed his tall black top hat, revealing his thick hair, and bowed before her.

"Wren, to what do I owe this pleasure?"

"I have a message for you."

Grandmother grimaced.

"Anton and David made it through today, despite the curse."

"What?" She could hardly believe what she'd heard.

"Today is May twenty-third, their birthday. I can see why you forgot. All I am permitted to say is that the curse was activated, but I assure you, they are still around."

"The twins! They're all right." Fresh tears sprang from her tired eyes. Grandmother clutched her heart. As she moved, she dropped her cane and lost her balance. The angel swiftly came to her side before she fell.

"The powers that be wanted you to know."

Once Grandmother was steady on her feet, he picked up her cane and looked at it carefully.

"Chief Qaletaqa did a wonderful job," Wren said as he looked at the little symbols carved into the wood.

"It's made of Indian rosewood, one of my favorites," Grandmother said.

Standing next to Wren was comforting. He smelled of roses and his hands were soft and cool to the touch. Her aches and pains faded.

"You aren't talking about my new walking stick, are you, Wren."

"Your Highness, you are as wise as you are majestic."

"Even with my new gray hair?" Grandmother joked.

Wren smiled. He handed her cane back to her. "I can provide you a little healing, although judging by the blessings from your people, you'll be back to your regular self before sundown."

"In between the kisses and the wishes I'm as happy as I could be," Grandmother said as she clasped her manicured hands together and smiled brightly.

Wren touched the sides of her face. His fingers were feather-light as they brushed her skin. Her eyes watered when the skin around her eyebrows and eyelashes pulsed. Her scalp tingled. There were no longer any random muscle twitches in her back, and the bruises from last night's events faded.

"I don't know how to repay your generosity," Grandmother said. "I don't know how to thank anyone these days, it seems."

"It is not needed, Your Highness."

Grandmother looked at the walking stick, realizing she would no longer need it to sit or stand.

"The symbols carved in your walking stick will provide some protection against negative energies, but I must warn you, the darkness you have nightmares of is still coming for you. It is not for a while, but it is coming."

Grandmother studied the angel's face as he spoke. He was surprised when she didn't react to him.

"I see that you already know this."

"I have known for some time that someone, or something, is coming for me."

"Your Highness, take to heart that just as he watches the sparrow, he watches over you. I must take my leave, but please, enjoy your family." He extended his long, elegant hand and pointed out to the meadow before them. Grandmother squinted. When she focused her vision, she saw two shimmering images. Syeira and Will were as happy as could be, dancing and laughing together in the sunlight.

With the blink of an eye, Wren was gone.

"This is one of the happiest days of my life," Grandmother said. She stood a bit taller and felt a little lighter. Will and Syeira waved at her before they faded away.

Laughter and music from the tent behind her beckoned her back to the Sunday dinner she had always wanted.

63319189R00229

Made in the USA
Lexington, KY
04 May 2017